A Soul's Final Journey

Everyone Calls Me Paige

A Novel

Steven R. James Productions

Steven R. James

i

Library of Congress registration number TXu 2-449-641

ISBN:9798344369440

This is For

Stephen King for unknowingly inspiring, teaching, and
mentoring me as a writer.
Alan B. for all his support.
Tory G. for his guidance and advice.
Linda C. for bringing out my creative side and teaching me
to trust my instincts.

Prologue

I never thought this day was going to come. I have spent thirty-five agonizing years punishing and blaming myself while suffering in silence. Those years were spent believing the events that happened, especially that one event that tore my soul apart, all of it was my fault. I was told it was my fault by the one who committed the act. No matter what was said or who said it, there was no changing my mind. She was right. It was all my fault. I felt like a total failure letting down the one person who needed me the most. The one person who needed me to protect him. I failed to do just that, protect him. Was it because I was a total fuck up or just so goddamned gullible that I believed she truly loved him as much as I did? How could I have been stupid enough to have believed her? She looked me straight in the eye and lied to my face. I should have known better. I chose to believe her because she told me the things I wanted to hear. I should have seen her for the true monster she was, (and I am willing to bet she still is). That is if she is still alive. I don't know if she is or not. I honestly don't care if she is alive. I can never forgive the cruel acts of deception and betrayal she committed. The very last time I spoke to her was the morning of August 14, 1987. The memory of that conversation has been burned into my brain, a wound that will never heal. Thirty-five agonizing years later, I still remember every cruel and evil word that came out of

1

her mouth. I can still hear the sound of her voice as if I was having that conversation with her right now. The ball and chain of grief and guilt made living and loving again next to impossible. Don't get me wrong, I did have a good life, and I did find happiness. I truly loved Mike with all my heart. He made me very happy. But it wasn't easy. I struggled with grief, and I struggled with guilt that I never talked about. I was too ashamed to tell Mike, or anyone else for that matter, what happened. I was afraid of their judgment and how they would verbally tear me apart and shame me. At least that is what I used to think. I was raised by a family that looked down on me. A family that used violence and verbal assaults coupled with mental cruelty, much like a schoolyard bully does. You don't realize everyone isn't like that. The ones who truly care about you love and accept you unconditionally encourage you, build you up, and support you. Those people are your true family. I know differently now and wish I had known sooner; maybe then I could have talked about it even though talking about it would not have changed the outcome. It would have been nice not to keep things bottled up inside. John, the man I looked up to as if he were my dad, was right about that as he was usually right about most things. Keeping things bottled up eats away at you and eat away it did. Some days it consumed me, those were the bad days. Other days not so much, those were the decent days. At this point, you are wondering what happened and what I am talking about. Is he going to tell us or just keep rambling on? I just didn't know where or how to begin telling you what happened. I guess I will start here. My name is Andrew Paige Turner, everyone calls me Paige. I lived in the small town of Tucker Maine. I owned a farm down a dirt road on the side of a little mountain called Mount Hollis overlooking the Bartlett River. I bought that place in April of '96. Mike would come out on weekends when we first met. I knew he loved it there too. One weekend in the spring of '96 Mike came to spend the weekend and never left. I was happy he stayed. If any place could have been my utopia that was the place. The farmhouse had the rustic charm I loved yet complimented with modern updates. There was not a room in that house I could not call my favorite. Attached to the house was the barn and as much as I loved my home, I loved being in the barn. We would spend hours in the barn tinkering on the choppers. Those old shovel heads needed a lot of attention and both of us were happy to give them the attention they deserved. Behind the barn was my other happy place. Mike and I fenced in an acre of land to keep the deer and other wild game out of the garden area. Since I owned a farm, it only seemed right to grow my own vegetables. Plus, the deer got to feast on the fallen apples in the small orchard on the other side of the property. From the very first day I moved in I would always start my morning with a mug of coffee while looking out the window over my kitchen sink. The shelf next to the window was the perfect spot for my herb containers. I loved to grow and cook with fresh herbs and always had plenty on hand. I had just yelled up to Mike that coffee was ready, and I had poured him a cup. I walked over to the sink, which no matter the season or how bare the trees, had an awe-inspiring view of the meadow that ran down the side of the small mountain stopping at the river's edge. I owned all that land that was the meadow, and I owned a lot of the forest on each side of the meadow. I had a parcel of land across the road too. In total, I owned 100 acres of land. This was my utopia. Mike came into the kitchen, walked up behind me, put his arms around my waist, planted his morning kiss on the side of my neck, and rested his chin on my shoulder holding me tight. Mike would do this every morning without fail. I loved being held in his arms like that but this morning it was different. The last time I felt this feeling was August of '88 long before I met Mike, the man who showed me it was OK to love again. I did not know that the weekend in August of '88 was going to be the very last time I would be held by him or ever see him again. This man is the one I fell in love with the moment I laid my eyes on him. I dismissed both the feeling and thought as the grief I never learned to live with. The grief I kept bottled up inside. I went back to enjoying my morning hug and view. What a view it was. We have always had beautiful autumn foliage that was picture-perfect without fail. This year it was as if the colors were more alive than I had seen in many years. I remember the year the colors were this alive. That was back in '87, but I digress. As the autumn breeze flowed through the trees the leaves in all their sparkling color magically danced in the wind as if they were alive. Mother Nature was putting on a spectacular show as only Mother Nature knew how. The meadow was filled with wildflowers, which were an incredible spectacle though the wildflowers have usually gone by after the first frost. This was now late in October with Halloween just around the corner, well past peak leaf-peeping season. I wondered if this is what heaven, if there was one, might look like. I lost my faith back in '87 and never really cared to find it again. But again, I digress. As I was saying. The last time I saw Mother Nature put on such a show was back in '87. I was sitting on a boulder looking out onto Rattlesnake Pond, being held by the man who I had a soul connection with. I had to fight to push that memory out of my thoughts. I just don't like my thoughts going there; the pain is too great. Mike sensed my mind was elsewhere and not in a good place, so he tilted his head to the side and gently kissed the side of my neck a second time. He always knew how to bring me back to the moment when I got lost. He always knew there was something that weighed heavily on me. But he never pried or asked about the cross I bore. I never knew he had one himself. All those past thoughts were gone and I was back in the moment, a moment I wished would never end. After a while, I could hear Mike's stomach growling like an angry bear. It was time to head out for breakfast. I didn't want Mike to let go, I just wanted a few more minutes. If I only made him hold me for just one more moment, then maybe just maybe…

The autumn air was fresh and crisp, and we both knew this year's riding season would be over soon. You could almost smell winter in the air. We gave the choppers a few minutes to warm up then it was off to downtown Cornish to our favorite breakfast spot. Rosey's diner has been a Sunday tradition for us since Rosey opened in 2000. Rosey even cooked breakfast for us during the pandemic lockdowns we had a few years back. From there, off to the Maine side of the White Mountain National

Forest and the Western Maine mountain roads, our favorite place to ride. We road up Rte. 25 then north on Rte.160 into Brownfield where we picked up Rte. 113 through Fryeburg then finally Rte. 5 to bring us to where we wanted to go: The Green Bridge in Gilead Maine. The bridge crossed the Androscoggin River where, other than scenic views of the mountains and the river, not much was there. Well, except for the large boulders we hung out on. That was our spot. We would stop and enjoy the picnic lunch Rosey at the diner would pack for us. This particular day, after our picnic lunch and resting for a bit, we both stood up to stretch. Mike was facing me. He put his hands on my shoulders and gently pulled me close to him. He took his right hand off my shoulder and caressed the back of my head pulling me closer until our lips met. At first, I was shocked and didn't know what to think. Mike was very affectionate but never in public. The shock quickly faded and I let myself get lost in the kiss. Mike was still caressing the back of my head and had his other hand on my shoulder when our lip lock broke. I put my hand on his chest then slid my hand down his midsection looking to see if he was ready. Damn! He was more than ready. I have never felt him this hard before. It was like grabbing onto an oak tree! I started coaxing him into the woods when he reached down and felt just how ready I was. Usually, I can get Mike to do just about anything with a little persuading but not this time. He had a place he wanted to go so we could be alone. I didn't want to leave just yet. I wanted to hold him for just one more minute. I didn't want him to take his hand off my readiness, nor did I want him to let go of mine. I just wanted one more moment. Then maybe just maybe…We were back on the road and cruising along with Mike leading the way. We had never been in this direction before. Usually, we head back the way we came. He seemed like he knew where he was going, so I just followed along enjoying the new scenery. Then it happened in a flash–the oncoming car with the careless teen driver texting away veered into our lane. It happened so fast that Mike and I didn't have time to react. The BMW, which I am sure was Daddy's, hit Mike head-on. Mike went right through the windshield head-first.

Mike was able to get his arms up quickly enough to protect his head from taking the full impact, which I hoped wasn't in vain. In that split second, people say you see your life flash right before your eyes. That isn't true. In that split second just before impact, I thought, what if he had just held me in his arms in front of the window a moment longer? What if I had just kissed him a little longer? What if I had just tried one more time to get him into the woods? What if I just held his readiness in my hand a moment longer? What if I had just one more minute, just one minute? As if he was standing next to me, I heard John's voice loud and clear. "Paige, there are no what ifs, there is only what happened." Then my chopper hit the car, I went over the roof and thought to myself what if we just wore our helmets? I Guess old habits die hard. I hit the pavement and lost consciousness. Then there was complete and total blackness.

Chapter 1

1

I remember blacking out for what seemed like just a few seconds. I remember hearing voices and a heart monitor beeping. The monitor suddenly stopped its rhythmic beeping giving off the ear-piercing flat line signal. Seconds later I felt a surge of energy bolt through my body that lifted me off the bed. I snapped my eyes open. When I opened my eyes, I was expecting to be lying on the pavement or in the sterile white surrounds of an ER. Instead, I was standing in a meadow like the one on my property, but I knew I wasn't on my property. I was hip-deep in the wild grass and flowers that filled the meadow. The air was filled with the sweet scent of the wildflowers. I wondered what type of flowers they were. I had never seen this type before. Some of the flowers were different shades of soft blue. Others were bright yellow with purple tips on their petals. The occasional orange flower reminded me of the daylilies around my farm, yet all the flowers were somehow different in this meadow. Some had hundreds of tiny petals surrounding the pistil center. Other flowers had one large petal with a type of pistil that seemed to be inverted. All held their own stunning beauty. Even the grass had a distinction about it that made it different. The differences were slight but significant enough to know they were not something I had seen before. The flowers and the grass were gently swaying in the warm breeze giving off their sweet aroma. In the distance, I could hear the soothing trickle of a gently flowing stream, and I could imagine just how clear and cool the water was. I felt the warm and gentle breeze on my back, and I turned around wondering what was behind me. I saw the lush green forest with snow-capped mountains reaching up to the clear blue sky. I loved the smell of the pine trees that lined the forest. Being surrounded by such beauty gave me a feeling of peace and the solace I had so longed for the better part of my adult life. The big sky and mountains reminded me of the road trip Mike and I took on the choppers out to Montana. Our journey took us through the Rocky Mountains riding on the Road to the Sun. What a time we had! I started reminiscing about our time at The Weeping Wall inside Glacier National Park. We both goofed around in the water at The Weeping Wall like two little kids. We even laughed about the wet ride back to the campsite. I remembered the day Mike and I had a little "adult fun" of our own on top of the continental divide. This was the one and only time Mike got adventurous outdoors. He even admitted I was right; outdoor sex in the woods is mind-blowing to the max! There is nothing like enjoying one another's nature while in the coddles of Mother Nature herself. I was so lost in that fond memory that I didn't notice the fog that was rolling in from the lake to my right till it was almost on the shore. When I finally noticed the fog, it was just hitting the shoreline. I thought about a story I read of this mist coming across a lake with all types of hideous monsters of death in it. The mist engulfs this little town and some of the citizens get trapped inside a grocery store. Then I laughed thinking to myself. *Man, I read way too much Stephen King.* Then again, maybe not. I saw a figure walking out of the fog. The figure walked upright and didn't look much like a hideous monster of death. It was a walk that I immediately recognized, but how could that be? The figure was still too far away to see who was walking towards me, so I couldn't be sure. As the figure drew closer, he spoke. "Hello, my old friend, it has been a long time. I have missed you." In an instant, I knew that voice. It really was him. I couldn't believe it! It was the man who I dare say literally saved me from my own self-destruction. He was one of the two people to whom I bared it all, who I told of a troubling past that was humiliating, embarrassing, and excruciatingly difficult to admit to, no less talk about. I felt ashamed about my past and quite frankly my subconscious mind wouldn't allow me to remember my past. That was me protecting myself from my past so I could survive. That is until that one fall evening, walking down the street in Old Port, Maine, when the memories of my childhood came flooding back to me. As John Williamson approached me, he put his hands on my shoulders in that fatherly way of his. I told him that I missed him too. Without thinking I blurted out, "You left too soon!" John could hear both the anger and hurt I still felt. John being John replied in his trademark non-confrontational way, "Paige, it wasn't by choice." I knew he was right and told him so. As we were talking, the fog engulfed us and the serene surroundings were no longer visible. I looked at John and said, "If I am standing here talking to you then I guess that was me who flat-lined." Again, without thinking I added, "Guess I should have worn my helmet." in the smart-ass way I was known for. John, rolling his eyes as usual, replied, "Turn around and take a look." As I turned around, an area of fog exposed a hospital room. There, I saw myself lying on a bed hooked up to all types of machines doing different things and making strange sounds. Once again in my smartass way, I said, "You know John, tubes and monitors are not the look I was going for." Once again rolling his eyes he responded, "Keep watching smartass." I chuckled because I knew he loved my smartass replies. John also knew being a smartass was a way for me to deal with the trauma in my life. I turned and looked again. I stared with confusion and shock which caused me to ask John, "Is that Mike standing over me? How can that be? I saw him get hit first." There is no way he could be standing there. I watched as Mike held me in his arms and kissed the side of my neck for what was going to become the last time. A bright light appeared. A light as pure and white as freshly fallen snow, yet it had a warm hue that wasn't blinding. I didn't realize I had said out loud, "What is that light?" until John replied, "It is Mike's time to go into the light." I told John he deserves to be at peace. I don't and I sure as hell didn't deserve Mike either. Our conversation began with John's statement.

"I see you are still blaming yourself."

" It was all my fault." was the only way I could reply. It was true. I did blame myself.

"Paige that isn't true, you know better," replied John.

Even though I never came out and said it, John knew I always blamed myself. For the first time, I finally said aloud what I had never said before.

" You were there! You know I fucked everything up. All I had to do was say one little word and none of it would have happened. I drove Tony away. My son never had a chance because I was a total fuck up! Protecting my boy was my job and I failed him. I should have…" I couldn't finish. I choked up so bad. There it was, the thing John had tried to get me to say so many years ago. He tried to get me to say how I really felt about what happened, but I never said it. Not to him anyway. With my head hung low and feeling ashamed of my failures, John again placed his hands on my shoulders and in his calm voice said,

"You failed no one. You were still a kid. It wasn't your fault." I tilted my head up, so we were both face to face and eye to eye and asked, "Have you forgotten the mess I created and brought into your life?"

In turn, John replied, "Have you forgotten the purpose and meaning you and Tony brought back to my life?

I didn't understand what he meant till he continued, "Paige, you have to understand, I was lost without my Alice. My daughter blamed me for her mother's death, and we became estranged. Helping you gave me purpose again. You and Tony made me feel like I once again had a family." John always felt like a dad to me, and I guess that is why I never really told him how I felt about what happened. I didn't want to disappoint my dad. As many times as John told me not to bottle things up, I kept that bottled up. I always felt like I let him down even though he said that I didn't I still felt that way. I couldn't help but ask,

"If I was so innocent and great, why didn't I just walk into the light with Mike? Why am I stuck here? Why didn't Mike come and get me?" I wanted Mike to come get me. I didn't want to lose him too. John told me that my time with Mike was over. "What are you talking about? Why do I keep losing the people I love?" These were my questions to him, and I wanted answers.

2

John removed his hands from my shoulders, took a step back, and then started to tell me, Mike and I were meant to be together to help fill the void in our lives we both had. We were guided to one another so we could complete our Earth-bound Journey. He said, "You needed to feel love and happiness. You both needed to raise your vibrations. Mike has reached that higher vibration. His soul is now free to follow the plan the creators of the Universe have for him." I told John I did find love with Mike, and he did bring happiness to my life. Which is why I don't understand the reason for being stuck here. John took a moment before answering. Maybe he was trying to find the words to say. "You are right. You felt love and happiness again with Mike. But there is something you still need to do. The powers that be know only I can take you down the path of your final journey. It is time you stop taking the blame, you need to forgive yourself. No one in the light blames you. We are going to travel back to the time and place where it all started. Do you remember?" Remembering hurt but I did say "Yes John, I do remember. How could I forget?" I told him how I remembered that Labor Day weekend back in 1986. It was my freshman year at Mercy College. I had just moved into the dorm the day before and met my roommate Josh for the first time. I remember how Josh introduced himself to me. He walked up to me and stuck out his hand so we could shake. As we were shaking hands, he introduced himself by saying, "Hi. I am Ben. My last name is Dover as in Bend Over." I released our handshake and thought, WOW, this guy is an asshole. I wasn't wrong. Before I could introduce myself, he said, "At least I didn't say I was Pat McGroin." He then told me about the opening weekend and as Josh put it, "The unofficial and unsanctioned cookout and mixer" between the two colleges, Mercy and State. That was Josh's code for a keg party. That was the day I met Tony. John once again placed his hands on my shoulders, this time it was to turn me around. When he did, I saw the place where it all started. Sandy Point Beach. Sandy Point was a small pond that was an equal distance from the two colleges. The colleges were so close to one another that it wasn't uncommon to have cross-over parties. As I stood there, I lost all physical feeling. I couldn't feel John's hands on my shoulders. I thought he let go of my shoulders. I turned around to talk to him and he wasn't there. I called out to him asking where he was. "I am right here by your side," he replied. I didn't know why I couldn't see him anymore. The fog hadn't thickened at all. I called out "Why can't I see you?" he answered, "You can't see me for the same reason you can no longer see yourself." I looked, and holy shit! He was right! My body was gone. How could that be? John continued "Paige, your higher consciousness, your spiritual self will remain here watching from above. My higher consciousness will be here with you. Your physical self is eighteen again. Your physical self has no memory of the past and will relive that time period as it happened." I was scared. I didn't want to do this. I was so scared of what I was going to see that I shouted at John, "Why are you doing this to me? I already know what happened. I didn't need to see it again." I didn't mean for that to be a question. I meant it as, "Hey! Fuck you pal! I am outta here!" John replied, knowing I had no choice in the matter, "Yes, you do know what happened. Now it is time for you to know the reality of what happened and why it wasn't your fault. Your final journey begins now." Just like that, my higher consciousness could not turn away from what I was about to see. It was like my mind was frozen and my eyes were stuck wide open. I had no choice but to watch.

Chapter 2

1

There was eighteen-year-old me sitting at the picnic table, thinking maybe Josh wasn't so bad after all. He told me about this cool party at Sandy Point Beach and what a great time it would be. I did admit to myself that maybe I was wrong about Josh. Maybe he wasn't an asshole after all. A few months later, I found out I was completely wrong. The dude was a complete and total peckerhead. I looked around because a few of the other freshmen I met the day before at orientation were going to be there. I noticed how cool this place was. It wasn't huge and didn't have very many picnic tables, but there was room to spread out on beach blankets and I noticed that is what Josh had done. He was about twenty feet or so behind me hanging with a couple of girls. One I recognized as his girlfriend Patty, who he introduced me to earlier that morning. I was surprised he didn't make some corny joke about her name like Josh did when he introduced himself to me for the first time. Then there was this cute blond with them I hadn't met yet. She had a pretty face and from what I could see she filled out her bikini top quite well. She had turned her head away from me, in fact, all three of them had turned their heads to look at something by the parking lot. They didn't see me looking over at them. I turned and looked out at the pond. It was a nice-sized pond. There was a swim raft about a hundred feet out. There wasn't a lot of activity on the pond which was odd since it was the last weekend of the summer, but then again, there were not many cabins on the pond either. When I looked forward, I saw a very tall Black man looking in my direction. He had to be at least six foot four. You could tell just by looking at him he was very fit and his tight-fitting tee shirt showed off his muscular chest and broad shoulders. Not to mention the jeans he was wearing left little to the imagination. I couldn't believe what I was seeing. He was the most beautiful man I had ever seen; I was awe-struck by the sight of him. Like most of my friends, I had dated and liked a bunch of girls in high school. I had my share of getting laid too. Unlike my friends, I never really understood why they got upset if they broke up with their girl or claimed to be in love. I liked the girls I dated and liked it even more when I got to fuck them. My first blow job was off the charts. Let's just say the girl who gave me several of those took it all the way to completion. But it never really bothered me when we broke up. Seeing this man was a different feeling. Of course, being a teenager, I didn't realize it right then, but I did shortly after. It was love at first sight. Then it hit like a ton of bricks. DUDE! Why are you thinking this? NOT GAY DUDE! NOT MOTHER FUCKING GAY! No sooner did I think that he started walking over to me. I thought, great he saw me staring and now is going to come over and kick my ass. I told myself to just be cool and act normal. It's cool, just tell him sorry. I was watching the guy trying to tap the keg behind you. The guy tapping the keg looked like he was already stoned out of his mind; it was hilarious watching him. But I was more interested in who was walking towards me. As he got closer, I noticed how dark his skin was. Being from the city I was used to being around Black people. I even dated a Black girl in my tenth-grade chemistry class. However, I never saw anyone as dark as he was. I found his skin beautiful. He was so black it looked like there was blue in his skin. He was smooth and his skin had a shine to it. I noticed I was starting to get a stirring in my pants. How can that be? I am not gay–I like girls. There was no way I could stand up and walk away now. He approached me, and to my surprise, he was very friendly. He greeted me with a smile and said, "Hello, I have not seen you around here before are you a freshman at University?" I noticed his deep African accent right away. How could you miss it? I told him that no, I am a freshman at Mercy College and asked if this was his first year too. He said he was a Junior at State University. I told him it was nice to meet him and introduced myself as Paige Turner. Even though my thoughts shifted, I still didn't think it was a good idea to stand up. But I did at least offer up my right hand to shake with him. His grip was firm but not overpowering and there was a gentleness to those large hands of his. I found his handshake and greeting to be warm and sincere. He said it was nice to meet me too then told me his name was Antonin Kofi Bedru Adama. I am usually relaxed around new people. I wasn't afraid or intimidated by him, no, it was something else I couldn't figure out. I was at a loss for words and didn't know what else to say besides, "That was one heck of a first name." My response didn't seem to faze him. He proudly told me that he has three first names, as you call them, and one surname. He wanted to know if I had just one first name. I told him my first name was Andrew, but everyone calls me Paige. That piqued his curiosity, and he asked why I'm called Paige if my first name is Andrew. I explained that I was named after my father, so instead of "Junior" or "Little Andy" everyone calls me Paige. I like being called Paige, so it worked. He said to me, "It is my family's tradition to call people by all their first names. I shall call you Andrew Paige." That made me laugh because when anyone called me by all my names it usually meant I was in deep shit with the 'rents. I told him what I was thinking. I could tell by the look on his face he didn't get what I meant. So I told him that whenever I heard a screeching shrill, which was like listening to nails on a chalkboard, "ANDREW PAIGE TURNER!" I knew I was in deep shit. I explained what deep shit was and who the rents were. While I was explaining this, he took a seat on the other side of the picnic table. I was glad he did. He seemed cool and laid back. I also figured out what I was feeling; I felt like I already knew him. It felt like we were old friends, yet we just met. I wanted to know more about him, so I asked where he was from in that smart-ass way of mine. "Besides Alabama, where is it customary to call someone by all their first names?" He told me he was from Africa and was here with his family who worked as part of an entourage for the dignitaries of the African Government that are on assignment at the United Nations in New York. He told me about all the hostilities in Africa and that he was relieved to be here in America. I said it didn't sound like a rad place to live. He gave me a puzzled look as if he didn't know what I meant. I guess he wasn't up on slang terms. He told me about the cabin he rents and how he loves it there. He told me how safe he feels living there, how he loves being in the US and prays that he never has to return to Africa. Just as he said that the guy tapping the keg shouted out. "It's in the hole! I got it in the hole!" From behind me, the blond girl who was with Josh and Patty shouted, "If you could do that with your girlfriend you might finally get laid." Which I thought was funny as hell. But Antonin Kofi Bedru–I don't think got it. He gave her a dirty look, but she didn't notice. I said to him, "Hey, looks like he finally got the keg tapped. Want to grab a couple of brewskies?" "Brewskies? What is a brewskie?" he asked with that puzzled look of his. Jokingly I thought to myself. *There we have it folks! It's confirmed. He isn't up on his slang.* I smiled and asked if he wanted to grab a couple of beers. He declined saying he did not drink alcohol. He offered me a bottled water he had in the ice cooler in his car. I replied, "Yeah, a bottle of granny juice sounds good to me." He looked at me and said, "Granny Juice? Wait now I get it!" He headed over to his car.

2

Just as Antonin left, Josh shouted over, "Hey Roomie, come over and party with us. I am rolling a fatty." I quickly shouted back, "Sorry dude not into it." I tried the stuff one time and just never really got what was so great about it. Same with drinking; I just didn't get what was so great about being drunk. But those three loved their weed. I overheard the blond say to Patty, "Who's that? He's hot." Patty told her I was Josh's new roommate this year. The blond told Patty she was shocked that Josh got stuck with a freshman who didn't get high. She told Patty she would fix that and said. "I will get him away from creepy jungle boy and get him to come party with us." Patty wanted to know how she was going to do that. She told Patty that she was going to offer me what all guys want, her pussy. The blond girl didn't think I could hear her, but I did, and she came over and introduced herself. I had my back to her when she walked up behind me. "Hi, I am Michele." Before I could turn my head, she started rubbing my shoulders and running her hands up and down my back. She wrapped her arms around my midsection and worked her way down to my crotch. By this time, I could stand again. She was a bit disappointed when she felt nothing going on down there after all her rubbing and fondling. I asked her what she was doing. She asked me to come and party with them, and she suggested that after a few hits of that nice fatty Josh is rolling we could go have our own little party. I gently removed her hands and said, "Thanks, but I am going to have to take a pass on that." Michele sat down on the bench next to me with her back against the table sitting the opposite way I was sitting. Michele was the type that didn't need makeup she just had a symmetry to her face that makeup would ruin. Being a natural blond went a long way in adding to her looks. Michele wasn't skinny nor was she overweight, but she did have a nice shape to her body that complimented her D-cup breasts. She reached over again and started rubbing my crotch noticing she still wasn't getting anywhere and asked. "What's the matter, don't like girls?" Normally I would have quickly risen to the occasion but with her, I couldn't even if I tried. There was something about her that just turned me off. I could see she couldn't take a hint. I told her that I liked girls just not what she was doing. It was bogus and I didn't even know her. Still, she didn't take the hint and tried a third time. "Ok fine, you can take me to dinner and stuff first." She giggled, thinking it would turn me on. It didn't. After the third rejection and being told I was hanging with my friend, her tone and conversation changed instantly. Michele got nasty and said, "You mean that guy you're talking to? He is like totally scary. Even his name terrifies me." I asked, "Scary? Terrifying? What do you mean?" Michele started telling me that Antonin was in one of her classes. She said he always sits up straight and just stares at the professor as he moves around the room during his lecture. It's as if he stalks him with his stare. She said he never speaks or laughs just has that creepy stare, and the only time he speaks is if the professor asks him something directly. She finished her short rant with, "And that accent is terrifying." I never liked it when people verbally attacked someone behind their back like that. I never knew how to reply to personal attacks. I didn't know how to reply to her except to say he seemed cool to me. Which was true. I didn't get any of what she was talking about, and he did seem cool to me. "No!" she proclaimed. "I mean it, the dude is scary! Total serial killer vibe." Now that I knew what to expect from Michele and her attitude toward Antonin there was no way I could take her seriously. I wanted her to leave so I gave her an attitude back. "Yeah, now that you mention it, I totally get that stalker serial killer vibe. NOT!" Maybe she thought I would believe her if she insisted, "NO! I mean he is horrifying. He scares me and totally grosses me out. Like pass the barf bag!" "Not even" was my reply. I just wasn't having any of it. Looking confused she asked, "Not even?" I told her "Yeah, not even going to have this conversation." Not only did Michele not like this reply she got nastier. "He needs to bag his face! He totally barfs me out!" At this point, I had about enough of this conversation and quite frankly had enough of her. "Time for you to bounce." is what I told her which pissed her off. She got up from the picnic table and was pissed. In what I came to know as her vile and mean-spirited way, she said, "If he goes all Freddy Krueger on you don't come crying to me!" Michele stormed back to where she was sitting with Josh and Patty. She didn't bother sitting back down she just ranted about what just happened. "I am going get him for that! I am going to get both of them!" Is how Michele began. By this time both Josh and Patty were baked off their asses. They just looked at Michele with that blank stoner stare and asked, "What did Paige do?" Josh and Patty were so high they couldn't help themselves and started laughing. That set Michele off even more. She became furious and with a bit more rage in her voice told them, "NOBODY blows me off like that

NOBODY!" She slammed her closed fist on her thighs and got red in the face with anger. I am not sure what Michele was expecting from her stoned friends but both of them just kept laughing. Josh told her to chill out, he has to room with me and offered her a hit off the joint they were smoking. Just when I thought Michele couldn't get any angrier, she screamed. "FUCK YOU! Just wait! I will get them and don't you ruin it for me either!" With that, Michele stormed off to the parking lot. Both Josh and Patty were really confused. I heard Josh ask Patty what was with her. He said to Patty, "One minute it was the Michele we grew up with and the next minute she is all psycho bitch." Patty had no idea what was going on with Michele. Josh started packing their stuff up claiming Michele was their ride and she was leaving without them. Off they went running after Michele. This was good because now Josh wouldn't expect me to give him a ride. I wanted to stay and talk more with Antonin. I didn't want them around while we were talking. I don't think Michele knew I could hear her rant, but I did—loud and clear. I didn't take it as a warning like I should have. I just figured she would blow off some steam and eventually, Josh would get her baked and she would forget about the whole thing. That was a huge mistake on my part.

3

I had my head turned watching Josh and Patty gather up their beach blanket as Antonin sat back down and placed one of the bottled waters down in front of me. He asked me who I was talking to and was wondering if she left because of him. I turned around to face him and said no, she didn't leave because of him. I just told him that she came over to say "Hi", but I think she is already shit-faced. I hoped he didn't hear or see her tantrum. I just didn't want to tell him what she said. It wasn't right and I didn't want to upset him. "Shit faced? I do not understand." He asked curiously. I told him she had too much to drink. I smiled and laughed because there was such an expression of confusion on his face that I couldn't see how anyone could find him terrifying. I just thought it gave authenticity to who he was and his character. Unlike Josh, Patty and Michele who seemed fake and phony from the get-go. That is one of the things I find so attractive about him. There I go again. Why am I having these thoughts? Not gay dude! I was starting to get that feeling in my pants again. Lucky for me a couple of Harley's went rumbling by and provided a distraction. "Dude check out those Hogs! BITCHIN!" I exclaimed as the motorcycles passed by. I could tell right away he liked that I was checking out the bikes as they passed. "You like motorbikes?" he asked with a bit of excitement in his voice. "Dude, I love Harley's. There's nothing like the rumble of a big ole hog coming down the road." I said this while pretending I was riding a motorcycle trying to look cool. I could see Antonin was getting a little bit more relaxed talking with me. At first, he was a little standoffish, guarded, and even cautious when talking with me. Even more so after he saw me talking to Michele. Since nobody ever tried to talk to him or make friends with him there was no way anyone could have known about the motorcycles he had. He started to open up a little bit. "I love motorbikes. I have two." At this point, I was like, "No way! Don't psych me out! You got a couple of hogs?" He gave me a glimpse of his beautiful smile and said, "No psych out. I have two totally rad and bitchin' hogs. I love American slang." I could tell he was softening a bit which made me smile a little too. Being the cool rad teenager I was, I said, "Dude that is bitchin and fuckin "A" Awesomeness!" Antonin was a very laid-back guy and because of his upbringing he was very reserved, but I was starting to see that melt away. He finally met someone who wasn't afraid of him and liked motorcycles too. He said, "Come to my place. I will open the barn doors and show you, my hog." I totally wanted to check out his Harleys. I told him that was a bitchin' idea, and we should blow off the cookout and get motorin' back to his place. Off we went with me following him in my car. I was glad Josh told me about this party. Yeah, maybe Josh isn't so bad after all.

4

The fog closed over the portal view I had of the past and started swirling and clearing around me and I started to take my physical form again. Existing only as your consciousness with no body, just floating, was the most eerie and unnatural thing I have ever experienced. To have your awareness exist outside of your own body is a feeling and experience I cannot explain. I could feel John's presence the whole time. Neither one of us spoke. I don't know if we could have spoken even if we tried. How could we? Without a mouth, how could we communicate? I thought. John was taking physical form again too. Once he was whole again like I was, he said to me, "We communicate through a form of telepathy. Our thoughts are an energy we can project. You project that energy to the consciousness you want to communicate with. That consciousness will feel that energy and sound just as if the person who projected it was standing there talking out loud." I looked at John not realizing I telepathed that out loud. He looked back and smiled when he said, "Yeah Paige, you telepathed that out loud." We both laughed and he let me know that his hearing all my thoughts was temporary and existing only as a consciousness was temporary. Those were the tools he needed to help guide me through this journey. Then he got that look on his face he would get when he wanted to talk so, I got right down to business. I told him I was so excited about those Harleys that I forgot about meeting Michele that day. I never knew why she or anyone else for that matter hated Tony. They never knew how kind he was. They would have if they just talked to him or simply said "Hi". "You and I were the only two friends he made." John was right in saying that. Of course, Tony and I were more than just friends, so much more. Tony was so damn attractive physically and his personality was the icing on the cake. I knew this by the way he interacted with me and the surprised look he gave me when he found out I liked Harleys. Everything about him was real emotion. He was who he was, and I loved that about him. John gave me a moment and then reminded me that we had a long journey ahead of us. The fog once again engulfed us and within seconds we were both back to just consciousness looking through a portal in the fog at the physical past.

Chapter 3

1

The drive to the cabin took us around the basin of the big lake
to the four corners intersection. At first, I thought he was going
to take a left and head over to the little village where the State
College Campus was. Instead, he took a right turn and headed
up the western side of the big lake. The ride was beautiful. The
road leading up to the four corners had a heavy canopy from the
hardwoods that lined the sides of the road. This created a tunnel
effect that blocked the sun. I had to take my sunglasses off to
see, it was like driving at dusk. A few miles before Big Lake
Village, Antonin took a left at the fork in the road and then a
right onto an old country dirt road. We drove about a hundred
yards down this dirt road that was surrounded by forest. I could
see why he found it very peaceful here. There were just a few
mailboxes at the end of long driveways leading up to the
respective homes of those mailboxes. The area was very sparsely
populated, giving the homes on this road plenty of privacy. He
turned by the lone mailbox on the right side of the road, which
like the other homes, had a long driveway. We drove in about a
hundred feet where the driveway split. Antonin turned to the
right and the narrow drive led to the front of his cabin. There
was room enough for us to park side by side. As I got out of my
car, I could see just how picturesque and peaceful it was here at
the cabin and I could easily understand why Antonin never
wanted to go back to Africa. The setting was something you see

on those "Wish you were here" postcards my parents would send to family when they traveled to the mountains of Vermont for vacations. The cabin had a screened-in farmer's porch on the front with a stone chimney protruding from the center of the steeply sloped roof. Around the perimeter of the cabin were wild ferns and daylilies surrounding pathways that led around to the backside of the cabin where the firewood was stored and the bulkhead for the basement was. On the other side of the cabin was a large sun-filled area. It reminded me of the small field where I used to pick blueberries as a child when visiting Vermont. That area next to the cabin was filled with wild blueberry bushes. We both would be spending a lot of time the following summer picking those blueberries to put in our pancakes for breakfast. Not to mention the several containers we would fill and freeze for future use. I would eventually make Antonin a blueberry buckle which he never had before and would, from then on, insist I make it for him every week because he loved it so much. There were a lot of tall pine trees around with young hardwood saplings growing beneath them which added to the serenity of the landscape. As Antonin was getting out of his car, he said to me, "Andrew Paige, come inside with me. I need to get the key to the barn. I will make us something to eat since we left the cookout before the food was ready." That worked for me. I was hungry and was ready to put on a feedbag. As we entered through the screened porch, I noticed an old sofa propped against the wall. Antonin said it was his spot to sit and read or study in the evening. As I stepped through the front door, I saw the cabin had an open-concept living space. To my left was the dining table with an L-shaped kitchen running along the exterior wall and the wall that separated the kitchen and bedroom. To my right was the living room. Along the front wall was another sofa, much newer compared to the one on the front porch. The interior walls were tongue and groove board the old Mainers called "Pickwick pine". The white knotty pine the Pickwick was made from had yellowed with age, like pine does, making the feel of the room warm and cozy. The living room had a low pile carpet that complimented the vinyl floor in the kitchen. In the center of the room was a large stone fireplace and to the right in the corner was the television set which Antonin admitted he didn't use very often. The back of the stone fireplace was the interior wall to the bathroom which was accessed through the bedroom just off the kitchen. At first glance of the outside of the natural cedar shingled cabin, you would have thought it was a single-story cabin. I saw there was a small loft above the bedroom and bathroom with a set of library stairs next to the stone fireplace as you headed toward the bedroom. There wasn't a ton of headroom up there but enough so it could be used as a sleeping loft. Antonin told me to take a seat, so I sat at the head of the table while he walked over to the refrigerator and started to tell me what he had to heat up. He told me he had lasagna, manicotti, meatballs, sausage and peppers, and lots of fresh rolls. "I am going to take a wild guess here; you like Italian food." I said this with a bit of sarcasm which got a thumbs up from him. I could tell he was still a bit guarded with me though. He said that was his favorite part of Italy, all the food. He told me that most of his childhood was spent living in the consulates his country had in Rome and Milan. I was wowed by the fact he lived in Italy. I said to him. "Living in Italy, that must have been awesome." I also told him sausage and peppers on those fresh rolls sounded good too, I couldn't forget the bottomless pit of a stomach I had in those days. As Antonin was heating the food on the stove he started telling me about life in the consulates. How sheltered of a life he and the other children had. They were not allowed to watch television, not allowed to listen to the radio nor were they allowed to read any newspapers or magazines. Their only exposure to the outside world was shown to them by their teachers. I guess maybe that was their parent's way of trying to protect them from the harsh realities going on in their home country. He brought the food over and as we ate he told me about the strict rules they had to follow. There were severe punishments when any of the children stepped out of line. One of the children was caught watching Italy's version of MTV on the TV in the common area which was only used for special movie nights. Otherwise, the children were only allowed to watch VHS tapes if they pertained to schoolwork. Not only was he flogged with a leather strap, but he was also confined to his quarters for an entire month. He was only allowed to come out for classes. He even had to have his meals alone. I tried to help him clear the dishes and clean up, but he insisted that I was the guest, and I was to sit and digest my meal. This was another custom I assumed, and didn't tread on that. As Antonin was cleaning up, he told me about the only time he spoke out of turn. He explained that in his culture it is considered rude if you are not paying attention to the person who is speaking to you. He told me one of his teachers said he was not paying attention. He said he made the mistake of saying, "No, I was paying attention." She took that as backtalk and slapped his mouth so hard that his lips bled. He bled on his white uniform shirt; the stain would not come out. He told me he had to wash tables in the cafeteria for an entire month to pay for a new shirt. That is in addition to the lashing on his backside with his father's belt when he found out. He was sitting back down when he told me about the violent clashes from the Apartheid resistance. There were brutal crackdowns with sectarian violence that caused thousands of deaths. Those who didn't perish in the resistance were sent to detention centers with horrid conditions that caused even more deaths. I could see he was starting to get upset and rightfully so. I chimed in with, "Well I can see why you like this place so much. It is totally rad." then added, "Where's the barn?" I was hoping that changing the subject would take his mind off of the difficult conversation we were having. It bothered me to see him get so sad. Luckily it did take his mind off things for the moment, anyway. Antonin told me the barn was just up the drive a bit more and his landlord's home was just up beyond that. He liked his landlord a lot. They quickly became friends right after Antonin moved in, which was good because of the way Michele and the others treated him. At least someone was kind to him. Antonin was sitting to my right. He scooted his chair a bit so he could look straight at me. He said, "Andrew Paige I have a serious question to ask you. Would you please give me an honest answer? I do not care what the answer is as long as it is honest."

I was a little confused at first. I didn't know what to think but I told him go ahead shoot, ask me your question. He did and he didn't beat around the bush either. He told me he knew the girl that I was talking with when he went to get the bottled water from his car. He wanted to know if I was part of Michele's group of friends. I told him I wasn't and then explained that Josh was my roommate, and I just met him yesterday and I only knew Patty because she was Josh's girlfriend. I told him that was the first time I ever talked to Michele so no, she wasn't a friend, and I wasn't interested in being her friend either. He seemed a bit more at ease when he asked, "So this isn't part of some cruel trick?" I said that I didn't understand what he meant by cruel trick. I truly didn't understand but I was starting to understand why he was so uneasy and guarded at first. I can't say I blame him either, I would have been the same way. I could sense the sadness coming back. Not like when he was talking about Africa, this time there was hurt in this sadness. He went on to tell me how he could hear Michele and her friends talking about him behind his back. They laughed at him and mocked him because he was different. I could see the hurt on his face and in his eyes when he said, "They think it is eerie the way I look at the professor during lectures. They call me creepy and say I am some sort of serial killer. They are cruel! I would never hurt anyone." I agreed with him that it was cruel. I added it was very childish on their part. He went on to say, "They don't understand that his culture was different and life in a consulate was different." Maybe they would understand if they just talked to him, but they chose to act like assholes instead. I assured Antonin that they were not my friends. I didn't know what else to say. He did ask what Michele and I talked about. I didn't want to upset him, nor did I want to lie so I just told him about Michele wanting me to get high with her and then go have sex. After what he told me I didn't want to make him feel any worse, so I just stopped right there. It wasn't a lie. That's what she wanted. He was curious as to why I didn't go with her. I still was careful when I answered him by saying that I like girls but took a pass on her because what she was doing was lame. I explained to

Antonin that I also told her I was hanging with you and it would have been rude to just blow you off. Still, he was curious to know more about my conversation with her. He did ask if that was all she said and added, "Please, it is OK. Just tell me if there was more." Reluctantly, I told him that she mentioned the whole serial killer thing. I also made sure I told him that I didn't believe her and that she needed to stop talking about you like that. When she wouldn't, I told her to bounce. I saw this made him feel better. He did ask why I didn't believe her and why I chose to stay and talk to him. I didn't know how else to put it, so I just went ahead and said it. I told him that Michele made me feel very uncomfortable. She gave me a bad vibe. I said to him that talking to him was different. I told him that I was comfortable talking to him. I continued to tell him how I got this weird, but a good type of weird feeling when I was around him. It felt like I already knew him; sort of like we were old friends. The vibe was good. "Yes Andrew Paige. I get what you mean. I felt that I already knew you too." He said this with a relieved look knowing now I wasn't part of Michele's group of friends. Of course, me being the smart ass I was said, "Come on, seriously. What are the odds of two serial killers hanging at the same party?" Antonin looked at me, smiled, and then started laughing saying, "Two serial killers. That is very funny." I was glad I made him smile and laugh. It was a genuine smile and the most beautiful smile I had ever seen. His whole face lit up and man he was hot! As soon as I thought that I had to remind myself that I am not gay, and neither is he. Earlier, when I got up to help Antonin with the dishes, he told me to sit back down, so I spun the chair around to sit facing Antonin, with the back of the chair up against the table. I had both my hands on top of the table. Antonin placed his hands on top of mine. At first, I thought that maybe this was one of those custom things like maybe this is how they show sincerity. When he did this, I got such a warm feeling. It felt amazing when he placed his hands on mine, I was starting to melt. He looked at me and said, "I have lived here for two years, and you are the only person who will talk to me. I am glad you talked to me". My heart skipped a beat looking into his eyes. Wow! He was just so incredibly beautiful! I kept melting until I could barely answer. "I am glad we talked too," came stuttering out of my mouth. He looked deep into my eyes and leaned a little closer when he said. "I am feeling a vibe right now" He started gently caressing my hands which drove me wild. "I am feeling it too," I said, as we both leaned forward and started kissing. I could feel my crotch trying to bust out of my zipper. We were locked in a deep passionate kiss. I had completely melted by this time and was mesmerized by him and what we were doing. He was exploring my mouth with his tongue rubbing my hands and forearms. I just couldn't help but submit myself to that moment. We interlocked our fingers and finally pulled back from our kiss. With our fingers still interlocked we both rose from our seats. I couldn't help but notice his crotch was bulging hard against his zipper and I was bulging hard against my own. This time I wanted him to see it. We started kissing again. I explored his mouth with my tongue and he released his right hand so he could gently caress what was going on in my pants. This caused my knees to buckle enough that I had to use my free hand to balance myself on the table. We released from our lip lock and Antonin started guiding me towards the bedroom. The only thing I noticed in the bedroom was the huge king-sized bed he led me to. I didn't take the rest of the room in, my eyes and my mind were busy elsewhere. We stopped at the side of the bed. He unbuttoned his blue jeans and unzipped his fly exposing what was pushing so hard against his zipper. I started to laugh; he asked me what was so funny. I asked, "Is this what you meant by opening the barn doors to show me your hog?" He shook his head and rolled his eyes at me. I watched him take his shirt off. It was like staring at a statue of a Greek God carved out of onyx instead of white granite. His pecs and washboard abs were perfectly formed and well defined. I couldn't help myself. I just had to rub his chest and feel his abs, it was like rubbing a statue. He let me run my hands down to the thing that caused the bulge in his pants. It was so round and firm and it just felt so good to touch him like that. I fondled his danglers with my other hand causing him to moan with pleasure. He reached down and unbuttoned and unzipped my blue jeans. I immediately thought to myself, he is opening my barn doors and checking out my hog. He slid his hands inside my jeans so he could slide them off me. As he did, his hands moved to my ass, and he started to gently massage my globes. I wasn't nearly the chiseled piece of stone he was but in pretty good shape in my own right. He slid his hands back to my waist and started to explore my torso while removing my tee shirt. I had to let go of him so he could finish removing my shirt. With my shirt removed and tossed to the floor, Antonin got on the bed and was kneeling. I followed suit and immediately took hold of his member and started caressing his danglers again. Antonin was quick to return the favor. He leaned in and tilted his head a bit. I thought he wanted to start kissing again, instead, he started kissing the side of my neck. Between his fondling of me and the sensation I got from his mouth on my neck, I moaned loudly and gasped, "OH GOD! That feels good!" I didn't care if he left marks, I didn't want him to stop. I leaned in and I started to do the same to him which caused a very audible moan. I was so turned on by his moan of pleasure I started sucking on his neck harder. In turn, he started sucking on my neck harder too, which I knew was going to leave marks. Thankfully, all the marks were just below the shirtline enough that no one would see them. He started to lay back on the bed pulling me down on top of him and holding me tight. Once again, we explored each other's mouths with our tongues. He wrapped his legs around me reaching down and taking hold of me. He gently and slowly guided me inside of him. The feeling was so intense I was clutching the bed sheets and tensing my body so I would last as long as I could. Once I was in, he held me tight, our lips locked and our hips started to rock back and forth. It wasn't long before I was thrusting faster and faster inside him. I was clutching the bed sheets even harder now–I wanted this to last. I went on for as long as I could, thrusting my tongue in his mouth and my rock-hard manhood into him. I couldn't hold back any longer. In the heat and passion of it all, I exclaimed, "Oh God I am going to cum!" and started to pull out. He quickly grabbed my ass and pulled me deep inside gasping "Keep fucking me I am cumming too!" I could feel him spraying his sex juice onto our torsos. Feeling his hot liquid hit me caused me to lose control. I started filling him with my sex juice. As many times as I have gotten off inside my old high school girlfriends, it was nothing compared to this. The orgasms I had with women provided a nice feeling between my legs and was limited to between my legs. The orgasm I was having with Antonin was vastly different and exceeded all other orgasms in the past. My whole body was shuddering with every thrust as I pumped my sex juice inside him. I didn't think it was ever going to stop nor did I want this whole-body experience to stop. I know it was just as intense for Antonin, our orgasms were in sync. He was matching me nut for nut, shudder for shudder, moan for moan. The intensity was from deep within our souls. When it was finally over, he put one hand on my ass holding me inside of him as he pulled me down on top of him with his other hand. Our lips locked together for the deepest, most passionate kiss I have ever experienced. I finally rolled off him and laid on my right side so I could nestle my head on his shoulder. I slid my leg in between his legs and we both reached up with our free hands and interlocked our fingers together. We lay with our legs intertwined. He was holding me close with the arm connected to the shoulder I was resting my head on and the fingers of our free hands interlocked. Neither one of us spoke; nothing had to be said.

2

I lay there thinking to myself that as much as I liked having sex with my old girlfriends, it felt wrong at the same time. Things didn't feel right when we were having sex, and I always had a feeling of guilt when we were done. The fact that I never wore protection made pregnancy a looming possibility, and the social diseases I put myself at risk for added to the guilt. I also thought that maybe we were too inexperienced and that is why sex didn't feel right. That is until I did it with my best friend's mom. James Richardson and I had been best friends since first grade; we did everything together and you rarely saw us apart. We were like brothers. It was the night of our Junior Prom and as usual, James was running late. I would always tell him he was going to be late for his own funeral. I was in the living room talking with his mother Donna, who I always called Miss Richardson. Miss Richardson was thirty-three years old and looked like she was twenty-three with a smoking hot body to match. Miss Richardson was the first female and youngest President of First Bank. Miss Richardson was just seventeen when James was born. She was a single teen mom who got a job as a teller right after her high school graduation and put herself through night school to get her degree. She quickly worked her way up the ladder at First Bank. It was Miss Richardson who noticed I had broken the zipper on the pants of my rented tuxedo and offered to fix the zipper for me. She said the zipper could be fixed without me having to take my pants off. I was a little embarrassed at first, but we were running late so I said sure, go ahead. She took me down to the finished basement where the laundry room and mending supplies were. As she was adjusting and fixing the metal zipper on my pants she kept brushing the back of her hand against me. Of course, being just shy of turning seventeen and having a hot woman at my crotch, it didn't take much for things to get stirred up down there. This was something Miss Richardson noticed right away. She wasn't shy about helping herself. She unbuttoned my pants, slid both my pants and underpants to my knees, and quickly went to town on me with her mouth. When we finished, we promised one another never to tell James. She said it was just an "in the heat of the moment" thing that wouldn't happen again. Needless to say, it was shortly after prom she and I had an affair that lasted all summer. She went places on me and did things to me that no high school girl would ever think of. The summer of 1985 was the summer I wanted to marry my best friend's mom. Just before our senior year in high school began, James came home and found us naked in bed just after we had finished fooling around. Neither one of us heard him come home. Talk about being pissed! The dude lost it, and I can't say I blame him. James didn't want to be friends anymore and in turn, he stopped speaking to me. He would avoid me at all costs. His mom had to buy him a brand-new Mustang GT just so he wouldn't tell anyone. At graduation, James walked up to me and said he forgave me for the affair I had with his mom, but we couldn't be friends anymore. I guess I was Ok with that. I still miss my best friend, but I don't blame him at all. My parents never found out about the affair of 1985 but then again, my parents never knew I had a best friend. My parents knew very little about me but that is a story for another day. I wasn't happy that we got caught and things ended. I did love Donna Richardson, and I was okay with becoming my best friend's stepdad. I loved the things she was doing to me sexually and I was even trying to get her pregnant. Yet things still felt wrong. The sex was mind-blowing, but still, there was a feeling that something was missing. The guilt was still there but I couldn't figure it out. Then Antonin came along and I now know what the feeling was that I had at the pond when I first laid eyes on him. It was the feeling of falling in love at first sight. For some strange reason, I knew he experienced the same thing. It was the vibe we were giving one another. I could feel his vibe and I knew he could feel mine. We were soulmates and our connection ran deep. We didn't have to say anything we could just feel one another's souls. Lying there with Antonin there were no feelings of guilt. Everything was as right as it could be. That missing puzzle piece was found, and it was the man lying next to me. I knew I was lying next to the one person I wanted to share my life with, the person I wanted to have a home with, and the person I wanted to grow old with. I knew this because of Donna Richardson. I knew the difference between being in lust and being in love. After a while, Antonin released our fingers and reached down to get me going again which he had no trouble doing. He pulled me on top of him and started kissing me while guiding me back in for more of the same. There were times I spent exploring places on his body with my mouth and doing the things that Mrs. Richardson had done to me the summer before. Antonin wasn't shy about doing the same to me. That is how we spent the rest of the weekend. We would get out of bed long enough to shower together and maybe grab a quick bite to eat when we got hungry. Other than that, we spent the three-day Labor Day holiday weekend in his bedroom.

Chapter 4

1

When Tuesday morning rolled around, I knew I had to leave and head back to campus. My first class started at ten that morning. We were up early, and Antonin made us a nice breakfast. He was a little on the quiet side that morning which made me wonder if something was wrong. While we were finishing our coffee, I told him I couldn't believe we spent the entire weekend in bed the way we did. He smiled and said he couldn't believe it either. He also admitted that was the first time he had ever been with anyone, which came as a shock to me because of how good he was in bed. He wasn't saying much, and I was beginning to think he regretted what we did so I asked him if he liked it. As soon as I said that the thought of being gay started to creep in and I wasn't even close to being ready to deal with being gay. So, I quickly added, "I mean "like" as did you have fun?" Antonin said yes, he liked it very much. He nervously asked if I liked it too. I told him yeah that was fun. He said he had something to tell me and he wasn't sure how to say it. He nervously tried to tell me it was more than just the sex he liked. He loved the sex but that he was falling in love with me. Before he could get it all out, I got scared. Not of him though. I was scared of being in love with a man. I was scared of being gay and people finding out. I cut him off and said I had fun but not in a gay way. In two friends being goofy way. With that, I could see the disappointment and hurt on his face. I realized that was why he was so quiet, he was afraid to tell me he was falling in

34

love with me because of how I might react. I was screaming in my head, "You idiot don't fuck this up you fell in love too!" There was also a different voice screaming just as loud, "You fucking idiot what are you doing? You're no queer get out of there!" The internal struggle began along with the self-loathing which worsened with the event that was to come. Before I made things worse, I quickly changed the subject. "Hey Tony, let's go check out those Harleys before I got to get motorin' back to campus for my first class." He gave me an eyebrow-raising look and asked, "Tony?" I smiled and said, "Yeah, Tony, it's short for Antonin. You lived in Italy, and you love Italian food, it fits." The next thing I said was in my head and I wished I had said it out loud *because I am in love with you too*. I so wished I said that. He smiled, pointed to his face and said, "I even look Italian too". We both laughed! I was so glad to see that smile that I hugged him and started kissing him. I couldn't say it out loud, but I did mouth, "I am so in love with you" while kissing him. I was trying to drown out the inner voice that said, " I hate myself for loving you and being a little faggot." We broke our lip lock, but I still held him tight. I leaned in and kissed him again mouthing, "I love you Antonin Kofi Bedru." I don't know if he realized I was mouthing that while kissing him however he did hold me tighter when I did. After the second time we kissed Antonin, who I now call Tony, said, "Andrew Paige let's walk up to the barn and I will show you the motorbikes. " I told him I would like that. I meant it too. I truly did want to see and hear about his choppers. We headed up the dirt drive that led up to the barn which was about a hundred feet up from the cabin. The barn was hidden from the cabin by all the foliage on the young hardwood trees allowing the cabin plenty of privacy. The barn was located on the left side of the driveway where it forked to the right. This led up to Tony's landlord's house a few hundred feet further up on top of a small knoll. Tony opened the barn door leading the way to where the choppers were parked. I followed Tony over to the choppers and he began to tell me about them. He said this one is the one I like to ride. He said it reminded him of the motorbike Peter Fonda rode in Easy Rider which he said was his favorite movie and he has watched it several times since moving to Maine. He explained that there were claims that the Captain America motorbike was a 1952 Hydra Glyde which Peter Fonda himself modified for the movie. The other claim was that the Captain America was a 1962 FLH adding that they were both panheads. He told me his motorbike is a 1962 FLH panhead and it looked just like the chopper in Easy Rider less the paint job. Both his choppers had flat black paint on the gas tanks. The other chopper was a 1969 XLH Sportster shovelhead. He was telling me about the modifications he'd made and how he loved restoring them. We were so engrossed in conversation about the choppers that neither one of us heard his landlord approach until he spoke. Good morning, Antonin Kofi Bedru, I see you have a visitor. In turn, Tony responded with, "Good morning, John Williamson. This is Andrew Paige. Andrew Paige, I would like you to meet my landlord and friend John Williamson." John stuck out his hand to shake mine and said, "Good to meet you, Andrew." John and I shook hands with me replying that it was nice to meet him also and I told him everyone calls me Paige. Right away I could tell John was a very kind and compassionate man. He was very friendly and warm in his greeting. I later learned John was a widower and living alone in what was to be his and his wife's retirement home. Little did I know this was the man who was going to have a huge impact on my life over the decade to come. Tony couldn't wait to tell John that I loved motorbikes and we were going to go riding next weekend. That surprised me because he told me he wanted to show me the choppers. I didn't realize he wanted me to go riding with him, no less ride one of his custom-built choppers. If you know anything about Harley owners, you never lay a hand on their Harley without permission. It tends not to end well if you mess with their bike. Here he was telling John I would be riding his Harley. I was speechless! This was the coolest thing ever! John thought it was great that Tony had someone to go riding with. Even though I had a sense that John would be supportive of us, I had to get out of there right away. Panic and irrational thoughts were dominating my mind and I was getting trapped in my fear of being gay. My homophobia was taking over. I was thinking thoughts such as, is he going to ask what we were doing all weekend in the cabin? Why didn't we come outside? What would he do or how would he react if he found out we were having sex? Would he kick both of us off his property and leave Tony homeless cause we had sex together? OH GOD! I am fucking gay! I can't deal with this. I had to get out of here now. I still had well over an hour before I had to be back on campus for my first class but thought this was a good time to make my exit. I told them both, "I would love to stay and talk but I've got to get motorin' I don't want to be late for my first class." I was surprised I said that as calmly as I did. The panic was setting in and I was afraid it was going to show. I had to get out of there right away. "Andrew Paige, we will go riding next weekend." Tony said with that huge smile of his. "Good luck with your first class." John said he was glad I was coming back to go riding with Tony. He also said, "Any friend of Antonin Kofi Bedru is a friend of mine." He let me know I was welcome there anytime. There was no doubt about the sincerity in John's voice and the excitement in Tony's voice was undeniable. I was welcome even if Tony and I were gay but because of my fear, I was blind to it. I told Tony I would see him later, thanked John, stepped out of the barn, and headed for my car. As sincere as John was, I still harbored the thought of what would happen if he found out we were gay. Even though those thoughts were dominating my mind I felt safe here and in John's presence. There was something warm and welcoming not only about the property but with John too. Even though our encounter was very brief, John made me feel welcome. Both he and Tony gave me a sense of belonging– they wanted me around. As I got in my car, I took a moment to look around and take in my surroundings. I felt like I finally found a home. It was the first time in my life I had that sense of belonging, of feeling safe and feeling like I belonged. My entire childhood my family, not just my parents and my brother Jeff but my entire family, made me feel like an outcast. They made me feel like I didn't belong, I was a burden to them. I wasn't wanted, I didn't fit in. I was even told that by both my parents on more than one occasion. I had one Uncle in particular say and say often," Fuck Paige. Who does he think he is? He sure as hell is not one of us. Paige is a dickhead." His name was Nico, and he was from Greece. I would always think to myself hey Nico I am blood you're not so fuck off. But I would never say it out loud. If I did, I would have gotten beaten and beaten badly by my parents. The truly sad part is that my parents would always side with him not their own son. Here it was completely different.

2

Looking through the portal I watched myself walk away, but my focus remained on John and Tony still standing in the barn talking. As I watched I heard John say to Tony, "Well there is a side of you I have never seen before." "What do you mean?" Tony asked with a bit of confusion. John told Tony he was usually a bit more subdued, he tended to be a man of few words. Tony was smiling, he was happy and more talkative than usual. John said he liked this side of Tony. Tony dropped his head a bit but not out of shame. He had that huge smile that I loved and was a bit red-faced. You could tell he was blushing even though his dark skin tone hid it well. Tony shyly replied, "I like him a lot." Catching himself and trying to rephrase, he tried to say that what he meant was he liked that I like motorbikes too. John, with a big grin on his face, a slight touch of sarcasm in his voice, and his head nodding up and down, reached over and patted Tony on the upper arm as he said, "Oh is that what you mean by liking him?" Tony made a futile attempt at being surprised by John's remark by asking him, "What else would I mean?" John reassured Tony all was okay. He knew what we were doing in the cabin, and it wasn't talking motorcycles. John and his wife Alice were therapists who worked with men of all ages who were struggling with their sexuality in a time where being gay was not only forbidden, but you could expect a leper to be treated more humanely than a homosexual. Alice excelled at working with the men who turned to drugs and alcohol to deal with being gay. Self-medication was a way to seek relief from the pain and suffering brought on by a society that believed homosexuality was not only taboo, but some believed being homosexual was a form of demonic possession. Alice seemed to have a knack for dealing with people who had a chemical dependency that she discovered back in her college days. Alice helped a very close friend of hers. Alice's friend and I ended up having a few things in common. You could see the relief on Tony's face knowing John was okay with us and had no problem keeping our relationship under wraps. In fact, John even encouraged Tony to talk about it. He was sincerely happy for him. Tony told John the moment he saw me he got a feeling he could not explain. John told him that was love he was feeling. Tony replied he knew one day he would find love, but he always thought that his mother and father would find love for him. That was the way his parents and generations before him had done. Arranged marriages were part of his culture. John told Tony he did not doubt that his parents loved one another. John also told Tony what he experienced was more on the lines of true love which tends to have a magical quality to it if you will. Tony told John about how we met and how happy I made him but was worried I might not feel the same way. He couldn't help but wonder if I would come back or if this was just a one-time thing. John did assure Tony I would be back. John knew right away I was a scared and confused kid. Even though I was scared and confused he could tell just by the way I looked at Tony that I was crazy about him. John had a feeling I would be back.

3

As I left and headed back to the campus, the last of the good feelings quickly slipped away making way for the irrational thoughts and self-loathing to come flooding in. I had been gone since Saturday morning, I wasn't at any of the freshman socials or at the orientations that were planned for the long weekend. I hadn't slept in my dorm room since Friday night. How would I explain where I was to Josh or anyone else for that matter? I can't tell anyone about Tony or what we did. No one can find out I am gay. I kept thinking, why do I have to be gay? I don't want to be gay, I hate it. I even tried to convince myself on the ride back that what we did was just a mistake; I like girls. Hell, I even kept my best friend's mom satisfied for an entire summer. I am not gay. But I knew deep inside the truth and the truth was I have always known I was gay. I knew I was gay and wanted to come out when I was twelve. I didn't come out because in 1980, the AIDS epidemic swept across the world. My parents were convinced AIDS was God's way of cleansing the Earth of the freaks, misfits, and weirdo queers. Which is exactly how they put it. They were convinced if you were gay, you automatically had AIDS and died. Knowing what my parents thought of gay people was the reason I convinced myself I wasn't gay. The President of the United States of America, the highest office in the land, wouldn't address or even help fund research to find treatments or a cure for HIV. It was a gay disease, and he wasn't wasting taxpayer money on it. I was convinced that is how everyone thought of AIDS and gay people, even John. Everyone hated the gays. I didn't want my parents to hate me any more than they already did. I had sex with as many girls in high school as I could and even welcomed the affair I had with my best friend's mom so dad would be proud of me and love me. Coming out wasn't an option. The internal struggle was real; I hated being gay. I hated being in love with another man, I hated the world for hating the gays. I even started to hate myself on that ride back to the campus. I didn't hate Tony, I loved him and wanted to be with him, and I had no idea how to deal with it. I felt very alone in my struggle.

Chapter 5

1

The fifteen-minute ride back to the campus felt like an eternity and then some. I was realizing my true sexual identity, which I was still denying but I admitted to myself I was in love with Tony. This, coupled with the fact that I didn't want to return out of fear that my secret would come out, made for a long ride back. I was afraid of guys in my dorm ridiculing me. They wouldn't understand I wasn't gay. We were just having fun. What would they do if they found out I spent the weekend in bed with another guy? How would my roommate deal with it? I kept thinking about the hazing my high school's football team did to their star quarterback Ray Phinney when they found out he was gay. That happened my sophomore year and I will never forget that Monday morning coming back from Thanksgiving break. The football team tied Ray totally naked to the flagpole in front of the school. They even duct-taped a dildo in his mouth. There was no doubt they gave him a beat down with the number of bruises he had on his torso. One of his eyes was swollen shut from the beating. Rumor had it he would never see out of that eye again. He was bound with so much duct tape that the top layer of his skin started to peel off when they tried to undo the tape. The whole scene and aftermath were horrifying. I just couldn't get that image out of my head. I couldn't help but think that was going to be my fate too. I was freaking out and so scared I could see my hands starting to tremble and my knuckles turning white from the panic grip I had on the steering wheel.

When I finally passed through the main gate, I drove right to the parking lot of my dorm. I parked in the furthest spot I could find from the entrance. I was taking a stealth approach or at least in my mind I was being stealthy with my return hoping no one would see me. I quietly got out of my car and closed the door as if I was coming home past curfew and trying to sneak into my room before the 'rents caught me. I crossed the parking lot and went into the dorm heading straight for my room. I was glad to find the halls and common room empty. I unlocked the door to my dorm room went in and was very relieved to find the room empty. Josh was nowhere to be seen.

Our room was small, maybe twelve feet wide and fifteen feet long. It was just enough room for two single beds, two desks with chairs, and two dressers. We each had a tiny closet on each side of the door as you walked in. The walls were painted cinder blocks with a single window on the opposite side of the door. The room had that minimum security jail cell feel. I was able to change my clothes since I still had on the same clothes from Saturday and get my books ready for class. I was just about ready to leave and thinking, cool at least I have avoided Josh for now, when the doorknob rattled and Josh came stumbling in from wherever he was. I tried to like Josh but the best I could do was tolerate him. Josh was your typical 80's dude sporting a Mullet and parachute pants. He wore Izod shirts with the collar turned up and never wore socks with his Miami Vice shoes. I don't know how he functioned. He was stoned 24/7. No question about it, he loved his weed. He was the total opposite of me. I wore Levis and tee shirts. In the colder months, I wore flannel shirts and a black leather jacket. I hardly ever wore sneakers and the only reason I had a pair was because of high school gym class. I mostly wore work boots or cowboy boots which my friends called shit kickers. I did the peer pressure thing in high school; I tried pot and hated it. I really hated drinking but I gave that a try too. Having a father who constantly dealt with his poor life choices by telling everyone to "shut up and get him another glass of whiskey," wasn't a good incentive for me to even want to try alcohol. Watching him get drunk every night turned me off from drinking altogether. I always knew my father was nothing short of an alcoholic no matter what excuse my mother came up with to justify his drinking. Josh also had an arrogance and cocky attitude about him like he was the coolest thing since James Dean or Brando. Who knows, maybe he thought he was Fonzie from Happy Days. Compared to Josh, I was a more laid-back and do-my-own-thing type of guy. With the door to our room still wide open, Josh obnoxiously blurts out, "HEY ROOMIE! There you are. Have you been avoiding me all weekend?" I didn't know what to say nor did I have a cover story to tell him. I had nothing. The best I could do was give him a blank stare and say, "What are you talking about?" "Nothing, just busting your balls. So, tell me, how did it feel having the room all to yourself this weekend?" I had no idea what he was talking about but it sounded like I didn't have to come up with a cover story. "Didn't even know you were gone. Just busting your balls back. Where did you disappear to?" I said hoping that he really was gone all weekend, and I was in the clear with him. He told me that Patty's roommate dropped out at the last minute, so he just spent the weekend in her room. YES! I was off the hook, at least for the moment, with Josh. He did bring up the cookout and how I pissed off Michele. I told him I was sorry, and I wasn't trying to upset her but I was not into getting high. She was being cruel too, but I didn't say that part I just left it at that. Josh didn't side with Michele but did say he found Tony creepy too. I told Josh they were wrong about him and that he was a pretty cool guy. I didn't want to take the conversation any further. I told Josh I needed to get to class. Josh wanted to know more, asking what he was like. I said that he is a pretty cool guy. I briefly told him about the Harleys. Then I said I had to go because I was late for class. With that, I left. I sure as hell didn't want to talk anymore. Even though the common room and hallway were still empty, I did run into a few guys I had met when I first moved into the dorm, walking towards Mercy Hall where the classrooms were. Just about everything here was named Mercy. Mercy College, Mercy Hall, Mercy Administration building, Mercy Gymnasium, Mercy Library, and so on. It was Joey Flanigan who spotted me.

"Yo Paige! Dude! How's it hangin'!" This was Joey's trademark greeting with everyone. I said, "Hey guys what's shakin'?" to them. Joey was the one who replied "Dude, massive bake over from partying all weekend. Like I saw you take a few hits off the bong the other night. Great weed or what!" I could tell Joey had partied all weekend. He looked like a car wreck. I thought it must have been exceptionally good weed or maybe it was laced with something since Joey "saw" me at the party and I wasn't there or even on campus for that matter. But I was glad he said that because all the people I was afraid of having to explain my whereabouts to this weekend, were stoned off their asses or sleeping in their girlfriends' dorm rooms. I was completely off the hook for the time being. "Yeah dude, the weed was totally rad!" That came from Billy Rogers a rotund and asthmatic version of Josh. Joint in one hand, inhaler, just in case, in the other. I am willing to bet he was voted most likely to have a massive coronary by age thirty. Joey was a deadhead and liked getting baked, but he was a self-proclaimed weekend-only toker. You could always find him in tie-dye tee shirts and jeans or cut-offs, both were good guys. There were others I was acquainted with and hung out with from time to time on campus and for now, they were the only ones I ran into. I told them I would meet them for lunch and headed to my first class. My first class that day was a literature class. Dr. McCord was a Vietnam Vet who had us studying literature from that era. Some were poems, others were novels. All, I found interesting. I had three more classes that day then I was back to the dorm to get started on studying and kill some time before heading to the cafeteria for dinner.

2

I got back to my room and found Josh and Patty hanging out there. Right away I could tell both had recently smoked a joint; the bloodshot eyes were a dead giveaway. I didn't care if they were constantly baked as long as they didn't toke-up in the room. "SHIT!" Patty exclaimed, "I can't find my Visine." She was standing at Josh's desk rifling through her handbag. She looked up at me as I walked in. "Hey, thanks for pissing off Michele at

44

the cookout." I just gave her a fuck you look, put my books down, took a seat at my desk, and started reviewing today's class work. "No, really Paige thank you for doing that. Michele was so pissed with you that she refused to come here and hang out. She said she didn't want to run into you. Josh and I got to spend the weekend together, well I am sure you figured it out since you had the room to yourself this weekend." With a very noticeable eye roll, I told Patty I was glad to be of service. "I told you I had a wicked cool roommate this year. Last year I had a lame roommate," Josh said as he lay on his back on his bed. Patty replied sounding like one of those high school valley girl Wanna-Be's you see in comedy movies, "Like duh, totally lame and grody to the max, Josh and I swear Adam Ant made that song about him. OH! Look! I found my Visine!" I just shook my head at Patty. I couldn't help but think this was going to be a long year. Before anyone else could say anything, Michele strolled in. Growing up, Michele was Daddy's Little Princess, who always got her way and never outgrew it. Michele could be downright mean and ruthless when she didn't get her way. I would soon find that out, as Michele would show me a whole new meaning of cruelty. She didn't even acknowledge me when she entered, she just looked at Patty and asked if she and Josh wanted to go into town for some burgers. She was starved and she was buying. Josh jumped right up, he never refused free food especially when he had the munchies from being high. Josh asked if I wanted to tag along to this place they go to in town. He said it has fantabulous burgers. The three of them were standing together now with Michele just slightly out of Josh's view. As stoned as Patty was, she saw the look Michele was giving me. The look Michele was giving me could have stopped a freight train. There was no doubt about it; she was still pissed and it showed. I knew she didn't want me tagging along, so I thanked Josh for the invite but declined, mentioning I was going to hit the cafe here and then the campus library. I had a few topics I needed to research. I told Josh maybe next time. He didn't take the hint saying, "Paige Dude" which is what he called me, "We're just getting food and coming right back." Josh still had his back to Michele so he couldn't see how pissed she was that he said that. Both Patty and I could feel the tension rising in a big way. Just as Michele opened her mouth to say something I quickly cut her off with, "No Josh Dude, I can't. I already told Joey and Billy I would meet them in the cafe and then hit the library to work on some research." That was a total bullshit lie but it worked. Josh didn't ask a third time. The anger didn't leave Michele's face, I was still getting the evil eye. As Michele was walking out, she looked right at me and spouted off, "Fuck you, Paige." and added "Bite me asshole." all while flipping me off. Patty tossed the Visine to Josh and then followed right behind Michele. Patty was silent as she left. Josh put a few drops of the Visine in his eyes as if he was oblivious to what just happened. He said, "Look, Visine gets the red out, bet you can't tell I was toking. Later Paige dude." Out the door he went.

3

Patty and Michele were standing outside next to the building's exit door by the parking lot waiting for Josh to come out. Watching things unfold, I saw Patty stop and say to Michele, " I get it you're pissed with Paige and I am not saying you're wrong to be pissed." Michele snapped back telling Patty I had blown her off for that fucking Nig–Michele stopped herself before she finished saying the word that makes Patty's skin crawl. Patty tried her best o ignore the racial slur telling Michele she "gets it." She told Michele she didn't have to like me, and continued, "Hell, you can hate his guts if you want but please just be civil. Josh and I think Paige is cool." Both Patty and Josh knew I wasn't going to narc on them like Josh's last roommate did for smoking weed. That did nothing to ease any anger or resentment Michele had for me. There was a real snare to her tone when she said she would try to be civil. Michele's angry outbursts were starting to frighten Patty, but she knew something was wrong with Michele and was concerned for her friend who she had always looked up to. She asked Michele what was going on because she never heard her use the "N" word before. That wasn't like Michele. Michele gave Patty a nasty look and told Patty she wasn't hungry anymore and was leaving, using the excuse she had to study. With that Michele, filled with anger, marched over to her car with her hands balled into fists, yanked the car door open, and threw herself into the driver's seat, slamming the car door. She started the car then slammed the gear shift into drive and sped off. Josh came out of the dorm and saw Michele spin her tires as she drove off.

4

Patty and Josh were in Patty's room settling for some Ramen noodles instead of burgers since their ride took off. "Hey, what was with the Duke's of Hazard smoke show Michele did?" Josh asked as he was rubbing Patty's ass while she stood watching the hot pot come to a boil for their dorm room delicacy of instant noodles and Boones Farm Strawberry Wine. "Stop doing that. I don't want to burn myself," she told Josh as she poured the boiling water over their instant dinner. Josh asked what was wrong. He had never seen Michele this pissed before. He said she had a cow at the cookout and then took off tonight. He asked Patty if she was sure Michele wasn't mad because we were a thing now. It was Michele to whom Josh lost his virginity when they were in the ninth grade. Josh was Michele's first too. Even though they had random sex throughout high school, they never really clicked as a couple. Patty shrugged her shoulders and told Josh that Michele was still pissed, saying to Josh, "I mean psycho pissed, PMS to the max pissed at Paige for blowing her off." Josh knew Michele didn't want to go out with me or have a relationship she just wanted to get laid, so Josh was confused with the way Michele was acting. Patty agreed she didn't get it either. Josh asked Patty if he talked me into doing it with her, did she think that would help? Patty rolled her eyes at Josh thinking maybe she just needs to cool off a bit more, and it will all be fine." She turned and handed Josh a steaming bowl of noodles which they scoffed down quickly. Both always got a bad case of the munchies and cotton mouth after toking-up. They guzzled the bottle of wine before they got into bed giving me the room to myself for another night.

Chapter 6

1

The rest of the week was pretty much uneventful which was fine by me. All my professors were cool. I even thought Professor Pearlman, aka Attila the Nun, was pretty cool too, in her own way. Professor Pearlman was my professor for music appreciation. Being a liberal arts college there were required courses you had to take. The administration felt this was so we would have a "well-rounded" education. Professor Pearlman was very strict with her in-class rules and a stickler for details. She was known for being direct. She was not known to sugarcoat when she had to critique your work. She was called Attila the Nun not only because she was strict, but she used to be a nun and a teacher at an inner-city school in the Bronx. The story I was told is that she holds a black belt in Taekwondo. One day, a gang banger pulled a switchblade on her in class. Not only did she knock the switchblade across the room, but she knocked the dude out with a roundhouse kick to the side of his head. Her students there nicknamed her Attila the Nun, which she wore like a badge of honor. Shortly after that, she left the convent because she wanted to marry and have a family of her own. As tough as she was, I enjoyed her as a professor. She was a huge fan of Beethoven and would often talk about his music. In my very first class with her, she asked if I had ever listened to Beethoven's music. She was very surprised when I said I had, and the reason was that classical music had a huge influence on Rock and Roll. "Care to explain that Mr. Turner?" she said to me

48

snidely. Not knowing her reputation at the time, I said I would love to. I told her that Ritchie Blackmore of the band Deep Purple created the riff for "Smoke On The Water" by using an interpretation of inversion. Basically, he is playing Beethoven's Fifth backwards. I explained how Randy Rhodes would blow Ozzy Osbourne's mind when he would play classical music on his guitar incorporating it into mad licks and riffs for songs they were working on. I went on to tell her Randy Rhodes, Elton John, Stephen Tyler, and other rock artists are classically trained musicians and that their training holds an influence over the rock music they create. While I was explaining this, she was looking at me with her typical stern and cold face. When I finished, her cold look warmed with a smile and she said, "Well done Mr. Turner. I applaud you." which I think shocked the class. She then added a challenge which I was eager to accept. She wanted to debate with me about which had the biggest influence on all genres of music, Classical or the Blues. I had a month to prepare for the debate and I was to be graded. Not only did she and I have a lively debate, but she had the President of the College, the Director of the department, the Dean of the College, and the Dean of Students as judges. We debated back and forth for forty-five minutes, then the judges tallied the score. It was a dead tie! We both had strong and fact-based arguments. Professor Pearlman patted me on the back and told me, "Well done Mr. Turner, well done." I was glad the debate happened when it did because if the "event" happened to me before the debate, there would have been no way I would have had the courage to debate her. Not to mention having done it in front of the judges the way I did. Even though I maintained a 4.0 grade for that class, the event that happened rattled me to my core. Towards the end of the semester, Professor Pearlman sensed things were very off with me. She approached me and wanted to know if she could help. I was the only student who could see past her gruff exterior and knew just how kind and understanding she could be. She was right, I did need help but with what I was dealing with there was no way I was going to talk to a Catholic Nun even if she did leave the convent and wasn't a nun anymore. I could no longer

49

face anyone without help, in the end, I wish I had at least tried to talk with her and accept her help. I did accept help from two people. I accepted help from the first person but unfortunately, it was the wrong kind of help. Thankfully the second person I accepted help from was the right person and whose help I wished I had accepted the first time he offered.

2

Classes were done for the week, and it was Friday afternoon. I had the room to myself all week. Josh was sleeping in Patty's room. He would come back only to take a shower and change clothes. That first day of classes was the only day I had a late start. The rest of the week I ended up having early classes, so I was always up and gone when Josh came back to shower. The only reason I knew he had been there was because his fudged-stained fruit of the looms were always left on the floor next to his bed. I guess he never outgrew the skid mark thing. I was glad I had the room to myself. I didn't mind having a roommate but was a lot happier when he slept at Patty's, which was nearly every night. I took full advantage of being alone with my thoughts. Every night that week, I would lay in bed thinking about Tony. I couldn't get him off my mind. Just as I was lying back on my bed to read some of the poems that were assigned to us before I headed to the cafe for dinner, Billy and Joey came crashing through my door. "Paige you total spaziod! Way to start the semester by getting in a debate with Attila the Nun! That was grody to the max! Like were you trippin' or something." My rotund friend Billy said this over the groans from Josh's bed springs as he sat down. "No way Jose, that was radical." Paige made the ice queen smile. I heard that was the first time she ever smiled. She doesn't even smile after getting laid." Joey made me laugh when he said that. He was seated at my desk with his feet up and his hands behind his head. As I sat up, I asked, "Okay what do you two ass wipes want?" They told me they were headed to Peach's Variety for pizza and wanted to know if I wanted to tag along. Billy was buying. He bet Joey that I would cave when Attila asked me to explain, so it's loser buys the pizza. I told Joey "Yeah, I do want to tag along." Pizza sounded better than the barf bag delights the cafe had on the menu. "Hey, if Bulimic Billy is buying, I am in too," came from the hall as Kenny Jordan headed down to my room to tell me his dad has an encyclopedia dedicated to the history of the Blues. In his words, he wanted to see me smoke the bitch in our debate, so I could borrow it if I wanted. Kenny was pretty cool and funny as hell. He was from the Miami area and ended up transferring to USF after one winter in Maine. He found out quickly that he wasn't built for New England weather. "Cool man, let's all meet back here in an hour." Billy said, as he leaned over and raised an ass cheek, blowing out one of his infamous Billy farts which cleared the room. A Billy fart could gag an elephant. I had to hold my breath so I could open a window before making a B-line to the door. The stench followed us out into the hall. With that, the three of them left me to air out my room. This took close to an hour, which was when my friends were due to return. An hour and a half later, we were sitting in a booth at Peach's Variety, and they had just brought the pizza to our table. I loved the variety stores in Maine. Most had a small sandwich shop, griddles, and a pizza oven. They also had tables or booths so you could sit and eat if you didn't want take out. Peach's had one of the best thick-dough pizzas around. My other favorite pizza came from Big Lake Variety which I would be eating on a weekly basis in the coming months. Out of a clear blue sky, Billy says, and quite loudly too, "Now I get it! Calling me Bulimic Billy is like calling a tall guy Shorty." Billy tended to be a little slow on the uptake. With that, we all burst out laughing. The look on Billy's face was priceless. You could almost see the light bulb go on over his head. We had a lot of fun that night. We stayed there eating pizza and drinking sodas till the place closed at nine o'clock. The owner didn't mind at all because we kept ordering food and drinks and he found us entertaining. When the bill came, we ended up going Dutch. None of us had the heart to stick Billy with the bill since we ordered more food than expected. We didn't expect to be there for four hours either. The four of us had a great night. They were cool guys that I still think about now and then. Hanging out with them took my mind off

Tony for a while and my dilemma about going back to Tony's and of course, being gay. It was sad that both Billy and Joey didn't return after the Christmas break for the second semester of our freshman year. Joey wasn't afraid to party and, as he put it, "get all fucked up". I will give credit where credit is due, he never got behind the wheel of a car when he partied. That New Year's Eve was no exception. He was home for the Christmas break and was walking to a friend's house for a New Year's Eve party. He was crossing the street when a car barreled through the stop sign and hit Joey as he crossed. The driver took off and was never found. Lucky for Joey another car wasn't far behind and stopped to help. It was too bad that neither the driver that stopped to help nor Joey could identify the car or plates from the car that hit him. The Police figured the reason the other driver didn't stop was because whomever it was most likely was pretty fucked-up themselves. He did fully recover, but because the damage to his legs was so severe he had to be put in traction for six weeks. Joey had to learn to use his legs again, so his recovery took well over a year. Billy never really took care of himself, to begin with. Being an asthmatic, choosing to smoke weed wasn't the best choice to make. His obesity wasn't doing him any favors either. Even after suffering a few severe asthma attacks during the fall semester which required an ambulance ride to the E.R., Billy kept on toking like a fiend. I swear there were days he looked like a smokestack. The new semester started on the 19th of January. On the 12th of January, a week before the start of the new semester, Billy suffered another severe Asthma attack. The attack was so severe that Billy slipped into a coma which he never recovered from. Billy died a week later on the morning of January 19th the day he was supposed to begin the new semester. Kenny came back for the second semester, but we didn't hang out as much at that time. Things were very different for me and not in a good way. Kenny was the one who broke the news to me about Joey the day before classes began when we arrived back on campus. It was the Dean of Students who called Kenny and me to his office to tell us about Billy. It was first thing Tuesday morning before I had a chance to do more than shower. Kenny and I both came up with the idea of going to Peach's for pizza as a way to say our goodbyes to Billy. Peach's Variety had become our Wednesday night hang-out spot, and for Billy, it was more than that. Billy admitted one night this was the first time he had real friends. All through school he was known as the fat kid. He was always picked last in Gym class, made fun of in the cafeteria for the amount of food he would eat, and always sat alone. He told us he tried pot in high school thinking the cool kids (as he put it) would like him. "Hey, look at me guys! I am getting high just like you," was his reasoning behind that. It didn't work out too well for him, people still made fun of him. He did find the pot made him feel better and numb the hurt from all the bullying. The verbal assaults on his weight and the bullying were a daily occurrence, so the pot became a daily thing for him. Our time at Peach's meant the world to Billy along with our friendship. I speak for the three of us when I say Billy made the group that much better. It was also the last time Kenny and I hung out together as friends. Kenny and I didn't have a falling out, it was the situation I was in that caused us to drift apart just before he went back to Florida. Because Joey was still in traction from being hit by a car on New Year's Eve, we called his hospital room to give him the news. We wished him a speedy recovery and to get his ass back to campus, we miss him. We talked with him for a while and it was the last conversation I had with him. He was busy trying to recover and I had already slipped into a toxic oblivion which I hid well from most people.

3

I got back to my room around midnight after hanging out with the guys for a while. Despite having to deal with Michele, my first week of college was great. I had made three new friends and liked all my classes and professors. The best part was my worst fear didn't come true. As I sat on my bed to take my boots off, I had to laugh, there was still a lingering odor. I didn't know if it was the remnants of the bodacious Billy fart or the stench of Josh's fudged stained tighty-whities. Sleeping with the window open was a must tonight. Since I had the room to myself, and no one was around to distract me, I immediately started thinking about Tony again. I got into bed and started thinking about the weekend I spent with him. They weren't erotic thoughts nor did my thoughts cause me to pitch a tent, they were warm thoughts. I thought about how even though it was my first time there, it felt like home. I felt like I belonged there, like I was supposed to be there. Tony made me feel wanted and I wanted to be with him and see him again. I felt safe there, it was like the harshness of the outside world and its cruel judgment didn't exist. I was longing for him. I had a hard time getting my mind to settle down. I just couldn't stop thinking about him. I wanted to, no I take that back, I needed to see and be with him again. As I finally drifted off, it was the first night I lay there thinking about him without irrational thoughts that would lead to self-loathing.

Chapter 7

1

I woke up the next morning after sleeping in till eight, which is late for me. I am usually up no later than six. Right away my mind started racing with irrational thoughts, not the good thoughts I had before falling asleep. I was filled with the same panic and anxiety that I had on the drive back from Tony's. I kept wondering what would happen if people found out I was gay. Will John kick me off his property and evict Tony if he finds out? Will I get hazed like Ray Phinney did? Why do I keep thinking I am gay? I am not gay! We were just having fun as friends. I don't want to be gay and I hate the idea I am gay. How could I be with all those girls and the older woman that I slept with and yet be gay? There was no way I was gay was what I was thinking. I was able to push those thoughts out of my head before the self-loathing and the internal war I was having with myself set in again. I headed to the showers to do my morning routine. After a hot shower and with the ability to think more clearly, I thought to myself that since I told Tony I would be back so we could go riding together, I could say that if anyone asks where I was, just tell them motorcycle riding. I didn't know if I should pack a change of clothes or bring some classwork with me. Was I coming back here, or would Tony want me to spend the night? Now that I was thinking more clearly, I decided to pack a bag and bring some books and just leave them in my car;

they would be there if I needed them. If I do stay, I will be sleeping on the couch but most likely I will be sleeping here. What we did was just a one-time thing. I was feeling pretty good about myself as I headed to my car. I once again convinced myself I wasn't gay. On my way out I made a stop at Peach's Variety for coffee and a breakfast sandwich. The owner was there again and as I brought my coffee and sandwich to the register to pay, he told me since we spent so much money last night, the coffee and sandwich were on the house. I could tell he voted for Reagan and Bush twice. The picture of #40 behind the register and the gun rack in the back of his pickup truck out in the parking lot was a dead giveaway. I told myself there was no way a guy like him would ever give a gay guy free food. I had myself convinced I wasn't gay. I had to keep telling myself I wasn't gay because it was the only way to keep the anxious feelings from coming back, the battle within was a brutal one.

2

"Look who is pulling in the dooryard. I guess there is no more worrying about Paige coming back." John said. He had heard my car as I turned in from the road. I saw Tony was very happy I had come back but did tell John he wasn't sure how to approach me or if he shouldn't say anything about last week. John told Tony not to mention what they talked about or that he knew what went on. He told Tony to just go with the flow and let things fall into place on their own. Tony agreed that was a good idea and that is exactly what he would do. He was sticking his head out the barn door to let me know where he was as John was heading back up to his house. It was still a month away from the leaves dropping so I couldn't see the barn from the front of the cabin where I parked. I heard Tony yell my name and tell me to come up to the barn. When I got to the barn Tony asked if I had ever driven a motorcycle or, as he would say, a motorbike. I told him that I used to ride dirt bikes with my friend James and still had my license but hadn't really ridden street bikes. Tony said, "Let's ride up and down the dirt road out here so you can get the feel for it." The road Tony lived on was about a mile or so long and looped around at the dead end. Since there was no traffic, it was a great place to do that. It didn't take long at all to get a good feel for the motorcycle and build up enough confidence to take a ride out onto the regular roads. We left the dirt road and turned onto the main road. That took us to the four corners where I would normally take a left to go back to the campus. Tony took a right and headed to Rte. 25. This took us to the little village that was on the opposite end of the paved road Tony lived on. That classic chopper's rumble and the wind in my face was incredible. I immediately understood what bikers meant when they said, "Four wheels move the body; two wheels move the soul." Riding a motorcycle is like flying with the clouds. As we were pulling back in, John was driving off. We rode back up to the barn and parked the bikes. Tony asked how it felt compared to what I was used to riding. I told him it was totally radical! I felt like I was flying. I told him I think I am going to like riding choppers more than dirt bikes. From the moment I turned my car into the dooryard, the feelings of belonging and being with Tony came flooding back in. The outside world and its judgment didn't exist. I wanted to be in his arms again. When I first walked up to the barn and saw him that morning, once again I wanted him right then and there. It took everything I had not to embrace him. The sexual tension was broken when Tony said, "Let's take a ride and stop at the far end of The Big Lake for lunch." I couldn't say no to that so off we went. We stopped at Six Shooters for lunch and grabbed a couple of Italian sandwiches. After lunch, we continued around The Big Lake coming down the east side to its basin and eventually back to the cabin. It was mid-afternoon when we got back. Of course, being eighteen and riding choppers was the coolest thing ever. My blood was pumping, I was so excited! I was so pumped up from the ride that I walked up to Tony saying "Dude that was totally fucking "A" awesome! It was beyond rad!" and without thinking, I hugged Tony and started kissing him. Just as quickly as I did that, I pulled away apologizing. "GOD TONY! I am sorry, I didn't mean to do that. If John saw us, he would kick me off his property and evict you. You would have no place to live!" Tony put his hands on my shoulders trying to calm me down. "Andrew Paige, we are alone.

John left earlier and won't be back till Monday night." "Tony, I am sorry. I know last week was a one-time thing. I promise I won't do it again; I am sorry." With his hands still on my shoulders, Tony steered me through the barn doors and started kissing me. That was all it took for me to tear his shirt off and unzip his pants so I could help myself and he was quick to do the same. We found a spot in the barn to do our thing with one another. When we finished, we got the choppers put back in their designated spots in the barn and headed down to the cabin.

3

Once inside the cabin, Tony got undressed and sat naked on the sofa with his legs stretched across. I followed suit and quickly got naked too, sitting between his legs with my back to him resting the back of my head just below his chin on his chest wrapped in his arms. He wanted to know all about my first week at, as he would say, "University". I told him about the upcoming debate and hanging out at Peach's with the guys. I told him about Josh spending so much time in Patty's room it was like I didn't have a roommate. I did leave the part about Michele out of it. He told me all about his first week too. We talked about the day's ride and the places he wanted to take me riding. I lay there, with his arms wrapped around me, without saying a word. After a while, I rolled over onto my side with my ear to his chest. Tony softly kissed the top of my head and laid back. As I lay there listening to his breathing and the rhythmic lub-dub of his heart, I couldn't help but think I was right about sleeping on the sofa tonight. Soon we both drifted off wrapped in one another's arms.

4

The mist that was surrounding John and I lifted just enough so we could see one another. The portal was still open and I was looking down at the both of us lying there sleeping. I said to John, "Why didn't I just tell him how I felt? Maybe if he knew before I failed everyone…" John cut me off. "Then what, nothing would have happened? Things would have been different?" I didn't reply.

Chapter 8

1

The peak foliage season in Maine was here. Tony and I had taken the Choppers out every Sunday for the past four weeks. Riding the back roads of Maine in the foothills of the Western Maine Mountains was nothing short of spectacular with the fall foliage. Nothing made me happier than being with Tony and riding the choppers. I had spent the past five weekends at his place and my love for him grew deeper. As happy as he made me and as much as I wanted to be with him, the inner turmoil with my sexuality was in full force. Not when I was alone with Tony but whenever I left his place to go back to campus that battle would dominate my mind. It was Columbus Day weekend and traditionally the last weekend of fair season in Maine. The campus pretty much cleared out the Friday of that weekend leaving next to no one in the dorms. Joey, Billy, and Kenny were gone too. Josh and Patty grew up in a small town just east of Augusta along with Michele where they were going to be for the holiday weekend. What I didn't know was Michele was their ride and they were not leaving till Saturday morning. I had headed out to Tony's as normal late Friday afternoon when the last class of the week was let out. This had quickly become our usual weekend routine of dinner and then some studying and always a bit of fun before going to sleep. We would take our time getting out of bed on Saturday mornings and spend the day doing odds and ends around the cabin or errands if any needed to be done. We would get some studying in before dinner so we could either rent some VHS tapes or, in the nicer weather, we would spend time together chilling on the sofa that was on the front porch. Sunday was our day to ride. This Friday night was no different except it was the holiday weekend and both of us wanted to go to the fair. We got up early on Saturday morning and were getting the choppers out of the barn when I realized I left my wallet with my license and cash in my dorm room. Tony suggested we swing by the campus so I could grab my wallet and then continue on by going up Rte. 302 and into Fryeburg, instead of me just going to get my wallet and coming back. I immediately thought that was a bad idea even though there would hardly be anyone in the dorms, but we would still have plenty of time to stop for breakfast at the new diner we saw in Bridgeton before the gates to the fairgrounds opened. Even though the campus was deserted, I went against my better judgment and reluctantly agreed.

2

There were only a few cars in the visitor parking lot. The campus was empty as I hoped it would be. We pulled into the dorm parking lot Tony decided to stay with the choppers while I ran in to grab my wallet. I walked into my room and was surprised to see Josh, Patty, and Michele in the room. Josh was throwing some clothes in a weekend bag when I walked in and said, " Hey Paige dude wasn't expecting to run into you. I thought you took off last night." I told him I forgot my wallet and just stopped in to grab it. I said to Josh that I thought he was headed home for the weekend, as I fished through the pockets of my jeans that were in the laundry, searching for my wallet. "We were just getting ready to head out when you walked in." Michele said to me in a very civil tone. "Found it!" I said, holding up my wallet. "Enjoy your weekend guys. I've got to bounce." I said as I tried to hurry out the door without any further conversation. "Where are you off to?" Michele asked as I was trying to leave. I told her I was off to go riding with a friend. Josh piped in, "He goes riding motorcycles every weekend with that Black guy that goes to your school". I opened the door to leave and as I was walking out Michele yelled "Paige wait, I want to ask you something" I knew I should have just kept going but I turned around and asked her what. Michele started with, "I wanted to ask if you have everything because I think you're missing something," I told Michele Antonin was waiting for me and I had to go. I turned around again to leave. "No really, Paige you hang out with the Nig every weekend maybe you are forgetting to bring knee pads with you too. "Riding Motorcycles" That's what you gays are calling it now? It's code for sucking it." All three could see my face turn red with anger and I turned around and snapped back at Michele. "Screw you Michele, we're friends and we like to ride motorcycles. Why would you even think that? Just because I won't screw a skank like you doesn't make me gay." "You can't talk to her like that." Josh said, trying to defend Michele. He quickly took a step back when I stepped back in the room and told him "Don't even go there with me." I flipped off Michele and walked out. Patty looked at Michele and said, "I asked you to just be civil to him." "I was just asking him a question," that's all Michele said in that sheepishly evil way of hers giving Patty an "I am appalled" look. Patty tried to tell Michele that you couldn't go accusing people of being gay. She also said, "For Christ's sake, don't piss off the guy that Josh has to room with," reminding Michele, I could easily get them all in trouble. Michele got in Patty's face taking Patty by surprise. The tone Michele had in her voice and the rage on her face scared Patty. "I already told you no one blows me off the way Paige did! I am going to get him for it and don't get in my way—back off! Josh, who I didn't realize at the time was afraid of Michele said, "We won't get in your way. Come on we are all friends here. Let's forget about Paige and just get going." "I need to pee first," Patty said and quickly ran out of the room. She didn't need to pee, she just locked herself in the guest bathroom. Michele had scared her enough that she needed to get away from her and calm herself.

3

As I approached Tony, he could see I was visibly pissed. Right away he knew something happened. "Andrew Paige what's wrong?" he asked. "Nothing!" I said, snapping at Tony with anger he didn't cause. Realizing that I had snapped at Tony, I took a breath, and while staring straight ahead I said to Tony," I am sorry. I didn't mean to snap at you. It isn't worth talking about let's just get out of here and go get breakfast." I said as I was kick-starting the bike. Tony started his chopper and off we went.

4

We enjoyed the new restaurant, and although it was a bit out of our way, it was worth the stop. We arrived at the fair shortly before the gates opened which was cool, we were able to easily find parking and avoid the long ticket lines. I was starting to cool off a bit but was still pissed at Michele for using the abbreviated racial slur and accusing us of being gay. We made our way around to all the booths, pigged out on fair food, and spent a lot of time in the agriculture center; we both liked the animals. The farmers were happy to tell us about their animals, and we were allowed to interact with the livestock which is something the general public wasn't allowed to do. It was early afternoon when we headed back to the choppers. We both noticed some guys standing around the choppers. As we got closer, we saw they were wearing their colors. They were members of a biker club. Tony was the one who said hello to them. We approached cautiously as we were expecting trouble from them but when we approached them, they were very cool with us. They had a lot of questions about the choppers which Tony was more than glad to answer. He loved to talk about the choppers. One of the bikers told us he was impressed with us. He said, "Guys our age usually ride what he referred to as "Rice Rockets". It is cool to see you both appreciate the old iron. After talking with us for a while, they invited us to go for a ride with them. I was in my glory riding choppers with a badass biker club the coolest thing ever. We left the fairgrounds, headed to the New Hampshire border, and rode the Kancamagus Highway up to Rte.10 heading north to the junction of Rte. 302. Once we were on Rte. 302, we headed south to Twin Mountains, then down through Bartlett picking up the Hurricane Mountain Rd. which eventually brought us back around to the fairgrounds. Here we parted company with the bikers and headed back to Tony's.

5

It was around nine o'clock by the time we got back to Tony's and got the choppers back in the barn. We were still in the barn when Tony walked up behind me and put a hand on my shoulder to tell me he was headed to the cabin and wanted to take a shower to get the road grime off. I pulled away from him and he sensed my tension and could tell I was still pissed from that morning. He asked if I was willing to talk about what happened back at the dorm. Maybe telling me what happened will help. "Fine, you want to know what happened I will tell you." The anger that I had earlier that day in the dorm came back as I was telling Tony what happened. I told him what Michele called him and how she accused us of being gay and asking if riding motorcycles was code for sucking it. I told him how I felt betrayed by Josh for trying to stick up for her. My voice was raised in anger when I blurted out, "We're not fucking gay! Gay guys don't ride with bikers like we did. I hate that she calls you that name too. What is wrong with her and why does she have to act like a fucking… (the word I used rhymed with hunt). Just because I hang out here on the weekends so we can go riding and we have become really good friends doesn't make us faggots!" Tony and I had stepped outside, and he waited till I was done venting before he latched the barn doors shut. We were walking down the driveway while Tony was saying how sorry he was that she did that to me. He told me he knows what she calls him and he doesn't know why she hates him because he has never spoken to her. As we started walking toward the cabin's front porch, I stopped at my car. Tony said he was going to head inside, and he understood if I didn't want to spend the night because of what Michele said and go back to the dorm. He told me if I changed my mind the door was unlocked, and he headed inside. I stood there knowing just how hurt he was over what Michele did which made me feel even worse. After a few moments, I headed into the cabin. Tony was already in the shower. I stripped down and joined him in the shower. When I stepped in, I wrapped my arms around him and held him tight. It wasn't long before we ran out of hot water and had to take things to the bedroom. I gave Tony a lot of extra attention because I knew how hurt he was by Michele's words. It was my way of making him feel good. We lay wrapped in one another's arms holding each other like we always do and drifted off to sleep.

6

We woke up the next morning still holding one another. After our good morning kiss, Tony rolled up on his side so he was looking down at me as I laid on my back. He said to me there is a silver lining to Michele's behavior. I propped myself up on my elbows bewildered by what he said. "Andrew Paige, think for a minute. If Michele was nice to you, would you be here every weekend riding motorbikes? I am very happy you spend the weekends here. I like it when you are here things are better with you here. In a way, I am glad she is being cruel if she was being nice, I may not have you." I laid back down knowing he was right if it wasn't for her being such a... (rhymes with hunt), I wouldn't be here. I let him pull me closer, I wanted to be held by him. I let my internal battle go for the moment and allowed my feelings for him to take over. When those feelings took hold, I started kissing him. As we were rolling around getting into our favorite position Tony looked me straight in the eye and said, "I can't hold it in any longer I need to tell you something. Please promise me you won't get angry." I told him if he needed to say something I promise, I won't get angry. Tony said, "I need to tell you even though you may not feel the same way. I have developed strong feelings for you. I meant it when I said things are better when you are here. I am falling in love with you." After he said that he reached down and started to guide me in. I pulled him tight to my body lost in the heat of the moment and told him I wasn't falling in love with him. I was already there and I was crazy in love with him. Both of us saying that just added to the heat of the passion as we made love that morning.

7

We went riding later that day. Tony took me to what became our favorite spot on the big rock at Rattlesnake Pond. The pond was located about a mile or so down an old logging road in an unincorporated area of Northern Oxford County. The old logging road was a bit rough, but we easily managed to drive in. There were no cabins anywhere on the pond. Besides us, no one hung out here. At the top of the pond was a huge boulder sticking out into the pond. The boulder's backside was sloped like a ramp so we walked up to the top where it was completely flat and large enough for us to sit side by side and enjoy the view. The top of the boulder was eight feet from the surface of the pond where it was deep enough for us to dive off in the summer months. We were sitting and looking out over the pond at the fall colors and enjoying the view when I turned to Tony and said, "I meant what I said to you this morning, every word. I fell in love with you the moment I saw you at the cookout. But I am having a hard time talking about it and dealing with it, a really hard time" I told Tony about the girls I dated and I told him about the affair I had with Donna Richardson. I asked him how I could be gay after all that... I told him about Raymond Phinney and what happened to him when his teammates found out he was gay. I was afraid if anyone found out about us, they would do the same to me. I was worried that if John found out he would kick you out of the cabin. Tony told me he completely understood. He admitted he didn't understand why he feels the way he does about me and agreed we would keep our relationship a secret. He also said he would like to talk about us more but only when I was ready. He admitted he fell in love with me the day we met. He told me he had no intention of going to the cookout but at the last minute, he just felt he needed to be there. Now he knew why. We hung out for a while longer at the pond enjoying our surroundings and just being in one another's company. After a while, we headed out to enjoy the rest of the day riding the choppers.

8

The fog cleared out and John and I took physical form. John said he remembered how Tony would talk about taking rides there with me. I told John how I used to love that spot. At times we just sat looking out onto the pond, existing together, or going skinny dipping in the summer, and taking long walks in the woods. Then I started laughing and John wanted to know why. I told John I was happy that deer can't talk. John just shook his head and rolled his eyes. Then he told me that he wanted me to see that I did tell Tony how I felt about him before everything happened. I admitted that I had forgotten that I had told him. John reminded me that I said, "If I had only told him how I felt maybe none of it would have happened." He said, "Paige, you did tell him and it all happened. You need to see that what was to happen was going to happen regardless." Then he told me there was more I needed to see on this journey and some of it was going to be painful, but I needed to see it–the fog engulfed us.

Chapter 9

1

A few weeks had passed since Michele was first in our dorm room. All three of them Josh, Patty, and Michele started hanging out in our room when Michele was on campus. This was done at Michele's insistence. Usually, they liked to hang out in Patty's room because she had no roommate and the R.A. on her floor didn't care if they were smoking weed in the dorm room. She was usually baked almost as often as Patty was. I did insist that there was no pot smoking in our room because the R.A. on our floor, Scott O'Malley, was out to get anyone who smoked weed. Josh was his primary target and since I was his roommate, in Scott's eyes, I was guilty of being a pothead by association. So, I was on Scott's shit list for no other reason than that. I had no idea why, but all of the sudden, they were hanging out in our room all the time. I didn't like Michele hanging out in our room period but there was nothing I could do about it since she was Josh's guest and had not done anything to get kicked off our campus. Avoiding them wasn't too difficult. I would just go to the campus library and study there. Of course, on Wednesday nights, me, Kenny, Joey, and Billy would hang out at Peach's Variety to take a break from the ptomaine treats that the campus cafeteria served. I still had a semi-private room though. After Michele would leave Josh and Patty would head over to her room to get baked and screw. What little time I spent in the room when Michele was there resulted in her verbal attacks on Tony and me. I was getting good at ignoring her but there were a few comments made that got under my skin. I tried not to show it, but she knew when she struck a nerve. I mentioned this to Josh a few times, but he would just try and make an excuse for her. That is when I figured it out; he was afraid of Michele. Josh said not only was I a great roommate, but I was a good friend because he could trust me not to turn him in. We were not fighting nor was there tension between us, but things were a bit on the cold side since Columbus Day weekend when Josh tried to defend Michele when she started shit with me. I felt I couldn't trust Josh. Later on that Halloween weekend, Josh would prove me right.

2

Halloween fell on a Friday night this year, Tony and I had made plans to hang out and watch movies. As usual he picked Easy Rider, and since it was Halloween, I chose the movie that was the name's sake of that holiday. It was forecast to be a rainy weekend which was fine by us, we liked it when it was raw and damp outside. It gave us an excuse to have a fire in the fireplace, curl up together on the sofa, and snuggle. I wasn't very good at snuggling. Usually after ten minutes or so I would reach for his private parts, and we would end up watching movies the following morning. This night was no different even though his all-time favorite movie, "Easy Rider" was on, resistance on his part didn't last long. After we made love, we talked for a while. Most of the conversation was about what was going on at the dorm when Michele came over. I did tell Tony I was glad we had the cabin because it was like the outside world didn't exist. It was cool to have a safe place to just do us. That is where I stopped. I still wasn't ready to admit I was gay even though I told him I was in love with him I just couldn't talk about it. We laid there on the sofa for a while longer, while the fire in the fireplace burned itself out, then headed off to bed.

3

The next morning, we sat on the sofa having coffee and watching the movies we rented. As the forecasters predicted, it was still raw and cold out today and it was misty as well. We spent the day studying since there wasn't much else, we could do. We had been inside all day, so Tony had suggested we go to

Old Port later that evening for dinner, which I thought was a great idea. Later that afternoon, I was still inside getting ready to head into Old Port for dinner when I overheard John and Tony's conversation out on the front porch. John had said to Tony he was glad to see that I had been coming out every weekend. Tony was telling John how we both love riding the choppers. He was telling John how some days we would leave around six in the morning and not get back till almost ten at night. John said to Tony, "I see you're also spending a lot of alone time together." Tony admitted we were spending a lot of alone time together but didn't finish his sentence. John replied, "Okay, there is a "but" here. Tell me what is going on. Their conversation went like this:

"I couldn't help myself I had to tell Andrew Paige how I felt about him. I just couldn't hold it in any longer."

"How did that go?" John asked.

"I was expecting Andrew Paige to get angry and possibly leave and not come back."

"Okay, I see. He is still here so it didn't end badly."

"I was not expecting him to tell me what he told me."

"Which was?" John asked as his curiosity grew.

"He told me he fell in love with me the day he met me at the cookout. I couldn't believe it!"

"That's great!"

"Yes, it is great, now here is the "but"." He told me he is having a hard time dealing with the situation, and he is very uncomfortable talking about it. He insists we are not gay. He told me how Michele was treating him. He told me about the horrible abuse a classmate from his high school was treated when he was outed. I am worried it is all too much for him and he will stop coming out here."

"Tony, I have counseled many young men like Paige. Admitting to himself that he is gay is a very scary thing. There will be people finding out he is gay. It is a frightening situation for him."

"I know, I am scared too. I want to talk about us."

"Paige is here every weekend, so he wants to be with you. For right now just keep going with the flow he will talk when he is ready."

Just as soon as John said that I came out of the cabin. "Hey Tony, you ready to get motorin' into town? You're driving! Hey John, would love to stay and chat but we're off and running." With that, I headed to Tony's car. I was not happy that John knew about us. His knowing freaked me out. Tony looked at John and said, "He calls me Tony now." "I see that," John replied. Tony asked John if he thought I might have overheard them. John wasn't certain but he did ask Tony to let him know how the night went. As we drove off, I didn't say much, nor did I say much the entire ride into Old Port. Tony reached over and put his hand on my leg like he usually did when he drove. I didn't stop him, nor did I reach over and rub his leg in return as I would normally do. I just sat there quietly. With the amount of time we spent together it should not have been a surprise that John knew. I was still surprised, and Tony knew something wasn't sitting well with me.

4

When we finally arrived in Old Port, Tony parked the car and we got out and started walking down the street. Tony said, "The Villaggio Cafe is just a short walk from here." "Let me guess, it's your favorite Italian restaurant," I said which came out more sarcastically than I intended. Tony stopped walking and turned to me asking, "Andrew Paige is everything OK?" He knew something was irritating me. "You can call me Paige everyone else does," was something I regretted saying. I loved it when he called me Andrew Paige. "I can do that, I will call you Paige from now on. What is bothering you? Did I do something wrong?" As soon as he said that I felt like shit because he didn't do anything wrong. Even if he did, I couldn't get mad at him and if I ever did, there was no way I could stay mad at him no matter what happened. The look he was giving me immediately melted my heart. All I could do was think to myself, how could anyone consider him scary or creepy? Why would anyone, meaning Michele, say he gave off serial killer vibes or be afraid of him? I very quickly came to know he was truly a soft and tender man.

He had a heart of gold and wouldn't hurt a fly. "No, you didn't do anything wrong," I tried to tell him I overheard him and John. I stopped myself right there not wanting to tell him I was freaking out over him telling John. I quickly tried to cover by saying I was sorry; I guess I just had a bad week with classes. Tony suggested we get take-out instead and go back to the cabin. I told him no, let's go have a nice dinner together. I have been looking forward to this all day. Just before he turned around to start walking again, he told me that John had known the whole time. He told me, "You can trust John, he is very supportive of us and is a true friend. He also thinks very highly of you. He is glad you are around as much as you are." I still didn't like the idea of John knowing. I wasn't ready for that. It still made me feel uncomfortable that John knew but I did feel a lot better after he told me. He promised me the Villaggio Cafe has the best cannoli in the state of Maine and started to walk in that direction. I hesitated for a second. Tony turned around and started walking again. I was thinking to myself, stop being such a damn idiot and get over it before you lose him. I started walking and before I knew what happened someone had jumped me from behind. He tried putting me in a choke hold by wrapping his arm around my neck. His other arm was waving in front of me, but I was too distracted by being choked to realize he was holding something in the waving hand. We struggled as I choked and gaged trying to fight back. Finally, I was able to spin him around and get him off me. I saw that Tony had grabbed the person's raised arm, which held a lighter. Tony was yelling for me to take my jacket off. It took a moment for me to get my wits about me and realize what was happening. I saw the lighter that Tony was trying to get out of the guy's hand and yelling at him, "drop the lighter!" The guy kept screaming at Tony "FUCK YOU FAG LOVER! Let me go I want to burn the faggot." The stench of lighter fluid started filling my nostrils, the front of my jacket was soaked with the lighter fluid. I whipped my jacket off and in an instant all the chaos, confusion and mayhem around me was gone; everything just went black. I didn't remember what happened next.

5

I watched myself intently. Even now, I still don't remember what happened. With my bird's eye view, I knew I would finally see what I did. I watched myself throw my jacket to the ground. Before my jacket hit the sidewalk, I tackled the guy who jumped me and I started punching him wildly in the face, head and wherever I could land a punch. I was throwing a fury of fists. I kept pummeling him, completely blinded by rage–this asshole tried to light me on fire! The guy kept screaming, "Get him off me!" Tony was trying to pull me off the guy and was shouting for me to stop. The guy kept screaming "GET THE FAGGOT OFF ME!" Tony kept trying to pull me off yelling, "Stop! You're going to kill him!" As big as Tony was compared to me, he needed help getting me off the guy. I was shocked to see that I had utterly lost it. Watching what I was doing horrified me. No matter how justified I was I couldn't help being upset about what I did to him, how I just beat this guy with complete disregard for his life. It was one thing to deck the asshole, but it was another to do what I did. Later John would come to help me understand why I did what I did. As I watched I saw the police show up. Two cops jumped in and the four of them, Tony, a witness, and the two cops finally got me off the guy. The next thing I saw was the two cops slamming me onto the hood of their car and handcuffing me. As I was watching this I thought, "How could I have forgotten being handcuffed like that?" The attacker was lying on the ground screaming, "Those fucking pole smokers attacked me, they tried to kill me!" The cop who handcuffed me grabbed me by the arm and forced me down to the ground. Both cops refused to take Tony's or the witness's statement. One of the cops went over to check on the attacker who gave a false account of what happened. He told the cop we tried to kill him. After hearing the attacker's side of the story, the cop came back over wanting to arrest Tony and the witness who tried to help Tony. Both Tony and the witness were berated then ignored by the cop whenever they tried to tell him what really happened. A third cop showed up with, what appeared to be Sergeant stripes on his uniform, and saw the reprimanding that was going on. He immediately ordered the cop doing the berating to stand down.

The Sergeant went over to the attacker to try and talk to him and right away the Sergeant could smell the alcohol on his breath. The Sergeant stayed with him till the arriving EMT's attended to him. I watched as he walked over to us to speak with Tony who had been trying to give the correct account of what happened. He spoke to the witness while picking up my jacket from the ground to not only confirm the jacket was mine, but he wanted to smell the lighter fluid for himself. The Sergeant allowed Tony to help me up so I could lean against the cruiser. He finally came over to talk to me, asking if I wanted to file a complaint so he could press charges against the guy who attacked me. I refused. I told him I just wanted to leave. He told us he would be right back, and he took the other two cops aside to talk to them.

6

The Sergeant wasn't happy with the officers who were doing the rebuking. He reprimanded both, letting them know loud and clear that he overheard what was said to us when he arrived. He was angry that they refused to take a statement from Tony or the witness. He couldn't believe the rookie error they made by believing a guy who was clearly drunk and known to be strung out on drugs. He told them there was no excuse for not being able to smell the alcohol on his breath, he reeked of it. He was pissed they both handcuffed, verbally gay- bashed and started berating the actual victim and the other two witnesses without getting their side of the story. He told them they were on their own if an excessive force, brutality or civil rights complaint was filed against them for the way he treated us. He asked if they even realized just how much the attacker had to drink and how high he was. Both cops remained silent while their Sergeant asked if they even checked my jacket to see if it was covered in lighter fluid. Neither of the two cops spoke. They both knew there was no defending what happened. The Sergeant gave the order, "Go take the cuffs off him and if he still doesn't want to file a complaint, let them go." He told both of them he will file the reports and handle the rest. The Sergeant turned and walked over to the EMT's who were treating the attacker. The EMT's had him seated on the back of the ambulance. The other two officers walked over to us. One of them asked me again if I wanted to file a complaint, then stood so the Sergeant's view of me was blocked. I told him I just want to leave and to take the fucking cuffs off me. The one who did the worst of the rebuking told me to shut my faggot ass mouth. He spun me around so he could uncuff me and wasn't exactly gentle about it either. He knew the Sergeant was out of view and ear shot. As the cuffs were being removed, I was told to take my queer little ass and my, (he used a word that rhymed with trigger), of a boyfriend and leave. He never wanted to see our faces in Old Port again. Tony grabbed my arm before I could even react to what the cops had said, picked my jacket up and got us out of there.

Chapter 10

1

Neither of us said a word. I just stared out the passenger side window of the car the entire ride back. I didn't realize it, but I was visibly trembling, which had concerned Tony. Before we drove off, Tony suggested I get checked out at the hospital to make sure I wasn't hurt. I think he knew I was okay physically, what he wanted was someone to check if I was okay mentally, which I wasn't. I was jumped by some total stranger whom I had never met, yet he wanted to burn me alive. I had lost all control. I had no idea what I had done or the beat down I gave the attacker. I was slammed onto the hood of a police cruiser, handcuffed, and forced to the ground. We were berated by the cops who used racial slurs on Tony and verbal gay-bashing on the both of us. There was no way I was okay. I was rattled to my core. I didn't want to go the ER, I just wanted to go back home to the cabin. Thankfully, he didn't push the issue and just drove back to the cabin. When we arrived, I stopped on the front porch and sat on the old sofa. I didn't want to go inside feeling like this. I sat with my elbows on my knees and my head resting in the palms of my hands. Only then did I realize how badly I was shaking. Tony had taken my jacket, laid it over the rail, and asked if I wanted to go inside. I knew he was as exhausted as I was from the horrific turn of events. I said to him that I just needed some air and told him he should go crash, I'd be in shortly. He put a hand on each shoulder and gave a supportive squeeze. He leaned down, kissed the top of my head, and went in the cabin.

2

I knew I had been sitting there for a while. I didn't realize it was all night until Tony came out of the cabin. He sat down next to me, put his hand on my shoulder and said, "You must be freezing. Come inside I will light a fire for you to sit by and get warm." I didn't respond nor did I move. I was too numb from the attack. After a moment or so, he asked how I was feeling this morning. I told him, "I'm okay," which was the furthest thing from the truth. He asked if I was sure. I knew he was concerned so I tried my best to reassure him I was fine. He told me how sorry he was about last night. I thanked him for that and wanted to thank him for what he did, but I couldn't get the words out. My mind just went blank mid-sentence. Tony was glad I was not hurt and even tried to get me to talk by mentioning how horrible the whole thing was. He couldn't believe how cruel the police officers were. I told Tony I didn't want to talk about it. I was starting to get annoyed; I didn't want to talk at all. He said that he was concerned for me and worried because I sat outside on the porch all night. Even though I was getting annoyed, I tried to calmly say, "I don't want to talk about it." I didn't realize it at the time, but now I could see just how scared Tony was for me. I heard the worry in his voice and could see the look of concern on his face when he said, "Paige, you could have been burned, your face could have been disfigured, you could have lost your life." I couldn't deal with it and needed him to stop. In a knee-jerk reaction, I snapped at him, "Would you please just STOP!" Tony said he was sorry, he didn't mean to upset me, and he would stop. We sat silently; I stared out at the rain. Tony kept his hand on my shoulder, and I saw a tear run down his cheek. I was now starting to realize how the things that were happening to me made me blind to those around me. I was not aware of how much time passed before Tony stood and said, "At least let me get you some hot coffee. I will be right out."

3

My gaze went from looking down at myself sitting on the front porch to seeing what Tony was doing in the cabin. I watched Tony walk into his bedroom and pick up the phone that was on his side of the bed. He dialed a number, and the person at the other end picked up instantly. "John, it's Tony," "Good morning. Tony, I see you're calling yourself "Tony" now too, so I guess it is okay for me to call you Tony." John was always happy to see and hear from people and it showed with his greetings. Tony said, "Yes," it was okay to call him that. John sensed this wasn't a social call. He could detect the concern in Tony's voice. He asked if Tony was calling him to tell him how last night had gone. Tony said he was calling because he wanted him to come join us for breakfast. John now sensed that something was wrong. He asked Tony if everything was okay, he sounded like something was bothering him. "Things didn't go well, did they?" he asked Tony. Tony didn't get into details he just wanted John to come down and he wanted to get back to me. "John, I think you need to come and join us for breakfast. Please John, I need you to join us. I have to bring Paige his coffee, please John." John could hear the urgency in Tony's voice and told Tony he would come down right away. They both hung up. Tony walked over to the kitchen counter and poured coffee for us, then headed back out to the front porch. As Tony was stepping out onto the porch, I reached up, took the mug of coffee, and grumbled a "thank you" to Tony. Tony suggested that since it was raining, and we couldn't go riding, he thought he would make us a nice breakfast. John is going to join us. I thought to myself right away, there is no way I can face anyone right now. I know Tony said John was supportive of us and a true friend, but I just couldn't face anyone right now. I immediately said, "I can't stay I need to get back to the campus." We all have that flight or fight response, and flight was kicking in. Tony begged me not to go he wanted me to stay there for the day. The was no denying his concern for me. I wasn't starting to panic but I wasn't ready to face John knowing he was aware of our relationship. I was hoping to get used to the idea first. I couldn't face John after the attack. I just couldn't and with that, the urgency to get away took over. I told Tony I needed to get back. I got up, grabbed my jacket and without thinking, tried to put it on. The jacket still reeked of the lighter fluid. The smell hit me like a baseball bat to the head, and I started to choke and gag. I threw the jacket to the ground and rushed to my car while still choking and dry heaving, trying to get away from the smell. I got in my car and took off as fast as I could.

4

I watched as John came down the driveway as I was leaving. He hurried over to the cabin to find out what was wrong. As soon as he saw Tony he knew something was terribly wrong. John immediately asked what was going on. He wanted to know if I was okay. The stress of the last night and this morning got to Tony. Tony's emotional side was starting to appear. He was choking up with emotion as he tried to tell John what happened. He managed to get the words out that I was attacked last night, and that it was horrible. John was shocked by the news. "Attacked?!" he gasped. Tony's emotions quickly overcame him, he said to John, "Yes attacked! Paige was almost burned, and the police tried to arrest Paige!" John knew he needed to calm Tony down. John told Tony to take a few deep breaths and head inside to sit down. As they went inside, they both sat at the table. Tell me what happened nice and slowly John said. Tony took another deep breath before speaking. He started to tell John that we were headed to the Villaggio Cafe when someone jumped me from behind, poured lighter fluid all over my jacket, and tried to light me on fire. John had a look of disbelief on his face when he said, "Light him on fire? Dear Lord! Is Paige, okay? Was he burned?" Tony told John how he was able to get the lighter out of the attacker's hand. "Why did he attack Paige like that?" John's concern for my well-being was growing rapidly. Being in his line of work, he knew the effects this type of trauma had on people. Tony told John how the attacker said he wanted to see what a real-life flamer looked like. He kept calling Paige a "faggot" and a "queer." "Tony, I am so sorry you both had to go through that," John said Empathetically. John was confused about me being arrested and asked, "You said the police tried to arrest Paige?"

Tony told John "Yes." He went on to tell John that after I got my jacket off, I tackled the man and started hitting him. He told John that I lost all control–I was like a wild man. Tony said he was yelling for me to stop, and it was like I didn't hear him. I just kept punching and no matter what he did to try and get me to stop, I just wouldn't stop. Tony went on to say it took him and three other people to pull me off the guy who attacked me. John was shaking his head when he told Tony that it sounded like I had a mental break of some sort. It made John wonder if this triggered some other past trauma. Tony could see how upset John was over what happened. Tony continued, even though he was getting choked up again. He said the whole thing was awful. Tony told John that two of the people who helped get me off the guy were the policemen who tried to arrest me. He said to John that they kept calling us names and one of them called him the N-word. John heard all he needed to hear for the moment. Standing, he said, "Okay, I get what happened." He stepped out onto the porch and picked up my jacket. He said, Oh Wow! That really stinks!" He stepped back inside and asked how I was doing. Tony told him I couldn't stop shaking. He told John that I spent the night sitting on the front porch just staring out at the rain. He told John I barely spoke, and my hands were still trembling when he handed me the coffee mug this morning. They were both silent for a moment. Tears started rolling down Tony's cheek as he told John he was scared for me and scared he was going to lose me now. John saw the tears and knew he needed to step in and help. He told Tony that he had something to get the smell out of my jacket. He will go take care of that, then he will return my jacket to me in the morning which will give him a good excuse to stop in and see me. He said to Tony that he would try and get me to talk and see what he could do to help. Tony thanked John and even though he felt better that John was going to step in and help, the visible worry was still there. I watched John leave and saw Tony sitting at the table by himself crying for me. I never knew he cried for me like that.

5

I didn't go back to the campus right away in fact, I didn't arrive back till mid-afternoon. I had gone down to Sandy Point Beach and was sitting at the same picnic table that Tony and I sat at that first day we met. All the camps around the pond had been closed till spring. The gate at the entrance of the parking lot had been locked at the end of the season too. I parked by the roadside and walked across the lot to the beach. I sat there looking out onto the pond thinking how this perfect Halloween weekend turned into a complete disaster in a split second. I knew someone was going to attack me if anyone suspected that I was gay. But why me? I'm not gay. We're just friends. That guy didn't even know me so why would he think I was gay? I sat there for several hours with the same thought going through my mind. Why me? I am not gay! Why did he attack me? Repeatedly, the same questions bombarded my mind. I couldn't stop thinking about it. I couldn't stop the screams in my head, "I am not a fucking queer!" I even yelled that out loud, I yelled so loud I could hear my voice echoing across the pond. The internal rage and battle exploded in the worst way, probably thanks to the asshole who jumped me. What made it worse was the way the two cops treated us. Being treated like that by people sworn to protect and serve us upset me. Those two actions were what pushed my internal struggle into overdrive and right over the proverbial edge. What finally broke my thoughts and brought me back to reality was a flock of ducks landing in the water close by. Their landing was so loud it sounded like something crashing into the pond. The entire flock of what appeared to be, a couple dozen or so ducks, flapped their wings on the water and quacked loudly before flying off again. Today was the second day of November, so this was odd. The ducks had all gone south by now or at least I thought they had. As odd as I thought that was, I thought maybe I needed to take that as my cue to leave too. It was still drizzling, which was now turning to a light rain. I was soaked to the bone and shivering. I needed to leave, go back to the dorm, and take a hot shower.

6

On the short drive back to the campus from Sandy Point Beach, the rain let up and finally stopped. I parked in my usual spot. As I grabbed my book bag off the passenger seat, I saw myself in the rear-view mirror–I was a total fucking train wreck. I had calmed down somewhat. I was still shaking partly from my wet clothes and partly from the attack. I just wanted to take a hot shower and maybe get something to eat from the cafeteria. I opened the door to my room and before I could even get my key out of the lock, I was greeted by Josh's stoner voice, "PAIGE DUDE! Rough night?" Michele chimed right in with,

"What did the Nig do to you?"

I didn't even think before speaking I just blurted out, "FUCK YOU! He didn't do anything! Stop calling him that. His name is Antonin."

"Who is the Nig?" Patty knew who Michele was referring to but she was back to being Michele's dipshit lap dog.

Michele said, "You know, the weirdo just sits and stares and walks like a robot," as she stood up and walked like a robot to mock Tony.

Patty responded with a shrill, "OH MY GOD! I know who you are talking about. Paige is right he isn't like that. NOT! That dude is friggin creepy and scary to the max! He attacked you, didn't he?" Her squealing voice was ear-piercing.

"I knew it. The serial killer in him came out!" Michele said, with all the cockiness she could muster. I lost my cool with the two of them and started shouting, "SCREW YOU! SCREW THE BOTH OF YOU! Fuck off and get out of my room, NOW!"

Patty jumped up from where she was sitting, put her hand on her hip, made a circle with her arm, and snapped her fingers at me saying,

"You can't kick us out Josh said so. We are the clique."

Finally, Josh spoke up. "Alright, alright, everyone take a chill pill, will you? Ladies give us the room."

Michele and Patty looked at one another then turned and walked out. As the girls were walking out, I was thinking to myself that Josh may have grown a set, but I knew better. As soon as the door shut, I turned to Josh "Give us the room? Lay off."

"Paige dude, what happened? You're a total mess." By the way he said that I knew Josh was stoned off his ass. I wouldn't have told him what happened even if he was sober. Because he was friends with Michele, I knew I couldn't trust him. I told him to get off me and mind his business. I thought to myself, better still, why don't the three of them go hang out in Patty's room and leave me alone. Josh walked up to me and put his arm around me like I was his bro or something, he reeked of weed. "Paige dude if you don't want to talk, it's cool. I get it. Here, take this. It will help calm your nerves." Josh was holding up a joint with his other hand. I said, "You know I hate that shit. I don't like getting baked." Which was very true. Josh said to me, "Come on Paige dude, you don't have to smoke the whole thing, just a hit or two to take the edge off. Hey man you got to get right just take it. Paige dude trust me you're going to thank me." as he stuck the joint in my shirt pocket. "Fine, if it gets you off my back," I said, as I was trying to shrug his other arm off me. I told Josh I needed some air and headed for the door. Josh shouted, "There are some wooded paths out behind the dorm that circle the campus, and no one uses them. Good place to burn one. I turned to look at him and said, "I just want to clear my head," and walked out.

7

I watched Patty and Michele go back into the dorm room right after my younger self left. Patty asked, "Like what's with Paige? Why does he have a hair across his ass?" Patty suddenly started whining and talking like a Valley Girl. Michele said, "I am telling you, the Nig did something to him." She took a seat on my bed and sat with her legs crossed facing Josh who was sitting at his desk with Patty in his lap. Josh held up a joint. "Don't worry, I gave him one of these, you know, for medicinal purposes of course." The three of them laughed thinking they were hysterical. With an evil grin on her face, Michele told Josh to keep feeding him those. "He's cute and if he is baked, he's all mine." Patty's voice was like nails on a chalkboard when she

82

said, "OH MY GOD, you're such a slut! But you are right. He is cute, but not Josh cute." Josh sat there feeling proud of himself saying, "You want me to keep him baked so you can have sex with him?" Michele was hell-bent on revenge over something so petty, "He hates me because I can't stand The Nig. So yeah, keep him baked so I can get into his pants. No one blows me off the way Paige did at the cookout. NO ONE! I am just showing him who is in control." Patty, who at this point just liked hearing her own voice said, "You're so evil! You're the coolest person, like totally rad!" Josh was pointing at Michele, "You get laid, and I get a toke buddy. I can do that." Patty popped up off Josh's lap with her hands on her hips. "Hey! I thought I was your toke buddy." Josh smiled and told Patty she was his toke and stroke as he slid his hand up Patty's thigh toward her lady parts hoping to insert a finger. Michele just rolled her eyes at the two of them. "Just go find Paige and get him baked. We will wait here."

8

Just like Josh said, no one used these trails at all. I hated it when that little asshole was right. I came across a small clearing and was standing there talking to myself not realizing I was talking out loud. "OH GOD! That guy tried to burn me alive! What did I do to deserve that?" I couldn't stop shaking. I was startled by someone calling out my name. "Paige dude, there you are." I looked up to see Josh walking down the trail. I was hoping he didn't overhear me. As he walked up to me, I was expecting him to ask who I was talking to but instead he said, "Paige dude. Glad I found you, let's burn one together. He pulled a joint and lighter out of his pocket. I told him, "Josh, I don't like that stuff, and I don't want to get high." He said, "Look at you Paige dude, you're a total wreck. Look man I get it you don't want to talk about it, and I can't make you talk. But you've got to at least get it together before you go all psycho on someone." I thought to myself, he is just trying to help the only way he knows how. I was so wrong. I said that I had already gone psycho on someone that's why I…I stopped myself realizing I wasn't thinking this, I was talking out loud. Even though it was a mumble it was still out loud. Josh heard me and asked, "What did you say?" "It was nothing." I told him, but he kept asking, "No Paige dude you said something." I didn't want to talk to him either I just wanted to be alone, so I said to him "It was nothing now get off me." Josh put the joint between his lips. "Come on Paige dude let's spark one together." Again and again, I told Josh, "I don't want to get high!" He wouldn't take no for an answer. "Come on Paige dude just take a hit." The sound of Josh flicking his lighter triggered me and I had a flashback to the guy who attacked me. I shouted at Josh, "Dude get the fuck off me!" I pushed him aside and got out of there and away from him. I hurried further down the trail trying to get away from Josh. I finally stopped at a little pond at the end of the trail. Josh didn't follow me, and I was glad he didn't. I just wanted to be alone. I still had on my wet clothes that I'd been wearing since the prior night. I didn't care how wet or cold I was I just needed to be alone. I hung out at the pond till well after dark before I headed back to the dorm. When I got back it was very late, almost midnight. I was surprised to find Josh sleeping in his bed. I quietly got out of my wet clothes and crawled into bed without waking Josh thinking to myself, why wasn't he sleeping at Patty's?

Chapter 11

1

I was so exhausted I fell right to sleep but I couldn't stay asleep. I couldn't get warm. I couldn't stop shivering. I would drift off for a bit then wake up shaking and shivering. It was like I was having spasms. I spent an ungodly amount of time in my wet clothes and the only thing that would get the chill out of my body was a nice hot shower. Finally, around six, I got up, wrapped a towel around my waist, and headed for the showers. It was still early enough that I had the showers and bathroom to myself. I got the shower nice and hot and stepped in. Right away I started feeling the chill leave my body. I stood there under the shower head letting the hot water do its thing. The hot water was helping relax away the tension in my body. Between all the shivering and trauma I experienced, my entire body was one big knot, but I was finally warm again. The trembling from the attack and the shivers from being cold and wet finally stopped. I was feeling somewhat better and a little more relaxed. I lathered up and then rinsed off the stink from the past few days.

I stepped out of the shower to a still-empty shower room, dried off, and headed back to my room.

2

I was finally warm but still felt like shit, not as bad as yesterday but still bad. I was dressed and sitting on the edge of my bed putting my boots on when Josh rolled over. "Hey Paige dude didn't even hear you come in last night." I was thinking, *that's probably because you were still wasted.* What I did say was I was trying to be quiet so I wouldn't wake him. I didn't want to talk so I stood up and picked my wet clothes up off the floor hoping that was the end of it. Josh asked me where I took off too. I thought to myself, great, he wants to talk. I kept the answer vague and told him no place special just walking the trails for a bit. Josh asked if I had been walking the trails all that time. I had my back to Josh and when I looked over at him, I saw the big shit-eating grin on his face. I knew he was busting my balls and trying to get under my skin by asking so many questions. I turned back around and started picking up my clothes again. "No, I hung out at the pond too." The joint Josh gave me yesterday fell out of my shirt pocket as I was picking it up off the floor, he said, "Paige dude, the pond is a great place to burn one and hang with the old lady if you know what I mean." I stood up, turned around, and snapped at him, " I was there just to be alone. Here, you can have this back too." I tried to give the joint back to him because I didn't want it. With a loud "PAIGE DUUUUUDE!" he told me to just keep it and that I would thank him later for insisting I keep it. I wanted to smack that fucking smirk off his face, Josh was being a total peckerhead. I told him to mind his damn business! Just as I said that someone pounded on the door shouting "HEY, TURNER! There is someone in the lobby looking for you!" I knew whose voice it was. It was Scott the R.A. on our floor. As I shoved the joint in my shirt pocket and buttoned the pocket I replied. "Who is it? " "I am the R.A. not your butler. How the fuck would I know? It's just some old dude asking for you." Scott could be a complete dick when he wanted to be. I shoved the arm full of dirty clothes into the laundry basket that was in my cubby hole of a closet and headed out the door to the lobby.

3

I wasn't thinking about who was looking for me when I walked out to the lobby. I was expecting it to be a cop because of what happened over the weekend. It was a relief to find it was John who was looking for me, not a cop. Still, the angst of seeing him had me trembling again, at least on the inside. I was super nervous that he was here on campus and inside the dorm. The apprehension was showing on my face and John noticed right away. John tried to break the tension a bit by saying, "Hey there, I was just heading into town and I wanted to drop this off to you. I was able to get the smell out." He was holding up my jacket. I took my jacket but before I could say "thank you", John asked me when my first class was. He said if it wasn't too early, he would like to take me to breakfast asking if we could talk. His attempt at breaking the tension didn't work and I nervously asked him, "Talk?" John could see that I kept looking around to see if anyone was coming; I was afraid someone might hear us. He took a step closer, lowered his voice, and used a concerned father tone when he spoke. He said that he heard I had a bad night and how sorry he was not only to hear about it but sorry I had to go through that experience. I tried to downplay it by telling John it was just a stupid fight. John questioned it, still using that concerned dad tone. "Just a stupid fight? Nothing else?" I was trying to downplay it again hoping John would just drop it. I said, "Yeah just a stupid fight." Looks like no one was going to drop anything today. John kept trying by saying. "I am going to be honest with you. Tony told me what happened, and I know that was lighter fluid I cleaned off your jacket. So come on let's go have some breakfast and talk." I knew I was being stubborn when I replied, "I don't need to talk, I am fine." I may not have been fine, but I honestly didn't want to talk about it. John tried again by telling me if that happened to him, he would be a total basket case, a real mess. He told me Tony was really worried about me. I made another vain attempt to downplay the situation by saying that Tony shouldn't have said anything, and it didn't involve him. I said it was just a stupid fight, hoping John would drop it. He didn't. John tried one last time to get me to talk by telling me that from what he understood, Tony was very much involved adding if it wasn't for Tony, I would have been seriously burned to say the least. He said that he heard about the cops being way out of line with me. He knew this was a very traumatic incident and tried to coax me into opening up a little by saying, "Let's just sit and talk." I got angry and nastily replied, "I don't want to sit and I don't want to talk about it! Is that OK with you? Do I have your permission not to talk about something that I don't want to talk about?" John was a true professional in his field. He didn't flinch. He remained non-confrontational and calmly replied that it was fine, and I didn't have to talk. He did ask if I would just hear him out a second. He pleaded, "Can you do that, can you just hear me out?" I looked around to make sure no one was nearby and saw we were still alone so I nodded my head to let John know I would listen without having to speak. He started his monologue with, "Paige, you were brutally attacked, someone tried to burn you alive. That is as serious as serious can get. It's OK to be scared, upset, and a total wreck, it is expected. Tony is really worried about you and so am I. He is upset that this happened to you. You are extremely important to him, and he is afraid you won't come back. He doesn't want to lose you. So please promise me you will consider talking to someone. It doesn't have to be me. Talk to the campus counselor. Don't bottle this up inside it will eat you alive. Will you do that?" I reluctantly agreed and told John I would consider talking to someone. It wasn't a lie I did consider talking to him several times. John had one more thing to ask before he left. "Paige" he asked. "Are you coming out this weekend like you normally do and go riding with Tony?" I didn't answer I just kept my head hung low. He wanted me to come out and was hoping to get me to answer so he said, "I tell you what, come out Friday night after your last class and I will treat you both to pizza. How does that sound? Good?" I hadn't even thought about next weekend. I hadn't even thought about how I was going to get through today, but I told him, "Yes, I will see them both Friday night." I added,

"Let Tony know I will be home this weekend." "Home?" John asked. I quickly tried to correct myself. John smiled and said that he was glad I felt at home at the cabin. He told me Tony was like family to him and that I was a welcome addition to the family. I tried to smile as best I could but what I wanted to do was break down and cry and just let it all out, but I was convinced that was a terrible idea. I thanked John for cleaning my jacket and told him pizza sounded great and that I would see them Friday night.

4

Walking back to my room I realized that I did feel safe at the cabin with Tony. It was the first time I felt like I had a real home to go to. John, saying what he said about being family, made me feel wanted. That was new to me too. I got back to my room with my jacket and John was right, the smell was completely gone. Josh was sitting at his desk in his tightie whities rolling some joints. "So, who was the old dude that was here to see you?" He caught me off guard with that question. I had to take a second to think. I told Josh it was my uncle. I thought, what the hell, John did say I was a welcome addition to the family. Josh told me he didn't know I had family in the area, as he wet the adhesive strip on the rolling papers to seal up the joint he just rolled. "Well, now you do. Are we done with the twenty questions this morning?" Man, he was getting on my nerves, and it was starting to show even more than before. He told me we have been roommates and friends for a couple of months and that we never talked. He just trying to get to know me. I thought, what a crock of shit. Josh asked again if I would tell him what John wanted. My back was to him now and I just rolled my eyes and replied to Josh. He wanted to know if I wanted to go to breakfast with him." Josh wouldn't stop with the questions, and I knew he was just being an asshole and most likely on Michele's orders. I was tired of all the questions; I knew he wasn't just trying to get to know me and this wasn't going to stop until I left. I told him I had something else I needed to do instead. I grabbed my jacket and left.

5

I hadn't eaten a thing since Saturday afternoon, and I needed to get some food so I headed to the cafeteria. Beatrice Mills, who everyone called Grammy B., was in her usual spot behind the serving line doling out the food. She stood about four-foot-five and was as round as she was tall. She was the sweetest lady you would ever want to meet. All the students and staff loved her. She watched me walk up to her serving station with her trademark smile saying, "There's my Paige." She called everyone by name and always used the prefix "my". She genuinely loved her job of feeding us and thought of all the students as her grandchildren. "Hey Grammy B., what's on the menu today?" I asked, as she lifted the lids on the steam table. She said, "I got your favorites bacon, breakfast sausage, and scrambled eggs." She told me there were fresh bagels out by the toaster too. Granny B. told me I looked like I hadn't eaten for days. Little did she know that was true. She made sure I got an extra helping of everything. She stacked my plate full of eggs and the breakfast meat. I said, "Thanks Granny B., you're the raddest" She smiled when I said that and came around the front side of the serving line and hugged me, telling me I looked like I needed one of those. I hugged her back knowing she was right. I did need that. It didn't fix anything but the band-aid that it provided in that moment, felt good. The cafeteria was empty. I was able to quickly find an empty table so I could sit and eat in silence. I kept thinking to myself that maybe John was right. I should talk to someone. The more I thought about it the more I knew I should. I finished breakfast and was feeling a little better now that I had finally eaten. I decided to grab another cup of coffee in a to-go cup and head over to Student Services to see if I could talk to someone.

6

I was walking over to the Student Services building as the campus started to come to life with its daily activities. Students were headed to the cafeteria for breakfast, professors were arriving for classes and the office staff began to show up. Seeing all this activity caused the angst about what happened to come roaring back with a vengeance, giving me the jitters. I was starting to get the shakes again and not just on the inside. The hand holding the Styrofoam coffee cup was trembling so hard that I was spilling coffee all over my hand. There was no way I could discretely enter and exit Student Services without someone seeing me. Who knows the questions I would get asked or the rumors that would spread. What would they say or do to me if they found out about me and Tony? Would I get attacked again? I could hear it in my head loud and clear, "Paige Turner needs a shrink because he is a sissy boy." Would one of the rumors be that I go to a halfway house for the insane on weekends and I lied about riding motorcycles? I started to panic saying out loud to myself, "I can't do this, I can't fucking do this!" I immediately turned on the path that led back to the dorm and rushed off in that direction getting as far away from Student Services as I could. When I got to the dorm, I saw both Patty and Michele heading into my dorm. I knew exactly where they were going and the last thing I needed or wanted was to run into bitchzilla and her whiny lapdog. I had an hour before my first class, so I decided to head down to the pond to kill some time and hoped to avoid the unwanted guests that were headed to my room.

7

No one was on the trails behind the campus and the area around the pond gave me some privacy so I could be alone with my thoughts. I knew I couldn't deal with this on my own anymore. I kept thinking to myself that John is right I should at least try talking to someone. Panic abruptly took over my train of thought. NO! NO! I can't do it here! People will find out I am gay and love Tony. Oh god, why do I keep thinking I am gay? I AM NOT MOTHER FUCKING GAY! I don't look gay, I don't act gay, I don't want to be gay. Just because I am in love with Tony doesn't make me gay! I started to pace around because I was engulfed with nervous energy trying to figure out what to do. I couldn't take it, I caved. I reached into my shirt pocket and pulled out the joint Josh gave me. I stood there staring at the joint cursing Josh for being right that I needed something to take the edge off. The first hit off the joint did nothing. The second hit made my brain tingle, and the third hit did the trick; the pain and suffering were gone. Yeah, that's better, at least I can make it through today. Later, when I found the joints Josh stuck in my desk without telling me, I thought to myself, it looks like I am going to get through the week.

8

I could feel myself taking physical form again as the fog cleared enough so John and I could see one another. I looked over at him and said, "No shit, I completely forgot how pizza night started." I told him that as a kid, I didn't like pizza at all. I wouldn't eat a single bite. I told him it was he and Tony who got me to like pizza and then to love pizza. John looked me square in the eye and said, "Seriously Paige, loving pizza is what you got out of that? That was your takeaway?". I did the best I could to reply calmly. "Well then tell me what the point was." John simply replied, "Paige, you know what the point was." He knew reliving this was going to make me angry, and it started to show when I replied, "No John, I don't! I don't know what the point is in reliving my fuckups. I get it! The moment I lit that joint is the moment I fucked up and fucked up bad!" "You are right," was John's reply. It was a relief to see that John knew I was right and there was no point to this. We are stopping here. The final journey is over. NOT! He was just taking a dramatic pause. He told me, "You're not getting it. Let's move forward a few months and see if you start getting it". Back into the fog we went.

Chapter 12

1

Before John moved forward a few months he said there were some things he wanted to show me that he felt were a necessary part of my journey. We were not in physical form when we were in the fog looking through the portal, he was in my head telling me he was doing this before he took me to the time and place he wished to bring me. John communicating in my head is the eeriest thing, I don't think I could ever get used to it. I was looking through the portal again. John brought me to when Josh saw me after I took a few hits off that first joint. Josh tossed me his Visine for my eyes. He was like, "See Paige dude you're feeling better already," then he said "Later, when that wears off, we should burn one together." I had an awesome buzz going and did feel considerably better than I had less than fifteen minutes ago. I told Josh that no, it was a one-time thing and that's it. Even though I felt good, I also hated the feeling of being high. The high feeling didn't last very long. By the time my first class was over, the high feeling was gone. The mellow feeling though, lasted all day and into the evening. I was feeling very okay.

Kenny and I were hanging out in his room waiting for Billy to get out of class so we could go to dinner. No sooner did Billy walk into Kenny's room when he blew one of his infamous bodacious Billy farts that got me laughing as always. A few tokes and I felt calm, no more trembling, and I was laughing at Billy and his gassy ass. I was back to normal. Everything was fine and I didn't need to talk to anyone. That night Josh slept in Patty's room which was good because between being exhausted from the past few days and the effects of the pot, I crashed early.

2

The next morning, I got up at my usual time and headed to the showers to do my usual morning routine. I ran into Scott the R.A. as I was leaving the showers to head back to my room. Scott usually doesn't do more than give me an awkward "Hi" in passing. This morning, he was full of questions. "Hey Turner, who was the old dude that was here yesterday?" I had to think for a second then remembered what I told Josh. I told Scott that it was my uncle just stopping by. Scott said he thought he overheard something about getting into a fight or getting jumped and asked if he heard right that someone tried to burn me. I froze right there. I could feel myself starting to sweat and I didn't know how to reply. I was too confused to think about what to say, my heart started racing. Scott looked at me and asked if I was okay. I didn't know it at the time, but I was having an anxiety attack. Scott asked again, "Paige. Are you Okay?" He even said that if I wanted to talk his door was always open. I went into panic mode and started shouting at Scott. I let him have it, "I am fine and I don't need to talk, so get off me! Who the fuck do you think you are listening to a private conversation! A conversation that was none of your business. Not only that, but it was also just a stupid fight. I kicked the guy's ass, end of fucking story. I don't know what else you think you heard but if you think I am a faggot you can get that out of your head right now. I ain't no fucking queer! Keep your nose out of my business and leave me alone!" I flung the door open and stormed out. I gave Scott one hell of a verbal beat down and I never felt bad that I did it. He was an asshole toward me right from the start. I had no idea why.

The both of us made it a point to steer clear of one another after that. I got back to my room, sat at my desk, and tried to put my head between my knees. I couldn't catch my breath. I was having a full-blown panic attack. When I finally started breathing somewhat normally again, I wondered how much Scott heard. Does he think I am fucking Tony? Does he think I am gay now? When I yelled, "I ain't no fucking queer", did he believe me or did I make it worse? I opened my desk drawer to get the bottle of aspirin that was in there. My head was pounding from the stress of what just happened. That was when I found the joints Josh had stuck in there. I put the aspirin back and grabbed a joint instead. I got dressed as fast as I could and headed straight to the pond. This time it wasn't a few hits, I had to smoke the whole thing before I felt better. Later that afternoon I finished off the joint from the day before. I ended up toking every morning that week, something I never intended to do

3

Friday after my last class, I couldn't wait to get out of there and be with Tony. The effects of my early morning toke session had fully worn off. The high feeling and the mellow feeling were gone. I was sober and I was feeling a little trepidation about seeing Tony because of last week, but I promised John I would be there. I figured this would most likely be the last weekend of riding season and I wanted to get in a good ride or two. Once I pulled into the dooryard and parked, the angst was gone. I felt safe. I had the feeling of being home. Once I saw Tony standing in the doorway waiting for me to come in, I felt something I hadn't felt all week. I got out and headed into the cabin. John had pulled in with the pizzas just as I was heading inside. Tony was so relieved to see me–I could read it on his face. John came through the door right after I did and set the pizzas down so he could give me one of those fatherly pats on the back. He said he didn't know what I liked on my pizza, so I got a couple of pepperonis. He hoped that was okay. I replied, "That's choice man. I like pepperoni." John motioned for the both of us to have a seat. Things were a little awkward at first, but John asked about my week. I gave one-word answers, didn't get into detail, and tried to change the subject so we could avoid talking about me. Knowing I didn't want to talk about it, the subject of the prior week didn't come up. The conversation was kept light but enjoyable. When we finished, Tony stood and said that he'd brought home fresh cannoli which he knew was my favorite Italian dessert. We ate cannoli, talked for a little while, and at about eight o'clock, John said, "Good night, I'm turning in." and headed up to his house. We sat at the table in silence for a few minutes. Tony and I were sitting close enough that I reached over and put my hand on his thigh and asked if he wanted to wheel the T.V. cart into the bedroom and watch a movie in bed. Tony got in bed and was lying on his back, I got in, lifted his arm so I could put it around me, and rested my head on that sweet spot, on his chest, near his heart. I loved listening to his heart beating. It always soothed me. I wrapped my arm around him and held him tight. I didn't even bother to turn the T.V. on. Tony turned his head so he could kiss the top of mine. Lying there with him made me feel safe, and being there with him felt as though nothing else existed. There was no outside world and no judgment because I was in love with a Black man. No hate, no one trying to burn me alive, no violence, and no abuse. We didn't make love that night, I just wanted to lie there and be held. Tony didn't want to let go of me as he held me in his tight embrace. He wanted to protect me from the outside world.

4

The next morning, we just lay there in the same position and neither of us wanted to get out of bed. We just wanted to stay like that. I don't think either one of us wanted to let go of the other. It was late morning when we finally got up. I got the leftover pizza out for breakfast while Tony made coffee. He was standing with his back against the counter wearing sweatpants and no shirt. I went up to him, wrapped my arms around his waist, and kissed him in the center of that rock-solid chest of his. He tilted his head down and kissed the top of my head. Tony kissing the top of my head the way he did meant more for me than any words could ever do. I rested my forehead on his chest so I could talk. I told Tony that John told me how important I was to him. I just wanted him to know he was just as important to me. I tilted my head back to look at him and whispered, "I meant it when I said I was in love with you. I want you to know that." Tony wanted to say something back and maybe I should have let him, but before he spoke, I gently cupped his face, guided him to my lips, and started kissing him.

5

The ride that day had no set destination we just went where the road would take us. We rode through the foothills of the Western Maine Mountains across a few mountain roads. We went up as far as Sugarloaf Mountain. Straddling the chopper, feeling the wind on my face and blowing through my hair, and the roar of those engines that Tony kept so finely tuned had a way of transcending my soul. Riding those choppers was so calming, an effect the pot couldn't match no matter how good it was or how much I smoked. This was heaven to me. I didn't need to talk, this was my therapy, and this was all I needed. At least I thought so, but others disagreed and in time, I would prove them right. It was late fall, which meant it got dark early, so around four we started making our way back to the cabin. I was feeling great when we got back to the cabin. Tony had just closed the barn door when I took him by the hand and said, "Come, let's go rinse off the road grime." As great as the ride was, there was no getting around how cold it was. It was a typical November day in Maine, which meant it was around forty degrees, so a hot shower was more than needed. We walked hand in hand down the driveway to the cabin. I led him into the bedroom, and we started undressing one another as I guided him to the shower. After we got cleaned up, I led him over to the bed and spent the night showing him just how much I loved him.

6

Sunday morning, we rode up to Rattlesnake Pond to our favorite spot. Tony sat on top of the boulder with his knees bent, and I sat between his knees with the back of my head resting on his chest. We were a mile off the main road in the woods, with no cabins around the pond, and there was never a soul in sight. This was one of the few places we could show our affection for one another outside the cabin. I was nervous and reluctant to come out to the cabin this weekend but glad I did. That Friday night in bed was what I needed. Being with Tony this weekend quieted my mind and helped me find a little peace and solace. Tony leaned over and whispered in my ear, "I want you to know you are the most important person in my life. I am deeply in love with you, and I will do everything I can to protect you and keep you safe, whatever it takes, so I don't lose you. I do have feelings, but I am not the type to wear my heart on my sleeve." What he said caused me to tear up. I shifted sideways so I could wrap my arms around him and hold him tight. Soon after, we got back on the choppers and headed back to the cabin. I normally would head back to the campus for the week late Sunday evening, but not this Sunday. I stayed over till Monday morning and would do this from that point on.

Chapter 13

1

John wanted me to see what happened that first weekend after I was attacked. He insisted that the first pizza night and time spent with Tony was important for me to see. At that moment, I didn't understand why he wanted me to see this. However, I did know, and I understood that if John said it was important then it was important, so I had that for the moment. John also wanted me to see a few other things along the way. One of the first things he showed me was just how much trauma getting attacked had caused. I kept replaying that night over and over in my head, I couldn't get it out of my mind. The more I let the trauma, as he put it "take over", the more I would turn to pot and eventually pot and alcohol together. My struggle with being gay was fueling that fire too. It was the reason the attacker jumped me. He claimed I was gay, and he wanted to see what a flaming faggot looked like. Whether it was a random attack or not, I will never know. What I do know is for some reason I was his target. John then showed me it was Michele who was getting Josh to find ways to trigger me. They may not have known what happened, but they did know how to irritate me and that is all it took. Patty was in on it too, but she was a very reluctant participant and even told Josh she was feeling guilty about what they were doing. Josh didn't realize just how badly Michele was manipulating him and Patty or what her end game was. He was getting free weed from Michele and even some cocaine which made it easy for Michele to get what she wanted from the both of them. I didn't know at that time that Josh had started snorting and of course, Patty got in on that action too. Since they were getting free drugs from Michele, Patty caved in and took part in her plan. Very quickly I started spiraling out of control without knowing or even caring that I was losing control. I didn't have the slightest clue as to where or why Josh was sticking bags of weed and rolling papers in my desk. I didn't care either, I was getting high for free. The other thing I didn't know about and never found was the vial of cocaine he'd stuck in my desk. Michele had planned on getting me hooked on coke in addition to her other plans. I didn't know why he did it or that someone else found it first. If I had found the coke, I knew I would have tried it and it would have been the death of me. The thing was, getting high made all the bad shit go away. Not dealing with all the bad shit made things worse, making me want to find a better high. Adding coke to the weed and alcohol would have been an accidental overdose just waiting to happen.

2

John took me forward to the time and place he wanted me to see my dorm room. Josh, Patty, and Michele were all there. Even though Patty still didn't have a roommate, the three of them would now hang out in our room. Josh and Patty were starting to screw one another while I was sleeping in my bed instead of Patty's room. When they started sleeping together in Josh's bed, I was passed out from being stoned or drunk, too wasted to notice their fuck sessions. I did walk in on them one morning after I got back from the showers. Regardless of how fucked-up I got the night before; I was still an early riser. I would go out onto the trails and find a place to get high before heading to breakfast. The morning I walked in on them, Josh thought I had already headed out to get high and wasn't coming back. Josh was lying on his back with his arms and hands over his head holding onto the metal bar that ran across the headboard of his bed. Patty was under the blanket with her feet sticking out at the bottom of the bed. The blanket was rising up and down. Josh turned his head towards me seeing I had just come back from the showers. He smiled at me and said, "Don't get dressed, your next." I honestly didn't know what to say. I grabbed my clothes, walked over to the front of my closet, and quickly got dressed. I wanted out of there fast. As I was grabbing my jacket and leaving, I could hear Josh's moaning getting louder as he blurted, "Paige dude, you're next. OH GOD, I'M GONNA CUM!" I didn't respond I just got the hell out of there. It wasn't right away, but Josh and I did have words over that and some other things.

3

I looked through the portal at the scene in front of me. It was just after the Christmas holiday break. It was Wednesday night; the night Kenny and I had gone to Peach's Variety for what would be the last time we hung out. We had gotten the news about Billy and Joey and wanted to go there in memory of Billy. Billy's death and the realization of his death didn't hit me till the drive back to the campus. Billy had told the group we were the only real friends he had ever made. We liked him for who he was, and he could be himself without judgment. I guess the last four months of his life were his best because of the three of us. It hurt bad losing Billy. Because of that, I was hurting miserably that night and could not wait to get back to the campus so I could smoke another joint and polish off that bottle of JD I had. Josh and Patty were on Josh's bed in their usual position with Josh lying on his back and Patty lying next to him. She was on her side, resting her head on his chest with her hand on his crotch. Michele had claimed my bed as her chill spot. I could hear their conversation. The conversation started with Michele asking where I was. "He is down by the pond getting baked". Josh replied assuming that is where I was. "Holy shit he has turned into a total party animal! He is like totally drunk, stoned, or both 24/7." Patty seemed surprised by that, like she was expecting a different result. Michele seemed pleased with Josh, and she had a huge smile on her face. "Josh, you have created a monster." I think that was the only time Michele ever smiled. "Yeah well, you seem to be taking advantage of him." Josh was starting to regret his part. "Yeah well, it's not like he doesn't like it," was Michele's justification for what she was doing. Josh said that he and Patty didn't mind helping her get even with me for the beach party thing, but she was over here just about every night, and I kept telling her, "NO." Michele was still smiling that evil smile. "I love that he keeps telling me "No" when he is way too stoned to resist or stop me. "Patty's regret was showing now. "Josh is right, we didn't mind helping you get even but don't you think you're taking things too far? I mean you're going to end up getting pregnant." Michele revealed her true plan to them, "That's the point! Then he will have to marry me. I will own him and the Nig will lose his boy toy. I win!" This horrified Patty. "What if it backfires and he doesn't want to marry you, or you can't get pregnant?" Patty didn't know what else to say. She couldn't believe she let Michele trick her into doing something this evil. Michele insisted, "Once you finish helping me get him hooked on coke he will marry me. You watch." I could now see the regret Josh felt when he said, "If I knew you were going to take things this far, I would never have gotten him high. This is so fucking wrong!" I never knew he said that, nor did I ever believe his regret but then again, he didn't stop what he was doing. His free weed and coke seemed far too important to lose. Patty was truly upset, and her normal voice was back. There was no more squealing. "Josh is right! I regret being part of this too. You made your point! You got even! Getting pregnant is going to ruin both your lives." Josh tried to demand that it was time to end this. "You've got to stop this with him. He isn't in his right mind," but he knew he had already lost this battle with Michele; she wasn't going to stop. Patty tried again by telling Michele, "You don't even go here. We do. I am going to call campus police and have you kicked out of here if you don't stop." Michele was getting nasty with them. "HEY! Screw the both of you! It's not like you weren't part of this, you both helped me." Josh tried to make another lame-ass attempt to get out of it by telling Michele they didn't know it was going to go this far. Michele got right in their faces. Gritting her teeth she told them, "Go ahead, try and stop me and watch me turn you two into campus police. I will tell them where you hide your stash. You both have enough coke and weed to get arrested and expelled. When Paige gets back just leave us alone." She told them both how it was going to be. Patty was feeling used and betrayed by Michele, she knew her childhood friend would turn them in and stab them in the back to get what she wanted.

4

While all that was going on in my room, I was driving into the parking lot with Kenny. Kenny liked to smoke weed too, so he and I sat in my car in the parking lot and smoked several bowls with the bong he had. I had about half a bottle of JD left. We polished that off too. As hard as Kenny fought to hold back the tears that night, he did end up shedding quite a few on the ride back. I would be lying if I said I didn't get a little misty-eyed. As the saying goes, you don't know what you have till it's gone. We both wanted to numb the pain of losing Billy, and knowing Joey wasn't coming back sucked too. Very quickly we both got fucked-up pretty damn good. Our little party got broken up much sooner than we wanted though. Kenny was packing another bowl when the main door to the dorm suddenly opened. We were at the far end of the parking lot but could still keep an eye on the main door to the building. As luck would have it out came my ole' buddy Scott the R.A. Kenny shoved his bong into his coat, and I put the empty bottle of JD back under my seat and out of sight. I saw Scott look over at us but for some reason, he just kept going. It wasn't like he couldn't smell what we were smoking. He knew what we were doing and he couldn't have had a better opportunity to bust me like he wanted to in the past. For whatever reason, he gave us both a free pass that night. After Scott was out of sight, we both decided not to press our luck and called it a night. When I got back to my room, there the three of them were. Before I could even close the door Patty got up off the bed and said, "Come on Josh let's just go". I was too fucked-up to see the tension between the three of them. Josh followed right behind Patty without saying a thing to me on the way out. Being in the state I was I didn't even realize Michele was still in the room. When I turned around, there she was right in front of me completely naked. She wrapped her arms around my waist and slid her hands into the back pockets of my jeans and started to rub my ass saying. "Hey Paige, looks like we're alone." I was so stoned I couldn't push her away even though I tried. Michele knew I was powerless when I was this fucked-up. "Come on get off me. I don't want to do this," I told her as I tried to push her away again. "Oh, come on Paige. Don't you like girls? You're not the Nig's bitch, are you?" Michele slid her hands into the back of my pants and continued rubbing my ass, flesh to flesh. "Fuck you we're not gay! Get off me I don't want this." Michele kept at it. "I told you I don't want you coming over here doing this." Michele guided me over to my bed. She had taken one hand out, undone the button, unzipped my jeans and started fondling me. She pushed me down on the bed and got right in my face when she said, "Look at that, Paige can't get a stiffy. Guess you don't like girls after all". "I hate you now leave." I snapped. I just wanted her to go so I could pass out. I was so fucked-up I didn't have enough control to get her off me. Michele knew it too. She wouldn't take "no" for an answer. She took my boots and socks off then slid my pants off so I was lying there on my bed naked from the waist down. Michele was lying between my legs. She looked up at me and said, "I know," then proceeded to take me in her mouth. That's all it took; within seconds I was hard as a rock. If I wasn't powerless before I was now. "Well maybe you aren't gay after all". Michele quickly straddled my waist, took a hold of me, and slid me inside her. I gave in and let out a moan of pleasure. Once again Michele got her way with me. No matter how long it took, Michele wouldn't stop till I came inside her. I didn't get a reprieve even when Michele's Aunt Flo came to visit. She would still have her way with me, she would just use her mouth. This had been going on since we got back from Thanksgiving break which was the time I had started spiraling out of control and continued through February. I was at my weakest point. She knew it and she took full advantage of me. I was drinking heavily when the pot wasn't enough. I was making things worse for myself. I was scared to talk to anyone or tell them what was going on. Even though Tony said he would protect me, I was still afraid of losing him and I was scared he would think I was a loser for getting high and that I was nothing but a burnout. I was weak and powerless, and Michele's plan was in full swing and working damn near flawlessly. She was getting what she wanted.

5

I don't know how I managed it, but I was able to slam the portal shut. I didn't want to see it anymore. I didn't know which was worse the anger, the hurt, or the humiliation I was feeling. All I knew was I wanted this to stop right then and there. The remaining mist had cleared. John knew just how upset I was, and he could sense all the emotions I was feeling. I still had my back to him when he put a hand on my shoulder in that supportive fatherly way of his. I said, "Look at what I did to myself. How could I have been so stupid!" John was as kind and compassionate as you could get. His soft tone when he spoke always helped to ease my tension. But not this time, not when he said, "No Paige, that isn't what I am trying to show you. You're not seeing it." It was one thing to have done what I did, but to watch myself go through that again and not be able to stop it knowing what was to come, was unbearable. Nothing John said could help. I turned around to face him. He could see my eyes were welling up with tears of frustration and humiliation. I couldn't hold back my anger and self-loathing anymore when I said to him. "I see that I got fucked-up every day on pot and booze! I see that as plain as day. How could I let that happen? Why did I let Michele do what she did? I let her do that to me! Why?" I was so upset I was huffing from anger and trying to catch my breath. How could I have let this happen? John tried again using his calming tone with more empathy than before. He said, "No Paige that's not it". I was so frustrated, "Then what is it I am not seeing?!" John took a deep breath and sighed. The mist returned to engulf us so the portal could open. John spoke, "I guess I will have to keep showing you more. Come on, let's keep moving forward." Having to do this hurt John just as much as it did me. I was like a son to him, and I considered him to be like a dad to me. He was there for me when my father wasn't. Even though I knew how much this was hurting him too, it did nothing for the anger I had in that moment. I snapped at him. "Great let's just keep throwing my teenage fuck-ups in my face.

Maybe, just mutha fucking maybe, I'll get it. We were both swallowed up by the mist as the portal re-opened.

Chapter 14

1

John wanted to show me another time when the attack had influenced my behavior. John had shown me how horribly Tony and I were treated by the first responding officers. At the time, I didn't realize just how much of a hold the attack and the abusive treatment of the first responding officers had on me. The internal battle I had going on was fueled by the trauma of the attack and the horrible way we were treated by the responding officers. John said it was important for me to see that before moving forward again. The battle was raging and exploding inside me with the force of a nuclear bomb. There were times when the battle and explosions would spill out. Scott the R.A. wasn't the only one that I had an encounter with that led to me losing my cool. Another person I attacked was Cory Miller. Cory transferred to Mercy College from the University of San Francisco in California where he was born and raised. Cory was a short guy. He stood about five foot two, was lean, and kept himself in very good shape. Cory wasn't what you would call, openly gay. He never really flew the pride flag so to speak and he never really denied it either. There were a few guys in the dorm that did ask him if he was gay. The only reply he would give is, "I am who I am, and who I sleep with is none of your business." Then he would just walk away. Overall, Cory was a good person and completely harmless. His flaw was that he couldn't read the room. A couple of weeks after Cory transferred in and the second semester started, he and I actually met and talked with him besides the, "Hey, sup dude," we would say in passing. Like myself, Cory liked to get up early, and until Cory transferred here, I was the only one in the shower that early every morning. I was usually done showering and headed back to my room when Cory would pass me, and we would exchange our "sup dude" and keep on going. I didn't give it any thought when he started showering at the same time I did. The shower room had four separate showers then an open sink area. I usually had a towel wrapped around my waist when I went over to the sink before leaving. Something else I didn't give any thought to was when Cory took a shower, he would walk over to the sink completely naked. The dude was hung like a Bull Buffalo and wasn't afraid to flaunt it. Other guys did this too, it wasn't like they were hitting on you it was just dudes being dudes. I didn't give it any thought. One morning he asked if I liked getting baked. He said he had some California Gold if I wanted to try it. I was surprised he didn't look like the type to get baked. I said, "Sure, let me get dressed and I will come get you. We can go to my spot." The first time we went and got high together he asked about the blond girl (Michele), who was hanging around my room. He asked if she was my girlfriend. I told him, "No," and of course being eighteen and cool I said, "She is just some random chic I bang regularly. Then, maintaining my coolness I said, "I don't even like her I just like being in her pussy." There was no way I was going to tell him the truth about what she was doing nor was I telling anyone about the real reason I am not around on weekends. So, I just told him what I told him. We got high every morning for about a couple of weeks until one morning Cory's roommate wasn't around for a few days. That morning, I walked down to Cory's room after I got dressed. I knocked on the door like I normally did but this time instead of Cory walking out so we could go get high he said, "It's unlocked come on in." I walked in and there he was, still naked from the shower. I said, "Sorry dude, didn't know you were still getting ready." He said "I am ready how about you? Do you want to try something different?" I looked at him and said, "Ummm, different?" That is when he walked up to me, grabbed my jacket, and pulled me closer trying to kiss me. There was no missing his boner it was sticking straight out. Needless to say, I didn't react well, and I shoved Cory away. I pushed him so hard I knocked him off his feet and he landed on his ass at the other end of the room. As he lay naked and sprawled on the floor, I lost my cool. He saw how pissed I was. I saw that he was afraid of me and when I approached him, he cowered on the floor. I went off on him the same way I went off on Scott. I told him I wasn't fucking gay, and he was to stay away from me, especially in the showers. "This dude's asshole is exit only and I only eat pie so back the fuck off." Even though I kept my voice low so no one would hear me, the anger on my face, the rage in my eyes, and the gritting of my teeth was more than enough to justify his fear. After I went off on Cory, I stormed out of his room and went to my car to grab the bottle of JD I stashed in there earlier in the week. Weed alone wasn't going to calm me down after that. I took three huge swigs from the bottle which hit me fast on an empty stomach. I put the bottle back under the seat and went to find a new spot to get high just in case Cory called security on me. Fortunately, he never did. Cory made it a point to avoid me and never showed up to the showers in the morning again. The couple of times I did run into him I wasn't nice to him. He tried to apologize but I wasn't having anything to do with it. Back then and even now, watching myself through the portal, I couldn't understand why I was acting like that on campus, why the internal battle was so strong, and why I got triggered so easily. If I wasn't with Tony, I would have loved to have dated Cory, he truly was a great guy. I was with Tony every weekend, the man I was in love with, so I couldn't understand my actions to Cory. I have always regretted doing that to Corey. I wanted to apologize to him, but he transferred out at the end of the semester, and I never got the opportunity to do so. Scott the R.A. was a total asshole to everyone, so I never felt guilty about going off on him. I wasn't the only one who couldn't stand Scott. When I was with Tony at the cabin, I was so happy and at peace with being with him and loving him. When I left and went back to the campus for the week the self-loathing and humiliation of being gay set in. I was in complete denial. I was a textbook closet case who would do anything and everything to protect my secret. Although I could easily be triggered, I didn't think I would react like I did. There was no conscious thought involved. The self-medicating was making things worse.

2

After John had shown me what he wanted me to see, he brought me to the next stop on my journey. It was March of 1987, and I was looking into my dorm room. It was the beginning of a week of midterms and we were heading into Spring Break. Josh and Patty were on his bed as usual with Josh lying on his back. Patty was lying between his legs with the side of her head resting on his crotch facing Michele who made herself all comfy on my bed. Josh was stroking the top of Patty's head wishing I would get back so he could take off to Patty's room so she could take care of the boner she was lying on. Things had cooled off a lot friendship-wise with the three of them since Michele threatened to turn them into Campus Police. However, that didn't stop Josh from sticking a small vial of cocaine in my desk earlier that day when Michele first showed up. Josh and Patty started sleeping in Patty's room together again and leaving when I would come in instead of spending the night in Josh's bed. Through the big chill, Patty tried to make small talk with Michele by asking if she wanted to go to the Spring Break bonfire this weekend to celebrate the end of midterms. Michele said, "No, not this weekend." Patty was curious because Michele never said no to a kegger. Patty, trying to be funny said, "You said no to a kegger. What? Are you sick or something?" Michele just shrugged and said, "or something". Patty lifted her head off Josh's lap and said, "Ahhh, you got a better offer this weekend. What's going on with your homies and cronies over at State?" Patty looked at Josh, smiled then kissed his protruding crotch and laid her head back down facing Michele. Michele nonchalantly looked over at Patty telling her, "Nothing is going on I just can't drink for like nine months" As soon as Josh heard this, he bolted upright and looked down at Patty who was propped up on her elbows. Josh said to Patty " OH FUCK! She's pregnant. This has gone way too far!" I could tell he was sickened by this. Patty was in shock and disbelief. She didn't think Michele was going to go through with getting pregnant. Patty thought Michele was just mouthing off when she said it because they went on the pill together back in high school and she didn't think Michele was being serious about having me get her pregnant. They had filled their prescription together before coming back from Christmas break. Patty finally spoke up. I could tell she was disgusted with Michele when she said to her, "I can't believe you did this. So, what you got blown off months ago! You are barfing me out. "Michele didn't like their reaction and was getting pissy with them, she started using that nasty tone of hers, "I told you from the start nobody does that to me and gets away with it. I own his ass now." Patty backed off a bit knowing the tone Michele was using wasn't a good one. She asked if I knew. Michele snapped back, "No I haven't told him yet." Josh tried to stand up to Michele by telling her that she needed to tell me. Michele snapped back at Josh, "I am going to tell the Nig first. I am going to rub it in his face and tell him, "I stole your boy toy." Josh, still not backing down from Michele, raised his voice in frustration and told Michele. "How many times does Paige have to tell you they're just friends. He isn't gay!" Michele leaned forward and with her nasty tone told Josh it didn't matter, she was going to force me to marry her. Patty tried, to tone it down by using a softer voice when she asked Michele, "What if he says no?" No, the word Michele hates hearing coupled with the revolt of her partners in crime who were now realizing what they had done, had Michele getting more defensive and nastier than before. "If he says 'no', I am going to tell everyone he has AIDS and the Nig gave it to him." Patty tried again to talk to her friend, the person she idolized and wanted to be like. There was hurt in her voice now. "Michele this isn't you. You have turned into a total monster since we got back from Mexico. What happened to you with that guy in the bar?" Michele was immediately triggered by this. She got right in Patty's face and was completely infuriated that Patty brought up the Mexico trip which was a high school graduation present from her father. Michele screamed in Patty's face, "NOTHING FUCKING HAPPENED shut your slut mouth about Mexico!" Josh had had enough of this. Seeing Michele go off in Patty's face was getting to be too much even for him. He jumped up off the bed and stood up to Michele. "You know what, screw you, Michele. Turn us in or whatever but this is so fucking wrong. We don't want any part of it or you. Get out and stay away from us, we don't want you around anymore." Patty finally had had enough too, and told Michele to go screw herself and get out. Michele had taken a few steps back from Josh when he stood up and confronted her. She wasn't expecting them to react like that. She thought she pretty much controlled them. Michele said, "Fine I will turn you both in later right now I am off to see the Nig." With that she left and headed over to John's.

3

Josh and Patty were staring blankly at one another in total disbelief at what just happened. Patty hugged Josh, buried her face in his chest, and started crying. "Oh god, what did we just do? What were we thinking?" Josh stood there holding her for a moment before sitting on his bed. Josh looked scared. I wasn't sure if he was scared for me, of me, or of getting caught, but whatever it was, I was seeing Josh in fear for the first time. I saw what I had suspected all along; the cool dude act was just that, an act. Josh asked Patty what happened to Michele in Mexico. Patty stopped crying and was able to pull herself together to tell Josh the story. They had gotten separated one night because Michele met this guy in a bar. Patty told Josh that Michele was gone for a few days and when she finally came back to the hotel, she was a mess and had bruises on her. Patty told Josh that she tried to ask what happened, but Michele refused to talk about it. Josh said, "This is crazy, she is like Jekyll and Hyde. One minute she is the Michele we grew up with and the next, she is this crazy woman." They both knew how badly they screwed me over and for what? Free weed and coke. Patty started crying again and buried her face in Josh's chest saying through the tears, "She is scaring me."

4

From there, John took me to his place. As I looked down through the portal, I could see he and Tony were standing in front of the cabin just chatting, like normal. The conversation stopped when John saw a car creeping up the drive as if the driver were lost. John said, "I wonder who that is?" Tony turned to look and immediately recognized Michele. "That is Michele the one who likes to start trouble for me behind my back." John noticed Tony tensing up. He could see Tony's wall of defense rise. "Oh, this can't be good," John said as Michele stopped the car, got out, and started walking over toward them. "Hey Nig," Michele said in such a sassy and mocking way that it angered Tony. "My name is Antonin Kofi Bedru, do not call me that racist name. What do you want Michele Gibons?" John had never seen Tony this angry and just as Michele was going to say something else that was only going to fuel that fire, John cut her right off. "Hey, listen here. I will have none of that on my property. He said his name very clearly and you will call him by his name, or you can leave." Michele tried her sass with John, "Like who's the rude old dude?" Without changing his tone John replied, "My name is John Williamson. This is my property and I will have none of that here." Michele put her left hand on her hip and thrust it to the side trying to add a physical element to match her attitude. "Like fine, take a chill pill. You're gonna want to hear what I have to say." Tony took a step forward, leaned in towards Michele with a pointed finger and said to her, "Then get to it. Say your piece then leave." I could see Michele was getting intimidated by John and Tony and nervously said, "You two are so warm and welcoming such gracious hosts, NOT." John could see Michele starting to realize things were not going her way and both he and Tony drove that point home when John said, "Last warning. Trust me, this is your last warning," Tony followed and was very direct, "What do you want?" Michele's plans were backfiring on her. Her two best friends stood up to her and told her to screw off, and John and Tony were not intimidated by her, so she dropped the attitude and got right to the point. "OK fine, I am here to let you know a few things about your 'friend' Paige." "Like what?" Tony asked, still not dropping his animosity towards her. Michele got nervous and flustered and blurted out, "I don't know what you did to him, something happened and he couldn't handle it, so he turned to drugs like pot and alcohol to cope. Paige is a total drunk and stoner. Who knows, maybe he is going to try coke too." This angered Tony. Watching this was the only time I ever saw Tony get angry and raise his voice. "That isn't true!" he shouted at Michele "Andrew Paige is never drunk or stoned when he is here riding motorbikes!" Michele, thinking maybe she struck a nerve and was again able to gain the upper hand, tried to get brazen and smart-mouthed Tony by saying, "OH, like motorcycle riding is why he comes here, NOT! I bet he is riding something else." John didn't like that one bit, and he told Michele point blank, "Don't, Just Don't. If there is nothing else, then leave. You have worn out your welcome here." No one has ever stood up to Michele, yet today four people have stood up to her and she didn't know what to do. Once again, getting flustered, she blurts out, " Paige is always drunk or stoned and forces me to have sex with him. Now I'm pregnant and he has to marry me." Tony shouted, "WHAT! That's not true! None of this is true!" A very scared Michele was barely able to utter, "Ask Josh his roommate. He is the one who got Paige high to begin with. I'm innocent." John had his fill of her and put an end to Michele's visit by telling her he was going to do just that, confront Josh and get the truth. He told her to get off his property and never come back. Michele turned and hurried to her car. As she was getting in, she told John and Tony that I had to marry her or else she was going to get an abortion and then tell everyone Tony gave me AIDS. With that, she wasted no time in getting out of there.

5

Michele showing up to the cabin and delivering the news to them like that made Tony furious. I had never seen him like that and neither had John. From my angle, I was looking down at Tony and I could see the tears welling up in his eyes from frustration. "John, she is a liar. Not Paige, NO!" John took a deep breath to help compose himself. He knew if he showed his emotions about the situation, it would just make things worse. When he spoke, it was with that soft fatherly tone we knew him for. "Tony, it may be true, Paige has been distant and not himself since he was attacked. He wouldn't be the first one to turn to drugs or alcohol to cope. I have seen it before." Tony said to John there was no way that I took advantage of Michele the way she claimed. John was quick to agree with Tony adding that it is more likely Michele took advantage of me when I was completely powerless. Tony asked John what they could do to help me. John needed a minute to think. He double-checked something by asking Tony if midterms ended this Friday and if Spring Break was starting. Tony said "Yes," that was correct and I was supposed to be spending the week there but now, after what Michele said, he didn't know if I was. John told Tony his idea of having pizza night up at his house instead of the cabin. John said he would stop by the dorm to confront Josh and see if he could confirm Michele's story before he confronted me. This gave him time to come up with a plan. Tony asked if this is what's called an intervention. John said, in a way, yes. Tony expressed his concern and was worried I would get kicked out of school if anyone found out. John assured Tony that he was going to do everything he could to prevent that. He told Tony they would take one step at a time. The first step was talking to Josh. With that, the portal closed so, John could take me to the next stop on the journey.

Chapter 15

1

We moved ahead a few days to the Wednesday of mid-term exam week. I was looking down into my dorm room. I had the room to myself again, and Josh was back to sleeping in Patty's room, I didn't know why Michele had **not** been around, but I wasn't complaining. I liked the fact I could study in my own room. As I looked down, Josh was alone lying in bed. He had just gotten back from Patty's room and with no morning exams, he decided to crash for a few more hours. I had already headed out to go to my spot. Looking down, I could see John entering the building and heading for my room. I saw John knock and heard Josh yell, "It's open." John entered the room. "Hi, you must be Josh. Is Paige around?" John's voice was friendly enough, but it lacked that warm fatherly tone John would use with me and Tony. Josh wasn't sure how to reply. He knew I went to get high like I did every morning since helping implement Michele's plan. He told John I must have had an early class or was at breakfast. He wasn't sure where I was. John, being a retired therapist, knew asking questions would get him the answers he was looking for.

116

"I guess I must have just missed him. Let me ask you something. How is Paige doing?" John started with a simple question to feel things out. "OK, I guess" wasn't the answer John was looking for but that is the answer Josh gave. He was hoping Josh would open up a bit. He probed a little deeper with the next question. "You guys are roommates and spend a lot of time together, so you would notice if something was off, right? Josh didn't like being questioned and was growing suspicious of John. He tried brushing John off by saying nothing seemed off. John gave him a questioning look and asked him if he was sure about that. Josh became nervous with the look John gave him and had a hunch John was a cop. Knowing John had to tell him if he was, Josh asked, "Are you a cop or something?" John was quick to respond by telling Josh that no, he wasn't a cop. Then he went on to explain to Josh why he was there. John's explanation left out the part where Michele told him it was Josh who was getting me high hoping to get Josh to talk. He told Josh about Michele's visit and what was said and as John put it, "I simply didn't believe her". He went on to say to Josh that he stopped by to check with him because he was my roommate, and he figured if anyone would know it would be him. Josh knew he was busted; John knew what was going on. Josh wanted out of there. In a panic to get out of the room and away from John, Josh got out of bed stripped down naked and headed over to his closet figuring hitting the showers was a good way to get out of there. He also thought being naked would get John all flustered and get him to stop asking questions he didn't want to answer. As Josh stripped down and tried to step over to the closet to gather his things he told John it was all cool there and he needed to hit the showers. Josh did add that nothing like that was going on as far as he could tell. John remained completely cool, calm, and collected as his past training taught him to be. He told Josh that was a relief, and he was very glad to hear that. John decided not to bring up Michele's claim of being pregnant. He wasn't going to get much else out of Josh and didn't want him running out of the room bare-assed naked and creating a scene. He told Josh he was going to leave a note for me and be on his way. John reached for my desk asking if it was okay to look for a pen and paper. Josh knew John would find the bag of weed and possibly the vial of coke he stuck in my desk if he went looking for a pen and paper. Josh grabbed a pen, tore a blank page from his notebook that was on his desk, and handed both to John so he wouldn't open my desk drawer. John smiled, thanked him, and said, "You could have put a robe on first." In his panic, Josh forgot he was naked. He stepped over to his closet, pulled out his towel, and wrapped it around his waist. He picked up his soap and shampoo and bolted out the door. John left a brief note saying he was on his way to town and stopped by to say "Hi" and see how midterms were going. Before John left, he checked my desk to see if I had any drugs in there. He saw the bag of weed which he didn't take, he knew if he did, I would know it was him and not show up to the cabin. He picked up the bag of weed and saw the vial of coke. I could see the disappointment on his face. Pot and alcohol were one thing, but coke was another. John also saw an empty bottle of JD behind my dresser which I didn't remember putting there. That was all the digging John needed to do and he headed out the door.

2

I was headed down to my new spot to get high. I had no idea what was going on in my room. When I got to my spot, with a shaking hand, I pulled a joint out of my jacket pocket. I didn't realize how bad things had gotten. For a long time now, I was at the point that if I wasn't high, I couldn't function mentally. It was showing on the outside without me even realizing it. I was visibly shaking but I didn't realize how chemically dependent I had become. If I had found the coke I would have gone from chemically dependent to full-blown addict, and snorting just one line would have done it. I reached back into my pocket for my lighter, but it wasn't there. I started patting my pockets trying to remember which one I put the lighter in. Coming up empty I said out loud to myself, "I forgot my lighter shit the bed last night." I had bought a multi-pack of Bic's and threw the extra lighters in my dresser. I forgot to grab a new one out of the top drawer where I kept them. Pissed at myself because I needed to get high,

I started heading back to my room to get a new lighter. I got back to the dorm and was walking down the hall to my room when I saw Josh bolting out the door with a towel falling off his waist and his shower stuff in his hands. We both stopped in the middle of the hall, and I couldn't help but laugh as Josh's towel fell off and he was standing in the middle of the hallway naked. "Laugh all you want but where have you been? There is an old dude in our room looking for you." I was still laughing at Josh because it was cold in the hallway, and it showed. "Old dude?" I managed to ask. Josh bent down, picked up his towel, and said to me as he walked away, "I hope you ain't baked cause we're both fucked if you are!" and off into the shower room he went. I stood there thinking, old dude in my room? Who the hell is here? I knew it wasn't my father because the 'rents were on vacation in the Caribbean. The cruise ship wasn't due back till next weekend which is why I didn't have to come up with a lie for the 'rents about not going home for spring break. I was excited about spending the week with the "Tones". I had no idea who was in my room or what to think. I was turning to leave, because going back to my room wasn't such a good idea now, and at that moment the door to my room opened.

3

In a way I was relieved to see John walking out of my room, at least I knew who it was. I was thinking maybe he was here to tell me I can't stay the week or that I am not allowed out to the cabin anymore. "There you are." He said as he stepped into the hall. I nervously replied, "Hey John, what are you doing here?" I thought to myself, this isn't a good time for him to be here. He told me he just stopped by to see how midterms were going. He also wanted to tell me that for a change of pace, he thought he would have pizza night in his house instead of the cabin. John wasn't staring but it was like he was sizing me up or something as he spoke. I had an awkward feeling about it like he was here looking for something. My reply of, "Yeah sure that sounds good," sounded as awkward as I felt. John asked if I was going to be spending the spring break week with Tony. I told John that was the plan if he was okay with it. John was completely okay with it. His tone got a bit more serious when he started to say that I looked to be in rough shape. I told him I was up all night studying and hadn't gotten much sleep the past few days with all the cramming I was doing. I know he didn't buy it, but he said he remembered those days of pulling all-nighters. Then John said he would get going and would see me Friday night asking me about what time I'd be there. I told him around seven o'clock because I wanted to crash for a while first. John thought that was perfect and told me to ignore the note he left on my desk. He wished me luck with my midterms and left. I watched John leave and thought to myself his visit was weird. Why didn't he just call if that's all he wanted? I was glad I forgot my lighter because if I ran into him after a few tokes that wouldn't have been good.

4

He left a note which meant he went into my desk to get something to write with and write on. It was like I could see the big neon sign that said, "BUSTED". I turned to go into my room to check if he had taken my stash and see what the note said. From behind me, I heard Josh ask if he was gone. Josh had been standing inside the shower room with the door cracked so he could listen to our conversation. "Yeah, he's gone. Will you put a fucking towel on or something," I said to Josh as he stepped into the hall. "Sorry Paige dude" he replied as he stepped back into the shower room and came out a few seconds later wrapped in his towel. As we were walking into our room, I asked how he kept Patty satisfied with that little thing. "Fuck you it's a grower, not a shower." "I'm sure it is," I said shaking my head at him. I asked if John went into my desk so he could leave a note. Josh told me he gave him the paper and pen to write with. He told me John didn't go into my desk while he was there. I double-checked to see if the bag of weed was still there, and it was. I asked if he said anything. Josh said, "No, he said he was just stopping by to leave a note". I believed his lie. "Paige dude, can I ask you something without you freaking out?" I wanted to say no. I wanted to grab a new lighter and go get high. "What do you want to ask Josh?" "I heard the old dude ask if you were spending the week with your buddy Tony," I told him yeah that's right I am.

Josh wanted to know if he could ask something else without me freaking out. I told him, "Just ask what you are going to ask so I can leave." He wanted to know if Tony and I had a thing because I was going there instead of going home for the week. I told Josh "Bite me you tiny dicked asswipe. I ain't fucking gay." I let him know I wasn't going home because my parents were on their twenty-fifth anniversary cruise. I didn't want to spend the week with my asshole brother, his girlfriend, and their two kids who lived with my parents. "Why would you even ask that?" Josh started to answer but I stopped him and said, "You know what, I don't even want to know why you asked, just go fuck yourself." I grabbed a new lighter and walked out. I didn't want to deal with him I just wanted to get high. The portal remained open. I watched Josh open my desk drawer and remove a vial. He unscrewed the vial and made a fist with his free hand. He turned his fist sideways and dumped the contents of the tiny vial on the side of his fist then snorted the coke, thinking he was getting rid of the evidence. Not only did Josh play hockey with a warped puck I swear someone blew his pilot light out because he left the empty vile on his desk: so much for getting rid of evidence.

5

The portal shifted to the cabin. Tony and John were sitting at the table. It was later the same day that Tony asked John if he stopped by the dorm and got the answers he was looking for from Josh. John had said "Yes," he got his answers and that he ran into me too. Tony was surprised John ran into me and wanted to know more. John told Tony he was glad he ran into me because it helped confirm his suspicions. I could see the mixed emotions of worry for me and anger for Michele when he said, "Your suspicions of Michele lying were true. Paige isn't doing drugs and Michele isn't pregnant. It was all lies just like I said." John said, "I am sorry Tony, but I think Michele was telling us the truth." Tony lowered his head; this wasn't what he wanted to hear. John went on to tell Tony that Josh wasn't very convincing with his denial of not knowing anything. When he ran into me, he didn't think I was high. He told Tony I had some of the telltale signs of someone who was using, though. He told Tony I seemed a little out of it (otherwise known as baked over) just enough that he could tell I was doing something. Tony told John that he still didn't believe it. He told John I never did any of that when I was at the cabin or with him. That was true. Whenever I was at the cabin with Tony, I didn't get high or drunk. He could not understand why I would do it at University. John told Tony the only way to deal with this was to be perfectly honest. He honestly felt that I was abusing, and he was afraid that I had already become chemically dependent. He also told Tony that I had the shakes when he was talking to me. Tony sat there silently listening with his head down staring at the tabletop. Normally, Tony would look at you when you spoke to him, but with his head down like that I saw just how scared he was for me. I knew that Tony was in love with me but now I was just beginning to realize how deep his love for me was. John was telling Tony that from what he had been told about the night I was attacked, I was using drugs like marijuana and alcohol as a coping tool because I didn't know how to deal with the attack and being gay. As always John was right. That was the reason, and he would soon find out there were other reasons too. John also talked about how he does think that Michele is pregnant but knows I didn't force myself on her. He believed Michele took advantage of me when I was completely powerless. They both sat silently for a moment. Tony lifted his head and looked at John with tear-filled eyes. "Then why isn't Paige using drugs when he is here?" John, doing his best to comfort Tony, said to him that I have referred to "here" as home several times. John said that most likely, when I am here, none of the bad stuff exists. John felt that maybe for me there is no judgment, no outside world trying to harm me, here at the cabin, I felt safe. Being with Tony made me feel safe. With the information John had, that is how he read the situation, and he wasn't wrong. Tony wanted to know what it was that they could do to help me. John felt that confronting me with an intervention may be the thing. He told Tony that sometimes an intervention can get ugly, and he is expecting things to get ugly with me. John let out a big sigh and said he wished his Alice was still here. That she would know how to keep things from getting out of hand. Alice had a knack for knowing what to say and when to say it to keep the ugly out of the intervention. Tony said he wished Alice was there too. He was nervous. He didn't want me to get angry and leave. Tony said, "I want Andrew Paige to get better. I want MY Andrew Paige back!" "I do too," John said, "I do too."

Chapter 16

1

After John's surprise visit, Josh stayed in Patty's room the rest of the week. I was glad Josh was hiding out in Patty's room and Michele was staying away for whatever reason. I needed a break from the toxic trio. He didn't even come back to shower which kept things quiet and uneventful. It was too funny watching Josh, who always tried to be the tough cool guy, cave like a bitch when John showed up. I always suspected he was a pussy. I was glad he didn't spill his guts, instead, he put his tail between his legs and hid in the showers till John left. I was looking down into my dorm room again and I saw myself entering. It was Friday, just around twelve-thirty in the afternoon. I had taken my last two midterms that morning, grabbed lunch, and was now ready to crash for a few hours before heading to Tony's for the week. Knowing how exhausted I was, I set my alarm for five o'clock p.m. just in case I overslept. That would give me plenty of time to pack a bag for the week, grab a hot shower, and be at the cabin by seven o'clock p.m. I was so exhausted from cramming all week long, that I didn't even kick off my boots before lying down. I just crashed face down on my bed, boots and jacket still on. I swear I was asleep before my head hit the pillow. I woke up to my alarm going off. Even though the effects of being high had worn off, I was feeling damn good. I was excited about spending the week with Tony. I got up and threw some clothes into a bag. I ran the bag out to my car. I reached under my front seat to take the bottle of JD back inside with me. Back in my

124

room I took the rolling papers and my lighter and threw them in my desk; I was not going to need them this week. I hid the bottle of JD on the shelf in the closet, got undressed, and headed for the showers. The dorm had pretty much cleared out and no one was around so I could just go about my business and get headed out. After showering and getting dressed, I headed out for Spring Break. I was glad I could leave all my books behind for the week, all except this one book I wanted to read. It's about these seven kids being terrorized by a clown holding a red balloon. It was still too early for the motorcycles, so Tony and I planned to just hang out and enjoy the downtime.

2

I was walking to my car when I saw that Scott the R.A. had parked next to me and the trunk of his car was open. Scott looked up as he was closing the trunk and saw me heading to my car. He caught me off guard because he was sincerely friendly towards me when he said, "Hi Paige, I hope you have a good week". I just nodded and waved as I said, "Thanks dude," trying to avoid an awkward confrontation with him. I didn't make eye contact. He tried to start a conversation by asking what my plans for the week were. I didn't want to talk to him I just wanted to leave so I told him I was headed to pick someone up and then home for the week. I said, "Gotta go, they are waiting on me". Scott told me to have a great week, and he looked forward to seeing me during the second half of the semester. Considering we didn't like one another, I thought that was odd. That was the last time I saw him too. We never ran into one another after that. I jumped in my car and was on my way. I made a stop at Peach's Variety to grab a candy bar. I hadn't eaten since lunch, and it was almost six-thirty. I was getting out of the car to go into the store, but I had to stop. I had been thinking about spending the entire week with Tony, aka "The Tones". Let's just say some of, if not all my thoughts about Tones, were impure and I was pitching a tent. Every time I thought about Tony, the way he would hold me in his arms when we were in bed or on the sofa, and his way of giving certain places on my body attention always got me to pitch a tent. The one-track mind of an eighteen-year-old never disappoints. After giving myself a few minutes, I went in and grabbed my favorite candy bar and a soda. I was quickly on my way again and, before I knew it, turning into the dooryard of the cabin.

3

I pulled up to the cabin but didn't see Tony's car. I had not forgotten that pizza night was at John's house, I just figured Tony had walked up to there. Tony would leave the cabin door unlocked on Friday nights for me if he was running late or up in the barn so I could let myself in and set the table for pizza night. Little things like that always made me feel like it was my home too. As usual, the cabin was unlocked. I threw my bag inside and walked up to John's house. I was surprised not to see Tony's car parked at the barn or John's house. I figured he might be in the barn tinkering with the Harleys if he wasn't up at the house yet. I got to John's, and as I was knocking on the door, I heard him yell to come in. John's house was a ranch-style home he built as a retirement home for both he and his wife Alice. Alice never got a chance to live in the house. She passed away just as the house was being completed. John never did talk about her death much. He would mention Alice from time to time but never really talked about her sudden death or even what she died from. I never pushed the subject; it was a sore spot for him. Alice's death caused a huge strain on John's relationship with his daughter. From what little he did say, his daughter Debbie blamed John for the premature death of her mother. I walked into the house, which had a cool layout. On the right as you walked down the hall, which ran the length of the house, there were three bedrooms. The master bedroom with its private bath sat at the far end of the hall. Separating the master from the other two bedrooms was the second bathroom. On the left side of the hall were the living room and dining room. There was a hip wall separating the two rooms. The house was L-shaped and on the other side of the dining room was the large kitchen with an oversized breakfast nook. Across from the kitchen was the mudroom and entrance to the attached garage. John was in the dining room setting the table when I walked in. I was very upbeat saying, "Hey John, where's The Tones?" I walked down the hall into the dining room and John was at the head of the table setting it with his back towards the kitchen. John said, "He went to pick up the pizzas, he will be back shortly. I bet you're happy midterms are over." He seemed very upbeat himself. "Yes, I am." I told him as I took my jacket off and hung it on the back of a dining room chair. John said I was looking a lot better than when he saw me last. He was right, I was feeling much better too. I told him that I crashed hard and slept most of the afternoon. John asked if I had any exams today which I did. I told John, I had two early morning exams and was glad to have been done early because I needed to crash for the afternoon. John thought it was great that I slept as long as I did and started asking me what else was going on when Tony came in with the pizza. I wasn't paying attention and didn't hear Tony come in behind me, plus I had my back to him, so I didn't see him. I don't think John heard him either. I turned around as soon as I heard his voice. "Paige, I am so glad you are here!" Tony had a huge smile on his face. He was genuinely happy to see me. Tony had always been a reserved and quiet guy. He never showed his emotions and always had a serious look about him. Since I came into the picture, his other side, the real Tony came out. John said he was a different person around me. Tony wasn't afraid to show emotions. His smile had always melted my heart. I loved seeing him smile like that. "Pizza is here so let me go grab some drinks and you two can say, 'hello'." John left to do that as Tony put both boxes of pizza on the table and wrapped his arms around me holding me tight and kissing me on top of my head. "Don't worry Paige we are here for you." Tony's emotional side was showing. "Here for me what are you talking about? It was hard to breathe he was hugging me so hard. "Trust me everything will be OK." I was struggling to get free. I was starting to sense something was going on. As I was struggling to get free from Tony's hug I said, "Tones what are you talking about, stop hugging me!" That didn't help, he didn't let go and he kissed the top of my head again. I was starting to wiggle free when I said, "DUDE! Like what's your damage? Why are you having a cow?" My voice was getting loud, and I was a little irritated and started feeling some anxiety because I knew something was very wrong. John quickly came back into the dining room and I knew he heard us. "Hey guys let's sit down and eat." John was trying to calm the situation before it got out of control. I very firmly said "NO!" Then demanded to know what was going on. John claimed nothing was going on just our regular pizza night and once again said to sit and eat trying to regain a sense of calm. I knew better. It was like my version of "Spidey senses" were going off and I could sense something was wrong. They were up to something.

4

As I was watching this, I could feel the same anxiety rising in me as I felt then. I knew just how scared I was back then. I watched helplessly as the evening's events unfolded in front of me. I wished I could stop it. I watched the fear rise in my eighteen-year-old self as John once again tried to calm the situation. "Come, Paige sit. Let's have some pizza." The fear was taking over I looked right at John, and with a raised voice I again said, "No I am not sitting down! What's going on? You came out to the campus to check up on me. Tony is saying he is here for me, and everything is going to be alright." John tried to deny he was checking up on me. Tony claimed he was just excited to see me, and nothing was wrong. I wasn't buying it, and they were not even coming close to selling it. They were up to something. I said, "Bullshit." Tony tried to say it wasn't bullshit but again, I wasn't buying it. I wanted to know why we were having pizza night here and not in the cabin like always. That's when John knew it was time to stop and just come clean and tell me what was going on. He said I was right something was going on and we needed to talk. He asked me to sit so we could talk about it. Tony asked me to sit too, "Please sit for me so we can talk," he said. With the pleading look he was giving, and his big brown puppy dog eyes, there was no way I could say no. I reluctantly sat down. I sat on the edge of the chair. They could both see how tense I was. I didn't realize it then, but I could see myself shaking. I was nervous and scared shitless because I had no idea what was going on. John said he was just going to come right out and tell me. He said they got a visit the first of the week from Michele and she told them what was going on. I damn near shit myself when he said that. I started shaking even more and got the uncontrollable urge to run out of there and get high so I could calm down, but there was no way that was happening. I tried to think of something but could only come up with, "She probably didn't say much since nothing's going on." John could see how scared I was and that I was hiding something. He said, "On the contrary, they got quite the earful. In a panic, I said, "Earful of shit maybe cause nothing's going on." John remained calm and used his soothing fatherly voice yet kept his professional demeanor. He said he begged to differ, and that Michele told them that I was doing an excessive amount of drugs and drinking. Tony was letting John do the talking at this point. I watched the exchange between myself and John. I was getting defensive in my interaction with John. I shouted at John, "Did I go to a few midweek parties on campus? Yes. That doesn't mean I am getting fucked-up all the time. Plus, Michele doesn't even go to my college she goes to State with Tony. She doesn't know shit. DUDE! I ain't a druggie." John assured me that he wasn't saying or even thinking I was a druggie. I asked him" If that's the case, then why are we even talking about this?" John's tone got less fatherly and more serious. "I am going to tell it to you straight Paige. I honestly believe you are having a hard time coping. You were brutally attacked I saw how badly that affected you. Someone tried to burn you alive. You know I think you tried some pot and maybe some alcohol to help calm you down. Then you used that stuff as a coping tool, and it has gotten out of control. That's what I think." John wasn't backing off in my mind, denial and running away was my only option. "Well, you're wrong! You want to know what I think?" The defensiveness was showing, and I was fucking terrified at this point–I was busted and knew it. It was time for me to bolt out of there. Tony put his hand on top of mine and said, "Yes Paige, we do want to know what you think." I tried to make my exit. "I think I need to bounce. It's time I leave and go find some new friends." Before I even finished my sentence I was standing, putting my jacket back on, and heading for the door.

5

Like a flash, Tony stood up and blocked me from leaving. Telling me he didn't want me to go. John stood up trying to get me to sit back down to talk but stayed where he was. He didn't make any attempt to block my path to the kitchen and mudroom door. In my terrified state of mind and in a complete panic, I was so focused on getting out through the front door, that leaving through the back door was something I didn't think of. I had tunnel vision. I started to lose my cool and I told John there was nothing to talk about. I hollered at Tony, "GET THE FUCK OUT OF MY WAY!" Tony said in the serious tone and look he had the day we met, "No". I needed out of there in the worst way, I had to get away from them. I needed to go back to my dorm and get my bag of weed. I desperately needed to get high. I wish I hadn't taken the bottle of JD out of my car. I had completely lost control and I screamed at Tony to get out of my way and lunged forward making a break for it. Tony grabbed the front of my jacket with both hands, one on each side of my shoulders. I grabbed his shirt the same way and started pushing back and trying to break free so I could run out of there. John shouted for us to both stop but it fell on deaf ears. Tony was much taller than me and larger and I don't think he was expecting me to shove him back into the living room the way I did. As our shoving match continued into the living room, I was shouting for Tony to let go of me, "I am outta here!" Tony would not let go of me and told me that I wasn't leaving. I kept at it trying to leave and yelling, "Let go of me!" Tony was shouting, "You're not leaving, we want to help you." I shouted back, "I don't want your help!" John had come into the living room at this point and yelled for us to break it up, but it was too late. Things started flooding back into my mind. Mentally I was flashing back to the night of the attack. What was making things worse was the things I had forgotten, the things my subconscious tried to erase from my memory that came flooding back as flashbacks, happening right before my eyes, just like the night of the attack. It was those flashbacks that caused me to go into a blind rage. I completely broke down and started screaming, "STOP HITTING ME!" Tony had no idea what was happening, he was confused. "I am not hitting you." I begged Tony to please stop hitting me and told him he was hurting me. My grip on Tony loosened as I collapsed to my knees. Tony's grip loosened a bit too, but he didn't let me go. His grip had changed. He held my head in a supportive caress as I laid the side of my head on the front of his legs while his other arm wrapped around me in support. This time the voice Tony used wasn't the serious voice he used earlier, it was the soft and loving voice that I brought out in him. "Paige I am not hitting you." John had approached us and tried to reassure me that no one was hitting me. My breakdown continued, "Why do you always hit me you're supposed to be my family. You're supposed to be my mother. Stop doing this to me! Parents aren't supposed to do this. I am sick and tired of being hit. STOP IT!" John once again tried to tell me no one is hitting me. It didn't help. I kept on saying, "STOP attacking me! Oh god, I'm in love with another man, that's why you're trying to burn me. Please don't burn me I hate being gay! I am sorry I don't want to be gay I hate it. OH GOD, I'm a fucking queer. Make it all stop!" My breathing was heavy, and I was trying to catch my breath. I was a total mess. John took me by the shoulders and guided me back to the sofa. He assured me I was safe there and no one was going to hurt me. I tried to shrug John off and told him to get off me. He instead put an arm around my shoulders and kept assuring me no one was going to hurt me. He promised I was safe there with them, and again promised no one was going to hurt me. I was starting to catch my breath and was slowly calming down. Physically I was fine, but mentally I was spent. Tony sat on the other side of me saying he was sorry; he didn't mean to hurt me. We sat in silence for a while, John now knowing the attack was just the tip of the iceberg, quickly realized there was an abusive past that I kept buried and didn't talk about out of shame and humiliation. Like others, I blamed myself for the abuse thinking the reason things happened was because of something I did. It was my fault. I was abused.

6

It took a while, but I finally calmed down. My breathing was somewhat normal, and I had stopped shaking. The fear and anxiety I was experiencing had lessened greatly but were not completely gone. John still had an arm around my shoulder but removed his arm and shifted himself so he could talk to me. Tony was still next to me, and I was leaning forward with my elbows on my knees and holding my head in my hands. When John finally spoke, he said it sounded like I had it pretty bad as a kid. Then he brought up the night I was attacked and just how crazy it was. I didn't answer him. I just sat there with my head down after what just happened, too embarrassed to look at either one of them. John spoke again saying it must have been scary for me growing up. I mumbled, "It fucking sucked." John said he didn't doubt one bit that growing up must have sucked for me and wanted me to tell him about it. I didn't want to talk about it, but John kept encouraging me and reassuring me nothing bad was going to happen; they only wanted to help. Reluctantly, I told John and Tony how violent my mother was. Her fits of anger always resulted in a violent rage. I told them of the time my mother grabbed the front of my shirt, slammed me against a wall, and started wildly hitting me with her free hand. I told them how I witnessed my mother shoving my brother up against a door, punching him in the stomach, and pulling his shirt over his head. Then she slammed her forearm and fist into his back. The abuse wasn't limited to just my mother, there was the time my father slammed a car door shut on my leg in a fit of rage. I talked about the times I hid in my bedroom closet or under my bed when the family gathered at the holidays. It always turned into an alcohol-fueled screaming match. I brought up my Uncle Nico. Nico was an immigrant from Greece. He grew up on the small island of Kalymnos where he and his father were sponge divers. After his father died in the Korean War, Nico came to America. Nico planned to live in Tarpon Springs Florida where he could find work as a sponge diver. His visa and travel papers got misfiled and Nico ended up in the same state I was from, where he met my aunt and married her. Nico was a verbally abusive and physically violent man. When he and my aunt fought, Nico got nasty and cruel. If they fought in front of me and my brother, he would holler in our faces, "Your Aunt is a douche bag" or "Your Aunt is a fucking... and he would use the "C" word." There were times I saw him grab my aunt by her wrists and shake her. We talked for quite a while about the abusive childhood I had and the alcohol abuse by several family members which shed a lot of light on things for John. At this point, John suggested we take a break. The night's events had taken a toll on all of us. John stood up and proposed we at least have some soda. Tony stood as well asking if I wanted to step outside a minute to grab some fresh air. I didn't move from the position I was in with my elbows on my knees and my head in my hands the entire time. I was still too embarrassed to look at them. With both off the sofa, I said, "No more talking, I am done," and laid face down on the sofa with my head turned so I was looking at the back cushions. I was spent and completely drained, so it didn't take long before I fell asleep.

7

I watched as John and Tony stepped into the dining room and I listened to a conversation I didn't know they had. John turned to look at me and told Tony that tonight took a toll on me, and it looked like I was down for the count. He was right, all the late nights including an all-nighter for midterms week, the pot and alcohol I had been consuming, and that evening shattered me. I was completely exhausted, and my mind and body shut down. Tony told John he had no idea there was so much abuse in my life; I had never talked about it. John wasn't surprised that I kept the abuse to myself. John told Tony how tonight shed light on things. Now he understood why I never mentioned the abuse or talked about my family. They both talked a little bit longer before stepping back into the living room. Tony said, "He is so exhausted." He placed a blanket over me and kissed the side of my head. John said they all could use a good night's sleep and best we deal with things in the morning. Even after Tony found out it was true that I was abusing pot and alcohol, and I was having sex with Michele even though it was against my will, he still laid a blanket over me, kissed me, and whispered in my ear that he loved me so much. Tony told John he would be by my side the whole time no matter what. Both of them had every right to kick me out and tell me never to come back, but they didn't. I didn't deserve either one of them.

Chapter 17

1

The portal closed briefly and although John and I didn't take full physical form, it felt as if he was putting his hand on my shoulder and giving a squeeze, like he used to, in that fatherly way of his. I needed that after seeing what I did to myself and to feel all those feelings again. I just wanted this to be over. I was glad for the break and the gesture of support. I needed a minute before watching more, but I didn't want to see anymore. I had my soul crushed once and I didn't need to see it or relive it again, but I had no choice– the portal reopened.

2

I was still looking down into John's house. It was the next morning, and John was seated at the dining room table. He had brought out a pot of coffee and mugs for all of us. I was still sleeping on the sofa. Tony let himself in through the mudroom entrance. I heard John say, "Good morning," to Tony and invited him to sit and have coffee. As Tony was pouring coffee and taking a seat, John asked him how he slept. Tony said he couldn't believe he had slept so late. It was around nine a.m. and that was very late for Tony. Like me, he was usually up by six. Then he asked about me. John told him I was still sleeping, and he was glad. He knew just how hard events like last night were on someone. Tony told John he was scared for me, and he didn't want me to leave. He was worried about the trouble I may get into if I did. He also said he wanted to help me. John knew Tony truly wanted to help and so did John. John said he really should be sending me to a facility but was worried they may reach out to my family. Getting the parents involved wasn't a good idea, he knew I needed to deal with the chemical dependency first. Tony agreed with John about not involving the parents after hearing about my childhood. He told John, "No, no, no! Involving Paige's parents is a very bad idea." John said that since I was eighteen, he didn't have to involve my family. Even though he could end up in a lot of trouble if the plan he was mulling over backfired, he was willing to try. Since we were off this week and hopefully, I'd be staying there, John was confident that the plan would work. Tony wanted to hear more but John wanted to wait for me to get up and then go over the plan.

3

I woke up just as Tony walked into the dining room. It took me a few minutes to get my wits about me; waking up in John's house with the unfamiliar surroundings was causing some confusion. I was still groggy but was beginning to remember where I was and what happened. I lay there not wanting to get up. I felt like a complete idiot after humiliating myself last night. It was the perfect time for me to get up and bolt out of there. Believe me when I say that is all I wanted. I couldn't though, and it wasn't from a lack of wanting or trying. I had never felt this awful before. My body ached all over and I had a killer migraine. The brain fog was the worst one I had ever had, and I couldn't think clearly. I couldn't even remember how to sit up or stand and when I tried to get up, I could barely support my weight. I could only lay there trying to hear what John and Tony were talking about. They talked for what seemed like an eternity. They finished talking and that's when I was starting to feel like I could get up and I thought this was a good time for me to leave. It took me a minute to rise, and when I finally did, I heard Tony say, "Paige you're up. Come sit and I will pour you some coffee." There went my clean getaway, I didn't realize Tony was sitting on the side of the table where he could see right into the living room. I didn't want to face those two, but I went over to the table anyway. I sat down, put my elbows on the table, and rested my forehead in my hands. Tony placed a mug of coffee in front of me. My throat was sore and my voice raspy, but I did manage to grumble, "Thanks." I supported my head with one hand as I reached for the coffee with my free hand. Tony made my coffee just the way I liked it, with a couple of splashes of cream. The coffee tasted great. I took a few big gulps, and it was just what I needed. I had a bad case of the zacklies–that's when your mouth tastes "zackly" like your asshole. The coffee helped wash that away. John asked me how I was doing this morning. I kept my head low and, not being able to look anyone in the eye, said I was okay. John said he was glad I got some rest and thought it was great that I slept for close to twelve hours. I gave him a head nod and said, "yeah," with my still raspy voice. John offered to make us breakfast or we could have cold pizza which was his favorite. I just sat there saying nothing. I just kept sipping my coffee. John knew just how bad I was hurting so he put a hand on my shoulder and gave a supportive squeeze saying, "Have some coffee and in a little bit we will talk some more." The last thing I wanted to do was talk. I lifted my head, looked him straight in the eye, and said, "No. I am done talking, leave me alone." John wasn't taking no for an answer, so he said, "Okay let's talk now then." I wasn't having any of it and told him again with a bit of an attitude that I was done talking. John looked at me and in his calm voice said, "You're right. You are done talking. Now you are going to listen." Tony spoke up and said, "John don't, he has been through enough." The Tones always had my back. John looked at Tony and said, "I will, and Paige is going to listen" I gave John a fuck you look and stood up to leave. This was the only time I ever heard John raise his voice in such a stern, commanding, and assertive way. "SIT," was all he said. I sat back down and didn't say anything.

4

Everyone was silent. I sat there staring at the table. John finally broke the silence. He started by saying, "You have been abusing illegal drugs and alcohol." I gave John a dirty look and attitude. "It's just weed," "Just weed?" he asked. With the same attitude, I said, "Fine, weed and JD." I knew nothing about the vial of coke and had no idea John saw it which is why he pushed it by saying, "That's it and nothing else. I lifted my head and looked him straight in the eye. "Yes, that's it. Just weed and JD, it's what college students do." With a direct and matter-of-fact tone, John told me, "It's still illegal. Do you get that, still illegal." I just frowned and put my head back down. His tone softened. "Paige, you have been abusing. It's beyond me how you haven't given yourself alcohol poisoning or ended up in the emergency room." I kept my head down and didn't respond. " I know Michele hasn't told you yet because you don't know." I was confused. What was I supposed to know? I looked at John and asked with my teenage attitude, "What don't I know?" John looked at me again. His hand touched my shoulder giving that supportive squeeze, so I knew the news wasn't good. He said, "Paige, Michele is pregnant." I couldn't believe what I just heard, and I was in total disbelief and shock. I was dumbfounded and stunned by what John just told me. I put my palms on my forehead, sat back in the chair, and let the news sink in. I leaned forward placing my elbows on the table and my hands on my head. If my world hadn't already come crashing down on me this bit of news surely made me feel that way. I was fucked. John's tone changed and became more empathetic when he said, "Paige, you need to stop with the drinking and drugs. It has to stop now." I felt so helpless. I told John I didn't know how to stop. John said he and Tony are more than willing to help me if I let them. I lifted my head and looked at John with defeat and despair written all over my face. I asked, "What if I fuck this up too?" John said I wouldn't, he believed in me. He said with his and Tony's help I will get through this. He told me to stay the week with Tony and if I wanted, I could stay the rest of the semester. He went as far as to say I could move in with Tony permanently if that's what I needed. He told me there were going to be set ground rules for me to follow to stay on track. This was all too much to handle, and I asked if we could just stop. There was too much being thrown at me all at once. John agreed and said it was time for a break. I refilled my coffee mug and got up from the table. I went to the kitchen, opened the refrigerator, and helped myself to one of the boxes of leftover pizza. I hadn't eaten a thing since I stopped at Peach's Variety for that candy bar. I needed to eat. I was starting to feel sick again from all the crap that went on and not having eaten a real meal since yesterday's lunch. I grabbed my coffee and headed to the front door. Tony asked where I was going. I told him to the front porch. I wanted to eat in silence. "The whole pizza?" he asked. In that smart-ass way I had about me, I replied that I was eating for two now.

5

The front porch of John's house was a decent size and was furnished with a beautiful outdoor furniture set including an outdoor sofa. I sat there on the porch sofa for a long time, eating pizza, sipping coffee, and feeling sorry for myself. I kept asking myself, "why now?" I fucked a lot of girls and never got one pregnant. Hell, even my best friend's mom, who I was trying to have a baby with, never got pregnant. Then one girl got pregnant, why did it have to be Michele? If it had been Donna, then I wouldn't be in this situation. I kept blaming myself for everything that went on because everything is always the abused kid's fault. Just ask the abusers, they will tell you that and so will the kid. We think that way because we are told everything is our fault by the abusers and children believe them. I was feeling so much shame for everything, especially last night's meltdown. I felt like a total fool. I thought Tony must hate me now because I was a loser, and stoner and I cheated on him. It wasn't like I wanted to or even went looking for it. She came to me. I was too fucked-up to stop her. Now, I would probably lose the only person I truly loved. I finally admitted and accepted the fact that I was in love with Tony, and he was all I ever thought about. He was the person I wanted to spend the rest of my life with, and I went and fucked it all up. I was scared and confused. I had no idea what to do. After giving me some alone time, John came to see how I was doing. He sat down next to me on the sofa. He saw that I had eaten the whole pizza. He was glad I did. Having an appetite was a good sign, he said. I couldn't bring myself to look at him I just stared in the opposite direction. John spoke, "I have been doing this for a long time, so I know you're hurting pretty bad right now. I know you're scared and confused. I am willing to bet there is some anger in there too." I didn't want to talk, I wasn't ready to talk, but I did anyway. "You left out humiliated. I made a fool out of myself last night. I am a loser for turning to drugs and getting drunk instead of talking things out." "Tony probably hates me now because of Michele. I told her "No", but I let her do it anyway. I screwed things up with Tony, didn't I?" The tears were welling up in my eyes. John took a deep breath to collect his thoughts so he could say the right things–the things I needed to hear. When John finally spoke, the first thing he told me was that I didn't make a fool out of myself and had nothing to feel ashamed about. "We all have a breaking point and sometimes it comes out like that. The important thing is you got it out. Nothing to be embarrassed about." He also told me I wasn't a loser I just made a bad choice. I was dealing with a lot and he has counseled many people who turned to drugs that were dealing with a lot less than I was. He used his serious dad tone when he said, "Let me tell you this, Tony doesn't think any less of you. He cares very deeply for you. He wants to be here for you and wants you to stay. Paige, Tony loves you." I know what John told me was supposed to help and most of what he said did. The part about Tony made me feel worse. I felt like I betrayed him. I told John that I didn't deserve him. John gave me a pat on the back the way a dad does when he is trying to comfort his son. He said "No Paige, you didn't deserve the things that have been done to you. You do deserve to have someone care about you and love you as much as Tony does." John was right I knew, but I still wasn't ready to face Tony. I sat there for a while longer and both John and Tony knew I needed a little space and time alone today and they gave it to me.

6

The portal closed and John and I took physical form again. I was still feeling the feelings and the emotions I had back then. These feelings were just as strong now as they were when I was that scared eighteen-year-old kid. I felt the same knot in my stomach and the same physical and emotional pain and suffering. I couldn't hold back the words; they just came out and they were laced with what I was feeling. "I told you it was all my fault because I didn't have the balls to say one little word! Just one stupid word and none of this would have happened! Look at what I did to myself. Look at all the crap I caused and what I put you and Tony through." John spoke, and this time it wasn't with that fatherly voice. It was his therapist voice. Trust me there was a very distinct difference, and I would react accordingly every time. "What was that one little word that would have saved you?" My rant started. "NO! If I had said, NO Tony, let's try something other than Italian food." We would have gone in the opposite direction, and I would never have gotten jumped. If I had just said "NO" to the stigma of a shrink and had just talked to somebody. If I had just said "NO" to Josh and tossed the joint away instead of keeping it. If I had just said "NO" to the thought of Josh being right and taking one or two little hits and thinking everything would be okay, I would not have become dependent on drugs and alcohol. If I had meant it when I said "NO" to Michele, then I would never have gotten her pregnant and I... " I couldn't finish that last sentence because it hurt too much to say what I was going to say. Instead, I said, "God dammit John, why can't you see it?" John's tone didn't change when he asked, " If you said no to Tony when he invited you to go motorcycle riding you wouldn't be gay either right?" The look I gave John was one of disbelief as though I couldn't believe he just asked me that question. "SERIOUSLY!" he saw how annoyed I was with that question. John said, "Yes Paige, I am being very serious." He asked if I would just hear him out for a moment. I nodded because even if it was something I didn't want to hear, or was extremely difficult to hear, I would always hear John out. "We have been through this. There are no what-ifs. If you went the other way, how do you know the guy who attacked you wouldn't have followed you or tried to jump you and light you on fire when you returned to the car? You don't know that. Just like you don't know what would have happened or if the results would have been different with the other situations if you had done something differently. What 'if' you did talk to someone else and they made you feel even worse about yourself? You have no idea what would have happened 'if'. We don't have that power. There is only what happened. Stop beating yourself up." I tried to respond, "Well I…" I tried to argue the fact but I couldn't because I knew he was right. I have known he was right since he said those things to me back in 1987. John's tone had softened when he reminded me how my choices were so heavily influenced by all the childhood trauma and people around me. I told John he was right, it was choices that "I" had made. John knew I still carried the guilt of it all. I was still blaming myself. He said I needed to understand the fuse was lit the day the abuse started. The night I was jumped, that's when the powder keg exploded. Everything from that point on was a result of the shock wave. Giving John a confused look I asked him what he was trying to tell me. He explained, "What I am trying to tell you is that your childhood was filled with violence and abuse. You were shamed, degraded, and torn down. You were made to feel bad about yourself so others could feel good about themselves and have power and control over you. The attacker took your power from you as did your parents and Michele. Because of that, you were not in control when you lost your cool with Scott and Cory. You felt attacked by them and you reacted, trying to protect yourself. I needed you to see this from a different view this is why I am showing you all this." All these years and all the times John tried to tell me this I never looked at my situation through his eyes. He could now see that I was starting to look at things his way and said, "Come on, your journey continues."

Chapter 18

1

Before we started back, John felt it was important for me to hear this. He told me he was so impressed with how quickly I broke my chemical dependency. He said he was proud of me not only for that but for my willingness to open up about the abuse and trauma I suffered noting how extremely difficult that is to do. He was impressed with the way I handled Michele. "Handled Michele? John she…" John cut me off before I could finish my sentence. He reminded me that Michele waited till I was at my weakest, my most vulnerable point, and completely powerless. That's when she dug her claws right into me. What impressed him the most was how I took my power back; I kept my cool not letting her bait me into arguments. I was assertive and took control when I needed to. Shaking my head, I asked John where it all got me. John reassured me that none of us, including himself, knew what she was thinking. The mist came back as he said, "Take a look." Before I knew it, the portal was open again.

2

I was looking through the portal. It was later that same day when I finally got off the porch and headed down to the cabin. I wanted to get out of yesterday's clothes and get cleaned up. A hot shower did feel good, but I was starting to get fidgety and couldn't settle down. It was getting close to six in the evening, and I was getting hungry so I thought maybe some dinner would help. I could barely sit still long enough to eat. I couldn't settle down. I paced around the cabin. John had told Tony that there was going to be a lot of nervous energy, and I would be very restless. I may experience irritability and have trouble sleeping. That is to be expected and don't be alarmed, it is part of withdrawal. John felt this could last all week. Saturday night was the worst of it. I tried to lay down in bed but that lasted all of thirty seconds. I couldn't settle down, my body ached, my head pounded, and my stomach was upset to the point I was starting to get the dry heaves. I got up, threw some clothes on, and went out walking hoping the cold of the early spring night air would help. I must have walked up and down the dooryard two dozen times before I walked to Big Lake Variety and back which had to be close to three and a half miles each way. It was late Sunday morning before I had finally worn myself out and I fell asleep on the bed. I slept well considering the withdrawal was kicking my ass and hadn't let up. I finally woke up Sunday night just as Tony was coming to bed. He crawled into bed next to me. I rolled over so I could rest my head in that sweet spot on his chest, over his heart, and pulled him close to me and didn't let go. Tony took me in his arms and held me tight. I heard him whisper, "We are going to get through this together I promise." He kissed me on top of my head like he always did and told me he loved me. I fell back to sleep in his arms and slept even better than I did earlier.

3

We both woke up at our usual time of six a.m. on Monday morning. We were in the same position that we fell asleep in. Even though I was still hurting on the inside, I was feeling a lot better physically. My body didn't ache, my head didn't hurt, and the restlessness was gone. I did have the shakes, but they were mild and didn't last. My cravings for pot and alcohol were gone too. Saturday night when I was doing all the walking, I was having the worst cravings. I could have very easily jumped in my car, shot over to the campus, snuck into the dorm, and grabbed my stash to get high. If I had done that, I would have lost Tony, and he was too important to me to lose. While lying there, I was trying to be angry at John for what he put me through the past few days and mostly for Friday night. I just couldn't get mad at him. It was the first time I felt like I had a father figure in my life. It was the first time I felt like I had a real family; it felt like I had a dad. There was no way I wanted to jeopardize that either. I knew I would have gotten high or started drinking if I wasn't at the cabin with them. I realized I would have never made it through the week without getting high because I was that dependent. What made things so bad so quickly for me was what happened Friday night. It was a huge trigger for me to want to get high. If Friday night had not happened, the withdrawal would have happened later in the week and who knows what the result would have been. I also realized while lying there that it wasn't the high or the being drunk I was craving. What I was craving was a calmness and a sense of peace which I got from the weed but sometimes I needed to add alcohol to get there. All that was gone this morning. I had a good night's sleep, and I was right where I needed to be, wrapped in Tony's arms. I never wanted to get high or drunk again. Being with Tony, this is what I wanted. Tony started stirring as if he wanted to get up. I held him tighter and just wanted to lay there for a while. He made me laugh when he said, "Paige, let go of me, I need to get up now or I am going to wet the bed." I leaned over, kissed him, and let him go. I got up and headed for the sofa taking the bed quilt with me. Tony joined me on the sofa. We lay there like we normally did with me in between his legs and my head on his chest. It felt so good to lay there like that with him. Later that morning John called to see how I was doing. He spoke to Tony who told him I was much better, and we were hanging out on the sofa. John was glad to hear that and before hanging up he told Tony he was going to stop down to talk with me. After Tony hung up, he said he would get dressed and give John and me some privacy. I said to Tony, "Please don't go, I want you here." I told him I was really scared, and I needed him to stay because he made me feel safe. That was the first time I willingly showed Tony my vulnerable side. He said he would stay. I sat up and Tony sat back down so we were sitting side by side facing one another. We leaned in and kissed. It wasn't a kiss of passion. Even though we hadn't dressed, when we got up and were still naked neither one of us popped a boner.

It wasn't a sexual kiss; it was nothing like the first kiss we had at the kitchen table. This kiss was so different. It was a soul kiss. A kiss that made us feel connected on a higher plane. It was a higher vibrational kiss. In that moment, in that kiss, we found a deep soul and spiritual connection. That's when we both realized we were soulmates.

4

We showered together, got dressed, and had coffee and a quick breakfast before John arrived. When John showed up, he made some small talk asking how I was feeling, whether I had any rest, and whether I was having cravings. It was small talk, but I was still very uncomfortable, and I knew that moving forward any talking we did was going to be extremely difficult and at times humiliating. But if that is what I had to do so I wouldn't lose Tony then so be it. I will do what it takes to not lose him. Then he got down to business with laying down some ground rules and conditions if I wanted his and Tony's help. The first condition was that I was to turn over all the pot, and any related drug items like rolling papers and bongs. This also included any alcohol I was hiding. There was to be no more using. Even if I chose to go back to the campus during the week, there were to be no parties: no using period, not even recreationally. I had to agree that if I was having cravings and uncontrollable urges to get high, I would call John right away. If he caught me using, then he would turn me in, and I couldn't come back. There were a few other rules too. He asked for my car keys and if I brought a weekend bag. He wanted to go through both to make sure I had nothing with me. My bag was still on the bed, and he went through it. I handed him the keys to my car and let him go through my car. I think it was more for show than anything else cause he didn't look very hard. John knew where I kept my weed in the dorm because he found it when he was there but never told me he did. He asked if I had anything in my dorm room. I was honest and told him where everything was. John suggested that after the break was over, he would go with me to the campus and turn everything over to him. I told him I hated that idea not because I was unwilling to have him take everything, but because what if any or all of the toxic trio were there? God only knows what problems that would cause. I asked if he would spare us all that potential drama by heading over now. Nobody was at the front gate or guard shack during the day. It was an open campus plus it was close to noon and the two security guards on the day shift were like clockwork. They would be in the cafeteria; the dorm would be empty. If we left now, we could go there and be back before Roscoe P. Coltrane and Barney Fife were done with lunch. It was Tony who said, "Yes that is a better idea, let's go." John cracked a smile and rolled his eyes as we headed out. We got on and off campus without issue. When we were in my room, I just sat quietly on my bed staring at the floor while John went through everything. It didn't bother me when he did that at the cabin there was nothing to find. My dorm room was different. That is where everything that he was looking for was. Not only that, but this was my personal space, my belongings, and I was feeling violated. Tony could see my flushed face and sat next to me for support. John took the bottle of JD and the bag of weed down to the bathroom to flush them. He threw the empty bottle and rolling papers in the trash along with my lighters. He spent some time digging through my desk. At the time, I didn't know he was looking for the vial of coke he saw when he was in my room the prior week. He didn't find it and never asked about it. We left the campus and headed back to the cabin. It was a very quiet ride back. I tried to be angry with John. I wanted to hate him. This was my space with my personal belongings that he just violated. I couldn't get angry at him though, he was doing what a dad does to help his son, and I loved him for that. I loved him the way I wanted to love my own dad and couldn't. I pulled into my usual spot and parked the car. I leaned back in my seat with my head tilted back on head rest looking up at the headliner. I was feeling exhausted already. John asked if I was okay. I told him this wasn't how I wanted to spend our spring break. John told me the hard part was over and things would get better from here. He was right, things did get better, for a while anyway.

5

It was Friday night of spring break our usual pizza night. I was not hurting as bad as I had been last week. I was starting to feel like myself again. I still had a lot to talk about and deal with but just being there with Tony did more for me than I realized. I know John was being a therapist, but it also felt like he was being a father figure too and that is something my father never was. I just don't think he ever knew how to be a father or a dad and sometimes I wondered if he had ever wanted kids at all. Having John be that proxy father figure to admire made a huge difference for me. John had just gotten back from picking up the pizza. We were seated at the table in the cabin. Tony said, "I can't believe spring break is almost over. This week went by so fast." To which I sarcastically replied, " Yeah, this week was a total cakewalk. NOT!" That made John laugh a little before he said, "This week must have felt like an eternity to you." With a mouthful of pizza, I replied, "You kidding me? This week was sheer agony, it dragged." It was true that I was feeling better, but the week was sheer agony. John admitted he was very impressed with how I handled everything. He thought I was going to go through heavy withdrawal, and it surprised him how by Monday morning the worst of everything had passed. I gave him a sheepish look and said I did have a little help. I told him there was this little stash he didn't find sooooo... Then I made a gesture as if I was taking a hit off a joint. The look on John's face and the "EXCUSE ME" that bellowed out, were enough to make anyone cringe. John was not happy. Tony dropped the slice of pizza he was just about to take a bite out of and exclaimed, "NO! you promised you wouldn't" I shrank back from Tony. I kept looking back and forth at them like I was in the deepest shit anyone could have gotten themselves into. John demanded I explain myself. I looked at them both one more time before throwing my arms up in the air and shouting, "PSYCH! GOTCHA BOTH !" Tony shook his head and said, "That was not funny. Paige, what in god's name am I going to do with you?" John didn't know whether he should laugh or throw something at me. He thought it was awesome that I was finding humor in the situation but pissed because I got him hook line and sinker.

"OK you little asshole, just for that you earned yourself a drug test." I was like "Come on dude you're putting me through hell can't you give me one free psych-out pass?" John grumbled "Fine, one free psych-out pass. "Now let's get serious for a minute, classes resume Monday. Are you going to stay here or go back to the dorm?" I didn't tell John or Tony that I made the decision Sunday night to permanently move in. Sunday was the night, Tony came to bed and whispered in my ear that we would get through this together and that he loved me. Hearing that, staying was a no-brainer. I did tell them that I would like to stay permanently if it was OK with both of them. I knew going back to the dorm wasn't good for me at all. Tony was excited by the news. This time he threw his arms up in the air. "YES!" His expression quickly changed. He looked at me in his serious tone and said, "This better not be a psych-out." I promised him that no, this was no psych-out, I was staying.

6

John had a feeling I would be staying. He did remind me that he was serious about one of the conditions which was random drug testing to make sure I stay on track. I told John, "Yeah, I know, pee in a cup I can't wait. Yeah me." I wasn't happy about this but it's what I agreed to if I wanted to stay. He gave me a shit-eating grin and said, "Good because you go for one next week." I was like, "Dude already?" John didn't hesitate with his reply. "Yes. And there will be no ifs, ands, or buts. Here is the time and address." I was a little bummed out about it as I took the appointment card from John. Tony said he would go with me for moral support. I couldn't resist, I just had to be a smart ass, so with a big shit-eating grin of my own I asked, "Oooo Tones, you gonna hold it for me too?" Shaking his head and rolling his eyes he replied, "Again, what in God's name am I going to do with you?" John was shaking his head and smiling. He knew I was going to be just fine. John wanted to know if Michele tried to contact me this week. I told him she hadn't and told John that when I saw Josh I was going to tell him she and I needed to talk, knowing he would pass that message along. Tony was curious to know if Josh was going to question why I was staying at the cabin. I told Tony that I would be hanging out in the dorm in between classes like normal. I said, "Josh is such a friggin space cadet that he wouldn't even notice. Besides, he was always sleeping in Patty's room". None of us realized how much time had passed and it was starting to get late. John said he had two things he wanted to talk to me about and then he was going to retire for the night. John felt I was ready to hear about what Michele had told him and Tony when she came to see them. He told me that Michele said if I didn't marry her, she was going to terminate the pregnancy. Tony let me know that she was going to tell everyone I had AIDS, and he was the one who gave it to me. I thought to myself she is a c... (rhymes with hunt), and that was something she would do. John wanted me to talk to a friend of his named Andy Harwich. He was an attorney who had a law practice close by. I thought to myself that if I wasn't a Jr., and everyone called me by my first name, I would insist on Andrew. I never liked being called Andy. Come to find out later, his name was Andy, not Andrew. John felt there was a need for me to do this and said he was willing to meet me tomorrow morning even though it was Saturday. I agreed to meet with Andy without hesitation. John then went on to talk about the other thing he wanted to discuss. He said, "This is what you need to hear so both of you just listen. I see the way you two look at one another. The way your eyes light up when you see one another or when I mention your name when the other isn't around. Since you two met, I have seen a side of Tony I didn't know existed; you both make one another happy. Don't be sorry or ashamed that you love each other. Your relationship is no one's business but yours." Tony reached over and put his hand on top of mine and said John was right. I knew he was right too. John slid his chair back and got up to leave. "I know this has been a rough week for you Paige, so I am going to head out and leave you two to do the dishes." Before John could walk off, I stopped him by saying, "John, about last week, the whole situation. I am sorry. I never meant for any of this to happen," John told me not to give it another thought and he was proud of me for the hard work I had done this week. He said, "Good night" and left.

7

Tony still had his hand on top of mine and as John left, he squeezed it. Turning around to face Tony, I put my other hand on top of his, I looked at him and said that I owed him an apology too. I told him I was so sorry that I said I hated being in love with another man and that wasn't what I meant. "You saved my life! Oh God Tony, I am so sorry." Tony placed his free hand on top of mine and squeezed. "Paige, it is okay, I completely understand," I told him I wasn't cheating on him with Michele and how it would never have happened if... Tony cut me off before I could finish saying that she took advantage of me. How it wasn't my fault she was attacking him too. She did it because she hated us for no reason. I knew he was right, and I told him I didn't want any of it to happen. Tony smiled as he rubbed my hand. "You know there is a way you can make it up to me." I was excited and was ready to do anything for him. I said, "Tony name it. I will do anything, just tell me." Still rubbing my hand he said, "Let's have some cannoli." I cocked my head to the side slightly confused and said, "You want dessert?" Tony removed his hand, reached over and started caressing my crotch. That's when I figured out what he meant. "OHHHH That cannoli, Antonin Kofi Bedru! What in God's am I going to do with you?"

8

Needless to say, dishes didn't get done that night and for obvious reasons. We hadn't had cannoli all week, so I made sure Tony got more than his fair share of cannoli and then some. After wearing ourselves out, Tony laid on his back like always and I started to lay on my side so I could rest my head in the sweet spot like I would always do. This time instead I kneeled over him straddling his chiseled abs. I looked down at him saying, "Last week when I was sitting on John's porch, I told John I didn't deserve you. He told me I was wrong, that I did deserve to be loved by you." Tony reached up and pulled me closer so we could kiss. After he kissed me, I rested my forehead on his. I told him this week proved to me that I found my soulmate. I told Tony I loved him in ways that I never knew existed. I told him I was so deeply in love with him that I wouldn't know what to do without him. I felt his hands rubbing up and down my back; I knew I was right where I belonged. Tony said he felt the same way I did, and he couldn't picture life without me. He said John was right, we do deserve to be loved like this. We started kissing again and before I knew it, he had flipped me over onto my back and was on top of me kissing me while rubbing my ass. I knew he was going to do to me something he hadn't done before and the thought of it drove me wild. I was ready for him. What he did brought me to a new level of ecstasy with a climax that neither one of us will ever forget.

Chapter 19

1

I woke up Saturday morning feeling the best I have ever felt in my just-short-of nineteen years. What Tony did to me last night was incredible. I saw that he was awake too so we both turned our heads to face one another. We were looking into each other's eyes without speaking. He rolled over on top of me and started doing it again. It was just as amazing as last night and like last night, I had my arms wrapped around his neck and his arms were wrapped around me holding me tight and kissing me while he worked his magic. Once again, I busted one without either one of us touching me down there. As soon as I started, Tony busted his own. Tony rolled off me and we both lay there, holding hands and trying to catch our breath. Finally breathing normally, Tony said, "Come on, we need to shower. I don't want us to be late for our appointment with Andy." "Our appointment." I still couldn't help but think I didn't deserve him.

2

I wanted to take the choppers even though there was still snow on the ground and the ice on the lakes was still thick enough to hold ice fishing shacks. Spring Break in Maine was a far cry from Daytona Beach in Florida where a lot of college students go in hopes of being seen on MTV. Tony rolled his eyes and gave his, what in God's name am I going to do with you, look. We didn't take the choppers. We took my car and as usual, I drove with one hand on the steering wheel and held Tony's hand with the other. We arrived at Andy's office right at nine sharp. Andy had just arrived too and was quick to get out of his car, greet us, and introduce himself. Andy was about the same height I was with a slender build. Unlike John whose hair was now white, Andy had salt and pepper hair and was clean-shaven. Since this was Saturday, Andy was dressed casually in jeans, a hooded sweatshirt, and a Members Only jacket. I was glad he was dressed casually. I felt more relaxed, and it helped ease the tension of the messy situation I was in. There was a bunch of small talk as we headed into his office. Andy told us how he and Alice became friends when they were both undergrads. They used to be the best of friends till she passed away. Andy told us how Alice always wanted a cabin in the woods to escape to when city life got too hectic. He told us how he and his lover found the cabin for them when they were out for a Sunday drive back in the late 60s. He took out his trusty Kodak camera, took pictures of the place and mailed them to Alice. She instantly fell in love with the cabin. It became her oasis. I was curious about something, so I had to ask, "You and your lover?" Andy smiled and said, "Yes I have a male lover. That is why John never got jealous of mine and Alice's friendship and part of the reason why John thought I would be the best one to help you out if need be." I was curious to know the other part of the reason, so I asked. Andy told us he had met a guy in law school and was crazy about him. Like me, he had an extremely difficult time accepting and dealing with being gay, so he turned to drugs to cope. It was Alice who got him sober again and helped him through his difficulties. He added that because of Alice, he and that guy he fell for in law school are still together. I was a little uneasy with someone besides John knowing about Tony and me and how I turned to pot and alcohol to help cope, and it showed. I will say it was good that he understood. Tony said he wished Alice was still alive he would have liked to have known her. I agreed with Tony that she sounded cool. Andy agreed, she was an amazing person and so was John. He told us they were still the closest of friends.

3

After the small talk and introductions, Andy said, " Let's talk about you and Michele, what's going on there?" I told Andy I had not seen or talked to Michele since I saw her last and that was just before midterms started. It was close to two weeks since I had seen her. I told Andy from what John and Tony had told me she was claiming to be pregnant, and I was the father. I went on to say Michele claims she is going to force me to marry her, or she will abort the pregnancy. Tony, who usually remained quiet and let John do most of the talking, spoke up and told Andy that Michele was going to start telling everyone Paige and I are gay lovers, and I gave Paige AIDS. Looking down and seeing Tony say that again, I could never understand why people chose to weaponize AIDS and use this deadly disease to destroy a person's character, reputation, or life. Andy had a great poker face, so it was hard to tell what he was thinking which I suppose is imperative in his profession. Andy asked if a blood test had been done to know if I was the father or not. I told him no, and I wasn't sure if the baby was mine to begin with. Andy wanted me to elaborate on why she would make those claims. I didn't get into a lot of detail but said enough about why it very well could be my baby. What details I gave made me feel like crap because I was saying them in front of Tony. I felt like I betrayed him and couldn't help but blame myself and think every bit of this was my fault. When it came to the AIDS claim, Tony spoke about that saying he had never been with anyone but me. There was no way he could have given me AIDS. Andy was getting a good sense of the situation. He felt that the first thing we needed to get done was a blood test to find out if Michele's claim was true. If the baby was not mine, we were done with her and would get her barred from campus. Then, we will decide how to handle Josh and Patty if I decide to go there. Until the test was done and we got the results, he didn't want me to say or make any claim that I was the father. I felt the need to tell Andy if the baby was mine because I had a weird feeling the baby was mine, I didn't want to marry her and I didn't want her to have an abortion. It's my baby too. Andy asked what I would do. Tony spoke right up, "Paige and I will raise the baby together, we will be a family." I

155

wasn't expecting that from Tony but hearing it made me fall deeper in love with him. I just wanted to wrap my arms around Tony and never let go. I had given it some thought during the week as to what I might do if the baby was mine. I had a lot of details to work out, but Andy thought we needed to have a very frank conversation first before I even went there. I had had my fill of frank conversations, and I could feel the anxiety building, but I also knew we had to have this conversation.

4

When Andy said we needed to have a frank conversation he wasn't kidding. He said to me, "Paige, I need you to understand Michele doesn't need your consent or permission she can just go and have an abortion if she wants to. There's nothing anyone can do about it. However, I have an idea that might work so hear me out." Andy went on to tell me that John told him about what Michele did or as much of it as he knew. John telling Andy about what happened pissed me off to the point that I yelled, "Isn't anything sacred with that man!" Andy told me John had to tell him everything. John knew he needed all the facts so he could effectively do his job. Andy had to have the whole story, so he needed me to be open and honest if what he was thinking was going to work. That didn't make me feel better, but he was right, so I let it go. Then I asked, "How does that help?" Andy explained that Michele had no right to force herself on me the way she did. He knew I told her "no" and she still forced me to have sex with her with the intent of getting pregnant against my will. He also stated that the fact I was under the influence of marijuana and alcohol, I had lost my ability to consent, and she knew it. Andy told me in a very direct way, "Forcing anyone to have sex against their will is considered sexual assault and possibly rape." My jaw dropped. I couldn't believe he just said I was raped. If I wasn't humiliated enough already, now he throws this at me. "I can't believe you just said that! Are you fucking kidding me! Dude! FUCK THIS, I am outta here!" I stood up and was ready to walk out. Both Andy and John had a feeling I wouldn't react well to him saying that. Although I didn't go off on Andy, he knew I wasn't a happy camper, to say the least.

"Paige, I don't believe there is another option so please just hear me out first." Tony stood next to me putting a hand on my shoulder and gently pulling me back, urging me to sit back down. Andy explained to me his plan in detail, which was the only way I may be able to gain some leverage over Michele. Andy also told me I would have greater leverage if I had someone who could backup my side of things. Someone who was a witness and knew what Michele was up to. After taking a few deep breaths to try and control my anger, I told Andy that my roommate and his girlfriend both knew. I told of how Josh kept pushing me to get high and all the pot he was giving me for free. I wasn't sure where, how, or even why he was doing this, but he was. Andy didn't think it would be hard to get Josh to back my side of things and with his advice on what to tell Josh it should be easy for me to get him to do what I needed him to do. Andy gave a few more details before wrapping up our meeting. He did say he was sorry to have upset me but there was no other way around this unless I married Michele. Even then, no one knew what she might do. Andy did say his plan had no guarantees, but it was the only leverage I had.

5

On the ride back to the cabin, Tony and I held hands with our fingers interlocked. My grip was much tighter than normal because I was realizing what I truly had with him and wanted to hold on to him and never let him go. We didn't talk like we normally did; it was a very quiet ride back. Tony knew there was a lot for me to process and knew how much tension there was with the whole situation. We got back to the cabin just around noon. I had put the car in park, taken the key out, and unbuckled my seat belt before Tony unbuckled his and opened the door to get out of the car. I refused to let go of his hand, I slid across the seat and got out his side of the car still holding his hand. We headed into the cabin hand in hand. We stood in the middle of the cabin, and I took Tony by the other hand, so we were facing each other. Then I asked if he truly meant it when he said we would be a family and raise the baby together. He was looking me in the eyes when he told me "Yes, I meant every word". He wanted us to be a family. I let go of his hands so I could hug and hold him. I told him just how much I was in love with him, and that I didn't deserve him. Tony kissed me on top of my head and hugged me tight. We stood there for a while just holding one another. I finally loosened my arms and led Tony into the bedroom. We got into bed and I completely submitted myself to him. Whatever he wanted to do, whatever he wanted me to do, I gave Tony complete control. Giving myself to him like that brought about feelings and emotions I never experienced. Our lovemaking was entering a whole new level. We were connecting in ways I just couldn't explain. We made love several times that afternoon and evening. Each time we finished, we held each other close. We couldn't get enough of each other. In those moments, nothing else mattered; there was no outside world, just us.

6

We both crawled out of bed early for a Sunday morning mostly because we hadn't eaten since yesterday morning. I was starting to feel the angst build up. This was the last day of spring break, and I had to face the toxic trio, or at least Josh, the next day. We made a big breakfast for ourselves and had a few mugs of coffee which did help me feel better, but the anxiety was still there. Just as we finished the dishes, the phone rang. It was Tony's parents making their weekly call. I decided to give him some privacy and headed outside. I started to get restless and fidgety again and thought to myself, great here come the cravings and withdrawal again. I promised John and Tony if this happened, I would find or call John right away. Walking up to his house I was starting to realize I wasn't having cravings or withdrawal. Something else was getting me worked up. I got up to John's house and saw he was out at his woodshed. As I approached, I said, "Hey John what's going on?" "Hey there, Paige." John stopped what he was doing and took a seat on one of the chopping blocks. I couldn't sit still so I started to take over stacking the wood John was working on as I walked up. "Tell me, how did it go with Andy Yesterday?" As soon as he said that, the knot in my stomach got even tighter and I started feeling flush thinking about what we talked about. I tried to play it cool telling John it was "okay I guess". John gave a little smirk and a quizzical head tilt. "Just, Okay? Tell me what you guys talked about?" Once again, I tried to play it cool telling John that Andy said they go way back to their college days, how he found this place for him and Alice, and how Alice helped him when he was abusing. I told him shit like that. John said, "Yeah. Andy gets what you are going through. So, after the small talk what else did you talk about?" I knew John already knew what we talked about, and I knew he was trying to get me to talk but this whole thing. I was too embarrassed to talk about it. I told John that I just wasn't comfortable talking about it. John reminded me that part of our agreement was not to hold anything in no matter what it is or how I feel. I was to lay it all out so we could work through it. I kept on stacking wood for a few minutes before speaking, trying to work up the nerve to say what was on my mind and how to say it.

7

I finally spoke and there was a bit of annoyance and crossness in the tone I used. "Andy wants me to file a sexual assault, possible rape complaint, against Michele. How can it be rape? She's pregnant so obviously I liked it." John replied that it didn't matter if I liked it or not that wasn't the point. He told me Michele had no right to do that to me. I crossed the line into anger. I slammed down the logs I was stacking shouting, "This is so FUCKING HUMILIATING! I wasn't raped! I am a guy; guys can't be raped!" John told me to take a minute and a few deep breaths. He knew there was more to this and wanted me to start from the beginning. I picked up a few more logs slammed them onto the pile and took a few breaths to collect myself before starting. I told John the first thing Andy wants is a paternity test done to make sure the baby is mine. Then I told him if the baby is mine, I don't want Michele to have an abortion or marry her. I told John that Andy had me go into detail about what Michele did along with Josh and Patty's role. I explained how I told Andy the whole thing. John already knew where the rape allegation fit in, but he needed to hear it from me to make

159

sure I understood everything. I explained to John what Andy told me about Michele not needing my consent to have an abortion. I told John that she can just go get one if she wants to. I reiterated my feelings about the abortion and marrying her. John nodded and told me he was with me so far. I told John how Andy wanted me to confront Michele and tell her I will file a police report for sexual assault and possible rape if she has an abortion. John asked if he wanted me to use that as leverage. I told John yes, and he wants me to confront Josh and Patty to see if I can get them to back my side of the story for even more leverage. Hopefully, that will get Michele to hold off on the abortion and buy some time so I can try and figure things out. John thought it was a good plan and asked if I was going to start by confronting Josh tomorrow. I told him yes, and I was going to try and track Michele down too so we could get the paternity test done.

8

Getting things out into the open with John did ease a lot of the angst I was having. I was glad to be more at ease and I spent the rest of the day curled up on the sofa with Tony. We talked about nothing in general, we talked about me living there, we talked about being a family. As I looked down, I wondered why John never brought up the cocaine that was in my desk. In my head I heard him say, he believed me when I said it was just weed and nothing else.

Chapter 20

1

I arrived back at the dorm first thing Monday morning. It was still early, and no one was up yet as I entered the building and headed for my room. I was expecting to find the room empty. To my surprise Josh was sitting at his desk in his tightie whities rolling a joint. Josh spoke first as I entered the room. I walked in and went over to my desk to gather my books for my first two classes. "Paige dude, you look different like..." I didn't know if he was trying to find the right word or just feeling things out. I replied, "Not stoned different?" Josh smiled "Exactly! Let's say we fix that." I had my back to him when he said that. I turned around and in a very serious and assertive tone said, "Let's say we don't." I opened my stash drawer in my desk to make sure it was still empty and thankfully it was. I turned my attention back to Josh. I guess my response caught him off guard and he wasn't expecting me to stand up to him. I told him Michele was pregnant and making claims I took advantage of her. I leaned in and was even more assertive when I told him we both knew that wasn't true. I also told him that I knew he and Patty had a role in the whole thing. Josh tried to push back and downplay it by saying in his fake stoner voice, "Dude it wasn't supposed to go that far." I stood my ground, stepped in a little closer and told him, "Well it did!" Josh shrank back again. He knew I wasn't backing off. I told him that he claimed I was a friend and the coolest roommate he ever had so instead of being that friend when he knew something was wrong, he chose to take part in

Michele's stupid plan to screw me over. After saying that I backed away from him. Josh tried to defend himself by saying not all of it was true. Yes, he did know something was wrong, but it was only supposed to be a prank where Michele got even with me. I asked Josh why Michele was getting even with me. I told him I never did anything wrong to her. Josh told me that I blew her off at the Labor Day weekend cookout and that pissed her off. He got up from his desk, stepped over to his bed, and started to pick up his dirty clothes off the floor and put them on. I figured he was going to try and leave. I stood between the two desks blocking him in so he couldn't leave before continuing, "So you're telling me you took part in Michele's plan because I didn't want to get high and have sex with her at the cookout?" Josh finished dressing and was standing up to leave when he told me he was only supposed to get me high the one time so Michele could have sex with me. He was very serious when he said he had no idea what she was planning, and I believed him. Josh tried to leave but I was still blocking him. We were face-to-face when he said it wasn't supposed to go that far. I wasn't letting him leave. I could tell I had him and I wasn't going to blow my chance. I pushed back "Well DUDE, it did go that far! You and Patty are in some deep shit for your role in this. Josh backed right off and sat down on his bed saying how sorry he was, begging me not to get him in trouble. He said he didn't know this was going to happen. Andy told me I needed to find a way to get Josh to side with me. Not getting Josh in trouble was what was going to get him to side with me. I told Josh that if he was really that sorry and if the baby is mine, he was going to tell my attorney everything he told me. That it was all Michele, and everything was done against my will. Josh did not like the sound of that at all. He told me, "No fucking way, it isn't going to happen." If he did that Michele would turn him into Campus Police, he would get arrested and his father would kick his ass. I wasn't expecting him to push back like that. I took a breath, kept my cool, and made sure I was still grounded before saying anything. I still had that assertive tone in my voice. Keeping my composure, I replied by telling him his choices, which were:

both he and Patty could either back up my side of the story or I could list them both as co-conspirators in the police report I am filing against Michele. That pissed Josh off to the point he told me to go fuck myself. I told him fine, have it your way. I wasn't playing games and Josh knew it. He quickly caved and agreed to my terms. I stepped aside as Josh was making his exit. I told him to tell Michele she and I need to talk. I reminded him that both he and Patty needed to keep their mouths shut if they wanted to be on my side of things.

2

After Josh took off, I gathered up what I needed for my first two classes and headed down to the cafeteria for a second breakfast. I knew I wasn't going to have to confront Patty, Josh would fill her in. I was hoping neither one would say anything to Michele to clue her in. Before heading to the cafeteria, I headed right for my smoking spot instead. I don't know why I walked down the short path that was behind the dorm to the small secluded area I used to frequent. I was thinking about nothing in general and was unemotional. Although my mind was void of thought, I did get a weird feeling; it was like this was the last time I was ever going to come here. I didn't need to come here anymore. In some way, I felt like I had broken free of the ball and chain, and a huge weight was lifted off me. I was no longer afraid to face what I needed to face and the inner war I was having was over. I found some peace within myself. I loved Tony and I didn't hate myself for loving him anymore. I took a deep breath, looked around, and headed back out the way I came in. I felt as if I closed a chapter and didn't need this place anymore.

3

The portal shifted so I could see Josh running across campus to Patty's dorm. I never realized when he took off like a bat out of hell from our room that morning, that he never put his shoes on. There he was in all his glory running across campus in his socks which were soaking wet from the melting snow. To say he wasn't the sharpest tool in the toolbox was an understatement, I swear his elevator didn't reach the top floor. He went running into Patty's room out of breath and in panic mode, while he was trying to tell her what just happened. Patty, who was still asleep, was startled awake by Josh who was now standing over her. Patty screamed and whacked Josh in the face with her pillow. I couldn't help but laugh as I watched the scene unfold in front of me. The comedy show came to a quick end as Josh caught his breath and Patty, now fully awake and sitting upright in bed, wanted to know what was going on. Josh was able to speak more clearly than when he stormed into the room but was still in panic mode because he knew they both were in deep trouble. He told Patty about our conversation. He was telling Patty about me talking with a lawyer and how I was planning on filing a police complaint against Michele, and if they do not back up my side of the story, they will be listed in the complaint too. Patty was starting to panic. They both feared Michele and what she might do if they sided with me but were just as scared of possibly being listed in the police complaint. Between all the pot and coke, she and Josh seeing jail time seemed like a reality for them. The thought of jail terrified them both. Patty started crying telling Josh how much regret she had for taking part in Michele's stupid prank. I could see Josh was shaking with fear. Josh told Patty that I wanted him to tell Michele she and I needed to talk. He explained to Patty I was going to force Michele to have a blood test done to find out if it was me who got her pregnant. Josh made it clear when he said, "There is no fucking way I am calling Michele." Knowing how bad the situation was and that there was no way out of it, the only thing they could do was hope I wasn't the one who got Michele pregnant. Maybe then they would be off the hook. They agreed with one another to side with me in hopes that would keep them from getting arrested. They also vowed never to speak to Michele again. They realized the only thing they could do was hope this all blows over.

4

The portal shifted back to later that same day. I was looking at myself sitting at my desk in my dorm room. I was going through some class notes before packing up some clothes and heading back to the cabin. I usually was done with classes by four in the afternoon and was hoping Josh would pass along my message. I didn't want to hang out much longer, so I started wrapping things up. I had just gotten up from my desk and was getting ready to pack up my books and clothes when there was a knock at the door. I shouted it was open and to come on in. I wasn't sure who to expect. I figured it might be Patty at the door begging me not to turn her and Josh in or make them talk to my attorney. I was half expecting them to try and weasel their way out of the situation. As the door opened, I heard, "Hey Paige," it was Michele. I wasn't expecting to see her today. In an instant the tension in the room grew so thick you could have cut it with a knife. John told me the best thing I could do was remain grounded and not lose my cool with her. He showed me a breathing technique which I used right away, and it worked. I looked at her completely unfazed and said, "Hi. If you're looking for Josh and Patty, I think they might still be in class if they're not in her room." Michele, with her sheepishly evil grin, was trying to be coy and said she was looking for me and was surprised I didn't come looking for her over break. I shrugged my shoulders and told her I was with family over break. I gave her a confused look and said that she was Josh and Patty's friend and didn't understand why I would be looking for her. Michele said she didn't know I was with family. She said, "Since you're always with the Nig and your Sugar Daddy, I figured they would have told you." She called him the name I hate and hate even more when she refers to Tony that way. That pissed me off, but I kept my anger in check. I turned to her using the same assertive tone I used with Josh earlier but this time there was a bit of resentment attached because of what she kept calling Tony. I told her, "His name is Antonin Kofi Bedru so cut the shit with the racist name-calling. Call him by his name. John and Antonin Kofi Bedru told me you're pregnant, you're claiming I am the father and you're going to get an abortion if I don't marry you." Michele was caught off guard. She was not used to having anyone stand up to her. She is too used to bullying the other two to get her way. Me standing up to her blew her mind even more than me blowing her off at the cookout. She didn't know what to do. Now I knew she hadn't talked to Josh. That little pussy would have told her that I knew. In a fluster, she tried to push back, "You said you were with family." I immediately shot back, "They are my family so you can knock off the gay crap too!" Michele was losing control of herself and it showed. It showed no one ever pushed back like this and stood up to her. I took her power over me from her, and she couldn't handle it. She screamed, "You have to do as I tell you or I will sue you"." "Sue me for what? I didn't do anything wrong so go for it, sue me. You will lose." I was matter of fact with that reply to her. I could see just how intimidated Michele was. She had no idea what to do or say; she had lost her control over me and she knew it. I knew I had to stand up for myself and I was doing it. As I leaned into her, just like I did with Josh to show a little dominance, Michele took a step back so she was up against the door and had nowhere to run, she was cornered. "I have already been to see an attorney. He is going to help me file a police complaint against you for sexual assault and possible rape. If that isn't my baby, I am going to sue you". Her jaw dropped. "You can't do that!" "Watch me." I told her. She demanded to know my attorney's name trying to call my bluff. I very confidently told her it was Andy Harwich who had a local office here in town. I just laughed when she said "You can't do that I own you! You must do what I tell you!" Then I told her this is what is going to happen. I handed her a piece of paper with the name and address of the clinic Andy suggested in Old Port. I told her they were going to do a blood test to find out if I actually was the father. Michele tried in vain to push back stating that she wasn't going. She had classes. I wasn't backing down. I told her I didn't give a shit if she missed any or all her classes, she was to get her ass there. It was a walk-in clinic but what the hell, I was on a roll, and I didn't want to lose my edge plus I had to get her there, so I told her one p.m. sharp and not to be late. If the test shows I am the father and she wants to save her ass, abortion was off the table. I would figure out what to do. Michele took the address from me and said, fine, she would be there. She tried to get sassy with me, "You can count on hearing from Daddy's attorney." I stepped back and returned to where I was standing when she came in. Michele stared at me and then reached for the door to leave. I stopped her by saying, "Oh yeah, and one more thing. What is this crap about you telling people I have AIDS?" Michele looked at me and shouted, "FUCK YOU!" and stormed out.

5

I finished gathering up my books and clothes thinking to myself I stood up for myself, I took Michele's power from her, and she had no control over me. I stood up for Tony and let her know the racist name-calling was done. She accused us of being gay and I set her straight without having to come out or having to deny our relationship. I was feeling proud of myself, and it felt good to take my power back. I was now in control, not the weed, not the alcohol, and not the toxic trio. Me, that's who is in control of me and no one else. Now it was time to go and get settled into my new home.

Chapter 21

1

The portal readjusted, and I was looking down into the cabin. I saw myself setting the table for pizza night. It was the end of that same week. I usually studied for an hour or two in my dorm room after my last class, or if I knew Tony would be late getting home, I would sometimes have dinner in the cafeteria before heading home for the night, except for Fridays. Friday, I left right after my last class ended. Friday was always pizza night. I loved pizza night because it felt like a real family dinner. I had just finished setting the table when Tony arrived with the pizza. "Hey, cool your back, I am starved. Where is Big Daddy Buzz Kill?" Saying that made Tony laugh and flash that beautiful smile of his. "Looks like someone is feeling like his old self again," I told Tony that taking my power back felt great. He was happy for me and asked about the blood test and if I got the results back. I told him I should have the results back in the first part of the week. He was curious to know if I was hoping the baby would be mine because we never really brought it up. We talked about being a family but never talked about if I was hoping the baby was mine. At first I said no, I was hoping the baby wasn't mine. Now that I had a little time to think about it with a clear head, I liked the idea of being a dad and us being a family. Tony said he loved the idea of being a family too. That man just melted my heart.

2

We both heard the creak of the screen door opening as John headed in. "There's John now," Tony said, as he took a seat at the table. I was still standing when John walked in. He entered the cabin, but he didn't have the laid-back happy guy look, with the warm friendly tone in his voice that was John. He had a stern look that said, I ain't taking shit from anyone. He looked right at me, and I immediately thought, Oh shit what happened. He had an envelope in his hand that he shook at me when he said, "Andrew Paige Turner." Tony looked up and said, "All three names you're in deep shit." I turned to Tony, "Seriously dude." John, still holding up the envelope continued, " I have your drug test results and we need to talk!" "Talk?" I asked. I was totally confused because I hadn't done anything wrong. "Yes, talk, now sit." Now I feared what was in the envelope. His voice was commanding when he demanded I sit. I tried to plead with him, "John..." he cut me right off and bellowed "SIT". Tony was now growing concerned too. You could hear just how worried he was about the test results when he said, "John, it has to be a mistake." John, not letting up told Tony to trust him, these tests do not lie. Then he looked at me using all three names again asking me what I had to say for myself. I was starting to panic–no this wasn't happening. I walked down to my smoking spot, but how could he know that? I didn't get high, I didn't get drunk, I took my power back. No, this can't be happening... kept running through my head. I told John that Tony was right. This must be a mistake. I told John I would take the test again to prove the results were wrong. He was still very insistent on telling me that these tests do not lie. My world was collapsing, it was all falling apart, and John wouldn't hear it when I said the test results were wrong. I knew they had to be wrong. I had no reply other than to say his name. "John!" He shook his hand with the envelope in it when he leaned in and let me have it. "You are not allowed to call me John anymore! Because of these results, you are to call me Mr... Do you hear me? You will refer to me as Mr... That's right, from now on it's Mr. Big Daddy Psych! Gotcha back!" It took a second for me to get what just happened and when it hit, I shouted, "FUCKIN A JOHN!" I got up and headed for the bathroom. John, laughing, asked where I was going. I told him to wipe because I think I just shit myself. Tony wasn't any help saying, "That was cruel, but I am laughing." The shit that ran through my mind, damn! I needed to take a second to recompose myself. I thought I was in serious-ass trouble.

3

While I was in the bathroom, I did check the Fruit of the Looms to make sure. I thought for sure John was going to ask me to leave and then turn me in. I was happy it was only a prank, and he got me good. I do have to admit what made the prank work so well is it was something you would have never expected John to do. When I came back out, the two of them were doing the best they could not to laugh. I looked at John and said, "Dude that was just plain wrong." I grabbed a slice and started eating. After they were both done laughing at me, John wanted to know how the week went for me. I told him about the talk I had with Josh, how I wasn't expecting to find him in the room the way I did, adding that I checked my desk to make sure he wasn't pulling any shit. I went on to tell him I got him to agree to back my side of the story if I needed him to even though I wasn't ready to talk or had time to think about what I might say. I told him about Michele coming to the dorm just as I was getting ready to leave that same day. I was able to get the blood test done the following day and was waiting for the results. After I told him all that, I sat quietly for a few minutes. I was debating if I should tell him about walking down to my smoking spot or not. I thought maybe I should, so I told John there was something else I didn't want him to be mad at because I didn't do anything. He told me he wouldn't and reminded me there were no secrets among us and if I had cravings, to tell him. I went ahead and told him about walking down to my smoking spot. I told him I didn't go there to get high, and I didn't even know why I went there I just did. I also told him about the feeling I had; that it was the last time I was going to see this spot. It felt like I didn't need to go there anymore. I told John it was something that I felt I needed to do and couldn't explain why. John knew I was sincere about that too. He said if he was to guess, I did that because that spot represented the power and control the substances had over me. He said that going there and not getting high and then walking away the way I did, was my way of taking back my power over the substances. He said I took control over the chemical dependency. It was my way of bringing closure. John said he saw that as a healing moment for me. He said by walking away from it physically, I could now move on from the dependency mentally. He was glad I did that. I felt relieved. I thought he would have gotten upset. I guess he was right too. When I thought about the way he put things, I was able to make sense out of something I originally couldn't. Until that point, I had no idea why I did what I did walking down to my smoking spot like that. Now I get it and now I know what that feeling was.

4

Tony and I spent an incredibly awesome weekend together. We spent time tinkering with the choppers, getting them ready for riding season. We spent some time studying together at the table sitting next to one another other holding hands. We spent time lying on the sofa, he on his back and me between his legs with my head resting on his chest, just thinking about nothing. We spent time, of course, doing our favorite thing in the bedroom. There was no doubt in either of our minds that moving in together was the right thing for us.

Chapter 22

1

The portal shifted again and now I was looking at myself sitting in Andy's office. It was the end of the following week. I had gotten the blood test results back, and the baby was mine. Andy had called me to get some information from me and permission to talk to John. I had come up with a plan that I thought would work and that Tony would like. I was waiting till our meeting at the end of the week to tell Andy the plan but thought maybe I should tell him beforehand. I hadn't run it by John, but something told me that he would be very supportive of the plan, so I went ahead and told Andy. Andy was glad I did and said he would see me Friday afternoon to discuss the plan in more detail. It was Friday afternoon and Andy and I were talking in his office. I was nervous and I was scared but I knew this was what I wanted. Andy told me he had a few conversations with Michele's father's attorney. I asked Andy to fill me in on what they talked about. Andy said that Attorney Foster had gotten a different story from Michele. Michele had told her parents the same thing she told John and Tony. I was abusing drugs and alcohol; I was an addict and had taken advantage of her. Andy let the other attorney know that wasn't true. Andy told him what I had told him in our phone call earlier in the week and that Michele had no one to back her side. He also let the other attorney know that the drug addict's claim was false and he had a professional in that field to support that fact. He told the other attorney that Josh had come clean about what happened, and he

172

needed to have another conversation with his client and let her know the police complaint was not an idle threat. I asked Andy about the second conversation he had with the attorney. He said Michele still wanted to have an abortion. Her father was pissed at me. I thought to myself, big surprise there. Michele's mother said abortion goes against her religious beliefs and wants you to give up custody to them or give the baby up for adoption. He said they tried to play the drug addict angle a second time which didn't work. I was quick to tell Andy neither of the two things Michele's mother said are going to work and they need to cut the drug addict shit out. Andy and I talked more. He told me he came up with an agreement that Michele has agreed to that he felt I would go along with but had to talk to me about it first. Andy told me to take the weekend and think about it. I didn't have to. I liked the plan a lot but agreed to think it over.

2

As I left Andy's office and headed home to the cabin, I had a sense of winning and yet I had a sinking feeling over the whole situation. My stomach was in knots and there was still a lot of uncertainty and a long road ahead of me. Even though everything was done against my will and didn't want to be in this situation, I was excited about being a dad and having a family with Tony, but I was still nervous. Something was scaring me. I was so terrified that I was close to tears. I knew what it was but kept trying to bury it in my mind so I wouldn't have to deal with it. I stopped at Peach's Variety on my way home. I figured maybe coffee and a snack might help. I was getting ready to get out of my car when I noticed my jaw was trembling and my hands were shaking. It took a few solid minutes before I calmed down enough to head inside. The owner was working like he always was, and gave me his usual, "Hey Paige good to see you," greeting. He and I always engaged in small talk but today he asked if I was okay. He said he noticed I sat in the car by myself for a while. He spoke with real concern in his voice. I cracked a smile and said everything was fine. Trying to come up with an excuse, I told him I was listening to that new Jefferson Starship song that was part of the soundtrack for the movie that came out back in January. The old man laughed and said he loved the old Jefferson Airplane music. He went on the tell me how he met Grace Slick at the Monterey Pop Festival back in '67. He told me how he and Grace got into an argument over who had the best cocaine. I looked at him and said, "No way dude that's bitchin." He told me he always thought his stuff was the baddest blow around till he tried her blow. Let's just say he was humbled. He said, "Her stuff was far out and trippin', as we use to say. After that, I got drafted and went to Nam, so my hippie days were cut short." That was the extent of our conversation and probably the longest conversation he and I ever had. I was driving back and thinking to myself I was glad I stopped. It felt good to get my mind off things even if it was just for the rest of the ride back home.

3

I got back to the cabin a little later than I normally do. I was expecting to find Tony and John and a couple of pizzas waiting for me. Instead, I found a note that said they were waiting for me up in John's house. I thought to myself, pizza night in John's house, great what did I do now? I threw my book bag down and headed up to John's house with the knot in my stomach even tighter than before thinking, What now? The walk up to John's house wasn't very long, maybe a total of fifty yards, but for some reason it seemed much longer. The things that ran through my mind only added to the angst.

4

We were sitting around the table with John and Tony doing most of the chit-chatting back and forth. I was nibbling on some pizza. I didn't have much of an appetite and wasn't saying much. John commented that I was awfully quiet tonight. Rolling my eyes I answered, "Pizza night in your house, what could possibly go wrong?" John and Tony both smiled and chuckled a little at that remark. "OK, smart ass, what is really on your mind?" I told John that my stomach had been in knots since earlier that morning, and because of the meeting with Andy. John asked how that went. I told him we found out the baby was mine, so Andy had a couple of conversations with the other attorney. Both John and Tony listened intently as I told them about the things Andy and I talked about. I filled John and Tony in on the plan that I had come up with. I told John how the company I was doing occasional work for was bringing me in full-time for the summer and then a permanent position once the baby was born giving me benefits. I would pick up night courses when I could, and finish school that way. John asked if I was going to file the police complaint against Michele. Both he and Andy knew I hated the idea of a police complaint which is why I was so willing to accept the agreement Andy had come up with. I told John the agreement was that I would not file the police complaint nor any civil suit if Michele agreed to carry the baby to term and then give up all her parental rights. I had no issue with Michele giving up her parental rights, giving me sole custody, and dropping the complaint and civil suit to get Michele to agree. I told John I guessed that is where the leverage came in. I explained how that didn't go over well at all with Michele's parents. I told them both that Michele's mother agreed with me about the abortion part but still insisted I either give up custody to them or put the baby up for adoption. She tried to play the drug addict angle again and I was unfit to be a father. Her father was pissed as all hell. Andy told me that they would be very hard-pressed to prove I was unfit, and they were just "pissing in the wind". I told John that comment made me laugh. John said that was Andy's favorite line. I told John I was expecting a lot more pushback and a bigger fight, but they did agree to work with me. Tony had asked about Michele. I told him she still wanted an abortion because I wouldn't marry her but has agreed not to as long as I held up my end of the agreement. John said that all sounded good so far. I told John and Tony that Michele's parents had made it a point to let both attorneys know they hated me right now. Especially Michele's father, because I stood up to him and threatened to file a police complaint. Tony quickly replied, "That's their problem, not yours," I knew Tony was right, but it still hurt. I told them that was about the gist of it all and I was well on my way to being a dad. This made Tony so happy he couldn't contain himself. "This is great news! We are going to be daddies! Now it is time to get the cabin in shipshape. We are going to need a cradle, a changing table, and diapers. I say we use cloth diapers. They're much better for the baby." His reaction brought a smile to my face and again I thought to myself I didn't deserve him. I looked at John and said that Tony was going to make a great mom. I asked Tony if he decided if he was going to bottle feed or breastfeed the baby. John burst out laughing at that which made me start laughing. Tony rolled his eyes and said, "Go ahead make your jokes Mr. Funny Man," and shook his head at me.

5

Despite all the laughing and the love and support from Tony and John, the real issue was still eating away at me and John picked right up on it. John asked if there was anything else I wanted to talk about. I told him no, but he knew better because I was so quick to answer. That somber tone and my facial expression added to that. John tried coaxing me by saying that there had to be something more causing my stomach to be so tied up in knots. "Tell us what's going on," he said. I sat there not saying anything just trying to force some pizza down my throat. Tony noticed I was barely eating and said we know something is bothering you. Tell us, we are family, we are here for you. I needed to swallow the bite of pizza I had taken before speaking. Even though it was just a nibble, it went down hard. It was like swallowing a brick. I finally admitted that I was scared. John assured me that was normal. He even told us how he was a nervous wreck when Alice was pregnant with Debbie. I did admit that was part of it but was holding back what was truly scaring me. Tony reminded me that I promised not to bottle things up and hold them in. I finally gave in and let out what was scaring me. I told them I was scared that I was going to be just like my parents. I was scared that if the baby cried too much or got into something I was going to hit that baby. I was scared that I was going to humiliate or tear down my child the way my parents would humiliate and tear me down. I told them both I didn't want my child to be afraid of me the way I was afraid of my parents when I was a child. I was choking up when I said, "I don't want to be like them." I couldn't get all that out without my

176

eyes tearing up–I was terrified. I never want to put my child through what I dealt with growing up. John could see just how upsetting this was for me and rightfully so. Both he and Tony were quick to say there was no way I would be like that with my child. They both knew the cycle of abuse was stopping with me and told me they had no doubts about that. John made sure to say it just wasn't who I was. The way I was stepping up proved just how good of a dad I was going to be. I am not sure if they realized how excruciating that was for me to get out, but I needed to get that out and hear their words of support. It helped undo the knot my stomach was in.

6

As Tony and I stepped off the porch and started walking down to the cabin I stepped closer to him so I could hold his hand and leaned in resting my head on his upper arm. We walked that way down to the cabin and stopped in front of the porch. I stepped in front of him letting go of his hand so I could wrap my arms around his waist and hold him close to me. I laid my head up against his chest listening to his heartbeat. I loved the sound of his heart beating. There were so many nights in bed I would rest my head on his chest listening to the soothing sound of his beating heart. I stood there in the darkness just holding him and wishing this moment would last forever. I never did ask why John decided to have pizza night in his house. I guess it didn't matter where pizza night was as long as I was with my family.

Chapter 23

1

The portal took me forward several weeks. Classes had just ended and I started working my summer schedule. I was working four, ten-hour shifts which gave me Fridays off. This was great because one of the finer details of the agreement with Michele was that I would be at all the monthly checkups during her pregnancy. This particular Friday, I had gotten back much earlier than my normal time and noticed Tony was home. He usually got home right at dinner time. I headed inside looking for him, but he wasn't there or in the yard. I figured he was up in the barn. I went walking up the drive to the barn and sure enough there he was seated on a milk crate tinkering with choppers. He was listening to his Walkman, so he didn't hear me walk into to barn. I slid my arms over his shoulders and rested my chin atop his head. He turned his Walkman off, slid his headphones off, and took hold of my hands. "You're home early," I said. Tony told me not much was happening at work so they let everyone have the day off. Since he was done with what he was doing he suggested we take the choppers out and spend the day at the falls. Spending the day riding the choppers and hanging at the falls; I was down for that. The falls were about an hour away just over the New Hampshire border. We came across this spot the day we rode with the bikers. We normally went to the rock at Rattlesnake Pond which was our favorite spot, but since it was pizza night, we were short on time and since the falls were much closer, we opted to go there. Being mid-May, most schools were still in session and the roads were not busy with summer traffic which made for a nice ride. As we expected, the parking lot was empty, so we were able to park at the base of the mile-long trail that took us to the falls. We wasted no time getting the choppers parked and heading up the trail that led us to the falls. It was so cool, we were the only ones that were parked in the lot, and not a single person was on the trail. We had the falls to ourselves. There was another trail at the base of the falls that led to the top of the falls. Since we had not been to the top of the falls before, we thought it would be cool to check it out. We reached the top and were standing at the side of the falls looking out at the forest. We had quite a view of the incredible White Mountains. I don't know what came over me, I had this uncontrollable urge, and I just couldn't help myself. I took Tony by the hand and yelled out as loudly as I could, "HEY WORLD! My name is Andrew Paige Turner and I am going to be a dad soon. This is Antonin Kofi Bedru Adama, and he and I are going to raise OUR kid together because we are in love, and we are going to be a family! That's right I am in love with a black man. Fuck you if you don't like it!" With my free hand, I held my middle finger straight up in the air flipping off the world. For a man so large in stature, Tony was very soft-spoken and a man of few words. Today he surprised me as he raised his free hand holding up his middle finger and shouting as loud as I did, "You heard him world! We are in love and we're going to be a family so fuck you!" We both turned to one another and kissed, right there in the open, at the top of the falls, for the world to see. I didn't care if no one heard me or even if they did, I didn't do what I did for their benefit I did it for ours. I did it because I needed to let it out. I did it because I wanted Tony to know I wasn't afraid to love him, and my internal battle was over. We were going to be a family and as far as I was concerned, my child was as much his as the child was mine.

2

The hike back down to the base of the falls and down the trail to the choppers took a lot longer than the hike up. Let's just say we made a stop; we both needed some pants-around-the-ankles fun. It's a good thing the trees and wildlife can't talk. I was feeling amazing as we held hands the whole hike back. The parking lot was still empty, and no one was around as we got on the choppers. I couldn't help but stare at him. He made me so happy. We left and headed back home. We got back just after three in the afternoon. We were in the barn. Tony walked over and latched the doors shut from the inside. He came over to me, lifted me by my waist, and sat me on top of the workbench. He stood in between my legs, wrapped his arms around me and we started kissing. It wasn't long before we were both naked and he started working his magic on me. We were both still naked when I poked my head out the barn door to make sure John wasn't home. I knew he wasn't due back till about six o'clock but wanted to be sure. Tony was right behind me when I told him the coast was clear so let's go get showered off. Tony asked, "Paige don't you think we should put our clothes back on first?" as I was opening the barn door. I said "Nope," grabbed him by the hand, and marched out the door. There we were strutting down the drive to the cabin buck-ass naked and without a care in the world.

3

We showered together like we always did. I was still in the bedroom dressing when John came in. I could overhear him and Tony talking. Tony was telling him we went for a ride today up to the falls and hiked to the top. Thankfully he left out the details about us shouting and flipping off the world and trotting around his property naked. I finished dressing and took a seat at the table, greeting John. John asked how the job was going and noticed I had picked up a lot of hours. I told him my four-day, ten-hour days schedule included having Fridays free for doctor's appointments or meetings with Andy. When there were no appointments, I would pick up an extra shift on Fridays. Tony said we had our minds so focused on riding today he forgot to ask how the doctor's visit went this morning. I got excited when Tony asked. " The appointment was awesome," I told them I got to listen to the baby's heartbeat. Then I told them I got scared at first because Michele kept complaining about something being wrong with the baby. So, they did an ultrasound, and I got to see the baby. John said that since I said the appointment was awesome, he assumed everything was fine. I told him the baby was perfect and Michele was just being Michele, trying to cause needless drama and draw attention to herself. I told them that I even had a printout to show them. I got up from the table to grab the printout and told them I even knew the sex of the baby. I handed the folder with the printout to John. He looked at it and said, "WOW look at that." I could tell Tony was excited to see the baby. He even told us not to tell him the sex of the baby because he wanted to see for himself. John passed the printout to Tony and said there was no question on gender. Tony took a look, "Holy shit" he said. There was no doubt about it; that is a boy, you can't miss it. Like father like son. I couldn't help but laugh. That's right we are having a boy.

4

After a few rounds of congratulations, I told Tony that I couldn't wait to take our son riding with us. Tony looked at me like I was insane and asked how I was going to take a baby riding on a chopper. I said I was going to duct tape the baby to the sissy bar so he wouldn't fall off. Tony looked horrified. "You can't duct tape a baby to the sissy bar." Tony had no idea I was joking, I just kept playing along. John picked up on it right away and since he and I had been doing a lot of talking, I got to know him and knew he had a devilish side to him. He was getting in on the joke. John chimed in with, "Come on Paige, duct tape? Everyone knows the adhesive isn't good for a baby's skin." I looked over at John and replied, "I didn't think of that. Guess I will just have to use a bungee cord." I had Tony hook, line, and sinker at this point. In a voice and tone that matched his large stature, Tony said, "Andrew Paige Turner, I am putting my foot down. There is no way you are taping or bungee-cording a baby to the sissy bar!" John was the one who kept the joke going by saying, "I am with Tony on this one. Tell you what, tomorrow we will measure the choppers for saddle bags. Those will be much more comfortable and safer for the baby." Tony was beside himself "John Williamson how is that helping!" We both started laughing. Tony now knew we were joking. "Another psych-out?

What in God's name am I going to do with the both of you?" John told Tony that he was going to babysit on the days we go riding and admitted he couldn't promise that when we got back the baby wouldn't be spoiled. I laughed and told John, "Spoken like a true Grandpa." Tony and I had already decided the baby would call him Baba, which was African for father. Tony was the one who came up with what the baby should call John. Tony said to John that we thought the baby could call him Opa, which was German for grandpa, because Alice was German and we thought it would be a cool thing. John loved the idea and was so happy we thought of him that way. Tony and I knew he would love it, and we were so glad he did.

5

John was using pizza night as sort of a weekly group session in addition to any one-on-one time we may have had during the week. John wanted to make sure we both were doing well with everything that was going on. We had wrapped up with that when Tony picked up the folder with the ultrasound and took another look. "It won't be very long before this little boy arrives." There was real excitement in Tony's voice. John remembered all the sleepless nights when his daughter was first born. Tony was smiling saying he knew a lot of lullabies and asked if I knew any. I told Tony I was getting pretty good at playing Stairway to Heaven on my guitar. Right on cue, John chimed in with, "I was thinking Black Dog." I thought it was awesome that John said that. I was like, "YES! I love it!" then sang the song very badly. "HEY HEY momma said the way you move gonna make you sweat gonna make you groove," then I threw in a little air guitar action. Growing up, Tony had a secluded and strict upbringing, so sometimes he didn't get it when we were joking. He said to me in a dead serious tone, "You cannot sing Led Zepplin to a baby. It is like living with a twelve-year-old and Opa isn't helping." John laughed as he got up. "Alright guys, it's getting late, good night." We both said our good nights to John. Once John was out of earshot, Tony suggested we head up to the barn and grab the clothes we left up there. I told him I had a better idea. I reached over and rubbed his crotch and said, "Let's have some cannoli instead." I could tell right away he liked my idea much better.

6

The next morning, after we finished breakfast, Tony headed up to the barn. I told him I would be up there shortly, I just wanted to clean up the breakfast dishes. After I got the kitchen cleaned up, I headed up to the barn. I could hear John and Tony talking. I guessed John had walked in just before I got there. I stopped just outside the door. John had said to Tony he wanted to talk to him alone just in case there was something he wanted to talk about without me present. Tony admitted to John he did some things yesterday that he would never have done with anyone else. John was curious as to what those things were. He asked Tony to tell him about it. Tony told John about what we did at the top of the falls. He said to John, "I held up my middle finger and said a bad word. No, I shouted a bad word." He told John about kissing on top of the falls and holding hands while walking back on the trail. For some reason, John wasn't surprised by me doing what I did but was very surprised that Tony did it. I couldn't see, so I didn't know if Tony and John were smiling or not. They didn't sound angry, so I thought that was a good sign. Tony told John about us fooling around in the barn and then walking naked down the drive to the cabin. John was laughing and telling Tony he never expected him to do that either. Tony tried to apologize to John, but John wouldn't hear it. He told Tony these are the things people do when they are in love. He told him that I was bringing out a side of him that he would never have guessed was there. "Don't be sorry, that's wonderful," he told Tony. Tony told John he was right. He would never have done these things if it wasn't for me. Tony admitted it was out of character for him and he didn't know what to think of it all. John asked Tony if he wanted things to be different; would he want things to be any other way? Tony didn't hesitate when he said, "Absolutely not! My home and my little family are perfect just the way they are. I can't picture life without Paige." John told him that I shouted it from the mountain tops so to speak, and I kept calling the baby "ours", so he was confident I felt the same way. John was right, I couldn't picture life without Tony. I took a few steps back and called, "Hey Tones you in there?" hoping they wouldn't think I overheard them. The portal closed.

Chapter 24

1

When the portal closed and the mist cleared, John and I were in physical form again. I had my back to John and could feel him place a hand on my shoulder. John felt the need to tell me again how proud he was of me. The way I broke my chemical dependency, the way I stepped up and took responsibility for my son. This time he added he was particularly impressed with how I took control of my inner battle and allowed myself to be who I was. I allowed myself to love who I loved unconditionally and without apology. He was impressed with the way I took my power back, took control of my own life, and started living my life my way. I didn't allow others to influence me. I, once again, asked John where it got me. John's hand was still on my shoulder, and I could feel him give a gentle squeeze trying to be supportive. John reminded me that I was too hard on myself, and that I was blaming myself. He reminded me that it wasn't my fault, no one could have seen that coming; we were all blindsided. I turned around to face John and said, "She looked me straight in the eye and lied to my face." John gave a heavy sigh and again told me to remember that everyone believed her, not just me. John knew just how hard seeing all this again was for me. I knew it was hard for him too. When I turned to face him, I could see the tears welling up in his eyes. I knew just how devastating what he was about to show me was. It upset him and he didn't want me to see it or live it again, but he knew I had to.

John allowed the mist to swallow us up again. In an instant, I was back looking through the portal.

2

When the portal opened, I was looking down into the small Bistro in Old Port where I took Michele for lunch after her monthly check-ups. Our conversations at the other appointments and lunches were small talk about nothing. Today Michele was on the quiet side at first. The waitress brought me the check and I was going to walk up to the front to pay when Michele spoke, "That appointment completely blew my mind." I asked her what she meant. She said that every time I talked to the baby he would kick. She seemed genuinely amazed when she told me the nurse tried and I tried. Nothing. You talked to him, and it was like a soccer game was going on. She was right, that is what happened–he knew my voice. I told her I couldn't wait to hold him. Michele knew and even said he was a daddy's boy and wanted to know if I had picked out a name for him yet. I told her I hadn't decided on a name yet. Michele knew I was excited for this baby and asked me why. I got an uneasy feeling thinking she was starting again like she did that one appointment when she suggested there was something wrong with the baby. I just flat-out told her I didn't come here to fight or argue. I told her if she was trying to bait me, it hadn't worked for the past six months, and it wasn't going to work now. She quickly said, "No, that's not it. That's not what I am doing." I didn't want to take things any further, but curiosity got the best of me, and I asked her what she was doing. She said to me, "Daddy and Mother were blown away by everything you are doing. It's like things are coming so naturally to you. They couldn't believe it and neither could I." I was shocked at the words and how sincere she was being. I didn't know what to say besides, "Thanks." She admitted none of them realized how good of a dad I was going to be. Michele also admitted if she knew what I was really like as a person she would never have done what she did. She said she was truly sorry. I again was at a loss for words. I couldn't believe Michele was saying these things to me. Apologizing! There had to be something more to this, but I was cautiously optimistic. Maybe she was realizing what she did and just how wrong it was. She said, "You do love this little boy." I guess maybe she thought I would have reacted differently when I found out she was pregnant. I did tell her that I do love my little boy. She was still sincere when she said she was happy for me. Looking up at me she said, "The baby is half me and I am his mommy." I was quick to cut in and asked where she was going with this. She told me that if I could love half of her then maybe I could love all of her. I knew right away that was a terrible idea. Trying to keep it civil, I simply said that isn't such a good idea. I felt like she was begging when she said, "Just hear me out. I have changed. I am not that person anymore," I wasn't buying it and told her the answer was no. Still pleading with me she wanted to get to know me for real this time. I wanted to end it right here and I tried by saying, "I told you I don't want to fight." She wouldn't take no for an answer and started pleading harder with me, saying how everyone misjudged me, that I was husband and daddy material and she wanted to try and be a family. I kept my cool and stood my ground. I told her she was right, I was husband material, just not her husband. She kept on trying to plead with me saying we didn't have to get married right away in case it didn't work. I tried to gently remind her that we have an agreement in place, and I just wanted to stick to the agreement. I asked her to please change the subject. Again, she pleaded with me. "Can't we just talk?" I didn't want to talk about it and told her, "Look tomorrow you will be officially in your third trimester. We are going to meet on August 14th to sign all the papers for the family court. Then our next appointment is on August 28th. We are going to start talking about a due date and birthing options. We both have a lot to think about so I really would like to stick to the agreement and follow the plan." Michele tried pleading one last time, but I cut her off. I told her again we both have a lot to deal with and that I would give things more thought after the baby is born. I told her I just wanted to get through the holidays, get settled in with the baby, and then we would talk. I asked her if we could do that for now. I even added a couple of pleases in there too. Finally, she let up and said, "If that's what you want."

I went up, paid the bill, and walked back to the table so I could leave a tip. Michele was still sitting there so I offered to walk her to her car. We got to her car and before getting in, Michele turned to me. She looked me straight in the eye when she said, "I am really glad you are doing what you are doing. I now know I would have regretted having an abortion. Thank you. This baby deserves to have a dad like you." I was once again, blown away by Michele. I told her thank you, and I needed to hear that. I even went as far as to kiss her forehead. After she got in her car, I watched her drive off. I didn't know what to think. I was glad she told me what she told me. It took any doubt I may have had as to whether being a dad was the right thing at this point in my life. This baby and being a family with Tony and John were the best things to happen to me. I had no doubts about that now. But I still felt she was up to something.

3

I got back home mid-afternoon. I knew Tony wouldn't be home because of work. I figured John would be around but as it turned out I was the only one there. I did some chores around John's house which I was doing as my way of thanking him for helping me. I was also doing it because John was being more of a dad to me than anything else. I liked doing things for my dad. My real dad never took any interest in me or my brother. In several of his drunken episodes, he was very vocal about wishing he never had kids. John was that father figure I never had. I finished what I was doing and headed down to the cabin to shower before John got there with the pizza. I had just stepped into the shower when Tony came home–I ended up having company in the shower. I was setting the table when I heard John's voice as he was coming through the screen door. "Knock knock, pizza is here." John came in, set the pizza down and I asked him where he had been today. He told me he went to his thinking spot; it was the place he would go when he wanted to sit, be quiet, and think things through. "Come on let's sit. I need to talk to you about something." Tony came out of the bedroom obviously overhearing our conversation. "What did you do now Paige?" I gave Tony a look that had "bite me" written all over it.

John laughed and said he wanted to talk to me about something I did. John said he had the latest drug test results. Right away I was like, "WHOA DUDE! Let's put the brakes on that hoe train. I ain't falling for that one again." Both John and Tony started laughing. I shook my head and rolled my eyes thinking to myself, now Tony finally gets a sense of humor and it's at my expense. John said no, your test results were perfect as always. Congratulations are in order; you have broken your chemical dependency. You have tested drug and alcohol-free once a week for the past five months and I am proud of you. This is commendable. Tony smiled and said he knew there were some nights I struggled and struggled badly but I kept my promise, and he was proud of me too. I was grateful for both of them and their help. If it wasn't for them, I probably wouldn't have made it. I told them both that too. I was also grateful that I was able to make my dad proud even if he was my dad by proxy. John said that moving forward I didn't have to drug test anymore unless I gave him a reason, which he was confident I wouldn't. I couldn't resist saying, "AWE. I am going to miss peeing in a cup! NOT." John shook his head "OK smartass. I do want pizza night to continue as our weekly session." I had no problem agreeing to that because even though it was meant to be a therapy session, I always looked at it as a family dinner. Family dinner was my favorite part of the week and couldn't wait for the newest addition to arrive and be part of our family dinner.

4

John wanted to know how the appointment went. I told him the appointment was great and I had the latest ultrasound. Tony reached for it right away. "Let me see." I handed the folder to Tony. He was so happy and excited. He said, "Hello baby boy! I am Baba Tony." I told them both I couldn't believe it in just three months he would be here. Tony passed the folder to John saying, "Look! he is so perfect." He asked me. "How did you make such a perfect baby boy." I told Tony the answer was simple, "I have super sperm!" John thought that was priceless. Tony shook his head, "Listen to Mr. Genetic Jackhammer over there." which got me laughing. There were plenty of pizza nights where we had some serious and tough conversations, so a laugh fest was always a welcome change. John was shaking his head and still laughing as he tried to again ask how today went. I told him today's appointment was mind-blowing to the max. "Mind-blowing to the max? How so?" he asked. I told him that every time I talked to the baby he would kick, it was like he knew me. I told them how Michele tried, and the nurse tried, and nothing happened. I talked to him again and he started kicking. It was so awesome. Tony said the baby knows who I am, and he and I will have a special bond. I told him Michele said he was a daddy's boy. John asked, "Speaking of the devil how is Michele doing?" I started to tell John what happened when I took her to lunch today. Tony quickly interrupted with, "I don't know why you take her to lunch like that. After everything she has done and put you through. She doesn't deserve your kindness nor your generosity." He was angry, not at me, but at the circumstances and how she tried to destroy our relationship. I knew he wasn't wrong to feel that way. I even told him he wasn't wrong, and I went on to tell him that I was doing everything I could to keep the peace. I don't want any fighting, arguing, or, to give her any reason to break our deal. I told him once the baby was born, I would cut all ties with her and her family. John agreed with Tony and even went as far as to say Michele didn't deserve me period, but he did like the way I was handling things. Tony knew I was trying my best to do the right thing in this very wrong situation, but he said it still wasn't right. I felt horrible knowing just how hurt and angry he was at the toxic trio for what they did to me, and Michele for purposely getting pregnant. I wanted to make Tony feel better so I asked him, "Would it make you feel better knowing the real reason I take Michele to lunch is so I can slip a big booger in her sandwich?" I pretended to stick a finger up my nose and told him I dug way up there to pick the biggest, greenest, and slimiest booger I could find and slapped it right on her sandwich. It worked. He started to laugh, and John chimed in saying he could picture me doing that. I decided not to tell them about the conversation she and I had at lunch, but I did want them to know what she had said. I said to Tony, "All kidding aside, Michele said a few things today." I told Tony how she looked me in the eye when she apologized for the whole situation. I told him that her apology doesn't help fix anything because it doesn't. But at least she realizes she was wrong. The other thing she admitted to me was how glad she was that I was doing what I was doing. She would have regretted having an abortion. I needed to hear that. I want to believe that she is truly sorry, and that she was being truthful. I also wanted to let Tony know that the apology and her telling me she would have regretted the abortion changed nothing. I am still cutting all ties with all of them.

5

It hurt to see Tony that angry and upset. I know he had every right to be. None of them was ever nice to him or treated him like he was a human being. I remember when we first met, he said they were cruel, and he wasn't wrong. Even though it was going to take a lot of time, I could deal with and eventually get past what they had done to me. I truly hated them for what they did to Tony even before I met him, now more so for trying to destroy our relationship. I tried to change the direction of the conversation. Not so much the subject but I tried to steer the conversation in a different direction. I said the question that came up was had I picked a name for the baby. I hadn't thought about it till today. Now I am racking my brain trying to come up with a name. John said it took forever for him and Alice to decide on a name for their daughter. He said he would never have guessed how much stress there is trying to decide on a name. I told them I couldn't stop thinking about it. Steering the conversation in another direction and not saying who asked about the name proved to be the right move. Tony asked if he could suggest a name for the baby. I was glad he asked and told him, "Please do. This is going to be your son too, and I want you to be a part of naming the baby." Saying that put a huge smile on his face. He proudly told me his grandmother would never name her children till they were born. She would wait till the baby was born and when the baby opened their eyes, she would look into their eyes and the name would be there. John thought it was a good idea. I told Tony that was a great idea and I loved it. I told him that was exactly what we were going to do.

6

Later that night, we were lying in bed in our usual position with my head resting in that sweet spot so I could listen to his heartbeat. Tony softly said, "This is going to be my son too and I can help name him. I am so honored. I don't know what else to say." His voice was so humble and sweet. I looked up at him. Tony turned his head to face me, and we started kissing. It was the same kiss that we had on the sofa that morning back in March. That deep soul connection kiss. The kiss that made us both feel we were bonding on a deeper level. The longer we held the kiss the deeper we felt the connection. I knew this man was more than just my lover and friend. Tony and I had a connection that ran deep within each other's souls. I could feel that we were brought together by a higher power. It felt as if divine guidance from a higher plane brought us together. I could tell by the clock next to the bed that we kissed for over an hour. As I rested my head back in the sweet spot and started listening to his heartbeat, I could feel our hearts beating in sync. I have heard the terms "twin flame" and "soulmate" in the past and knew there was a difference. When it came to us, I knew we were both to one another. I had been told that it was highly unlikely that someone could be both. I knew with us they were wrong. Our connection, our vibration, and our bond were on a level that being both twin flames and soulmates was the only explanation there could be.

Chapter 25

1

Once again, the portal opened and brought me forward a few weeks. Tony and I were lying in bed. Since we had moved in together, we would wake up around five every morning and just lay there together. My head was resting where it always does, my arm was across his chest holding his hand, and my leg was lying over his midsection. We would start every morning lying there like that till right around six when we would get up. I would go start the coffee before joining Tony in the shower. I wasn't sure why I was seeing this, but then I realized what day it was. I knew, because that same feeling of dread and the foreboding thoughts resurfaced. Even though I was in a state of higher consciousness all through this journey, I could feel everything. All those feelings felt as strong now as they did back then. It was Tuesday morning, August 11, 1987.

2

Tony had just left for the day, and I was on my way out the door when this feeling of dread washed over me. I didn't know what was wrong or why I was having this feeling, I just was. I felt like I lost a connection to someone or something. I felt this massive empty void that I could not explain even if I tried. I headed out the door hoping I wasn't getting the summer flu. We had a few guys at work out with it yesterday, so I thought maybe I picked up the flu bug or something from work. I arrived at work. I didn't have a fever or chills, and my stomach wasn't upset which in my mind, ruled out the flu. I loved my job and usually being at work took my mind off things for a while. Today that didn't happen. I got my work done but was distracted and had a difficult time concentrating on what needed to be done. Around lunch time I had lost my appetite. I had to force down my Italian sandwich, I didn't even finish my bottle of Moxie and took a pass on the Humpty Dumpty chips and Whoopie Pie. I did get a little hungry around afternoon break time and was able to finish my lunch but still had not felt any different than I did that morning. I got home that evening and Tony was starting dinner. Besides both of us loving Italian food, we both loved the red snappers from Jordan's Food. Every so often the cafeteria at the college would serve them and anyone who wasn't from New England would refuse to eat the red-hot dogs we called red snappers. Our favorite way to cook them was on a charcoal grill, served on fresh rolls topped with mustard, relish, diced sweet Vidalia onions, and a side of Tator Tots smothered in ketchup. I just picked at my dinner much like my lunchtime meal. These were going down hard too. I hadn't regained my appetite. Tony noticed something was off with me and that I wasn't myself. He asked me if something was wrong. I told Tony it was extra busy at work, it was hot, and several people were out so it was just a long hard day. He said to me, "I know what will help. Let's take the choppers over to Sandy Point Beach and cool off in the pond. I wanted to tell him, "Not tonight." Normally all Tony had to do was say choppers and I was out the door to the barn before he could finish the sentence. Tonight, I had to force myself to go.

3

We had an awesome ride. The swim we took in the pond was refreshing; it did feel good to cool off. We stayed there for quite a while too. Just a few people were there when we arrived, but they cleared out shortly after. We swam out to the raft anchored about a hundred feet out in the pond. Since no one was around, we swam under the raft and had a make-out session. We took our time riding back home. We were just enjoying the moment. The lovemaking that night was so intense we both climaxed twice. But somehow, through it all, I felt this huge disconnect from everything. I just didn't feel anything not even for Tony. We were lying in bed together and I couldn't shake this horrible feeling I had all day. Listening to Tony's heartbeat and the sound of his breathing when he slept always helped ease any discomfort I had. Not tonight. I laid there for hours and found no comfort or solace like I had before. It was around three in the morning when I sat up and shifted around so I was sitting on the edge of the bed looking out the window. There had been a full moon two nights ago and tonight the moon was still just bright, as it was Sunday night. I didn't want to disturb Tony, so I got up and went out to the front porch and sat on the old sofa hoping to find an answer. I looked out into the blueberry patch on the side of the cabin then shifted my gaze to the edge of the dooryard where the forest began searching for an answer in the moonlit predawn hours. I was looking out at the dooryard wishing I could find an answer as to what was wrong.

4

I was lost in my thoughts of trying to figure out what was wrong, I didn't hear Tony step out onto the creaky wood floor of the porch. "Paige, what are you doing sitting there? he asked. I had to sniff and clear my throat before I could speak, "Nothing, I guess I couldn't get comfortable that's all." I was so frustrated and scared that I felt like I wanted to cry but I couldn't. He asked if I had been sitting there all night. I tried to answer but I couldn't. He sat down next to me asking what was wrong. I told him I didn't know what was wrong and it was the truth. There was something wrong, but I didn't know what it was. Tony knew the summer flu had been going around at work, so he asked if maybe I was sick with the flu. I told him no, I was sure it wasn't the flu, and I was not sick. I did tell him I wasn't feeling right and knew something was wrong. Tony asked again if I was sure

I wasn't sick. I reassured him I wasn't. "If you're not sick, are you..." then he stopped mid-sentence. I knew where he was going and as much as I hate to admit it, it was a legit question to ask. It irritated me that he asked and it showed when I said to him, "I am not drunk, I am not high and this isn't withdrawal." He slid his arm around me and pulled me closer saying, "I know, I know. I shouldn't have even thought that way." I told him I had been sitting there for a few hours and I just had a feeling that something had gone horribly wrong. I think it has to do with the baby. We both knew the baby was perfectly fine at the recent doctor's visit, but I knew something was way off. He did ask if I knew what was wrong. I told him I didn't know what was wrong or how I knew I just knew something wasn't right. The longer I sat there trying to figure out what was wrong the more I was convinced something went wrong with my unborn son. Tony thought it best to call John and ask him to come down to the cabin. He asked if I was okay with that. I nodded my head in agreement.

5

Tony went inside to call John. I could hear him tell John he needed to come down to the cabin. I also heard him say Paige thinks something is wrong with the baby and I needed him. Tony hung up the phone and said, "Please, please Sango, I pray to you. Please don't let anything be wrong with our son". Later, I learned Tony was praying to the most powerful African God of protection to keep our son safe. Within a few minutes, John was walking up to the porch. As he opened the screen door and came onto the porch, he greeted me and asked what was going on. I told John I didn't know, I just knew something was wrong in a very bad way. I know John was being supportive and trying to help when he said the baby was healthy, had a strong heartbeat, and even kicked for me. I was so frustrated at this point and it showed. I said, "How many times do I have to repeat it? Something is wrong." John took a seat next to me and went into dad mode. "Paige, I know you have had a lot to deal with. I know things have been very unfair and have caused more stress than anyone should have to deal with, so I am going to have to ask a tough question." I immediately said, "No." John replied that he was going to ask anyway. John and I were sitting next to one another on the sofa and Tony was in the doorway. We were seated across from each other so we could talk face-to-face. I looked right at John and said, "The answer to your tough question is NO. NO, I am not using, NO I am not high, NO this isn't withdrawal again. If you don't believe me, I will piss in a goddamn cup right now. Both of you stop with that, I am not fucking high!" That was the first and only time I ever raised my voice at all with them. I was not angry just upset that John said I had earned his trust yet here they both were questioning if I was using. I knew it wasn't out of line for them and they did have a right to ask. Looking back, I was mad at myself because it was my past behavior that gave them cause to ask. I took a couple of seconds before I spoke. When I was ready I told him, "I know this sounds crazy, but I can't feel him anymore, I just can't feel him. It's like…" I had to take a moment to search my head for the word to describe what I was feeling. I found the words I was looking for… "It's like he is gone." John tried his best to provide comfort. He said we don't know that anything is wrong. How about we find out? This way we can put your mind to rest. John said to call Michele. I didn't have to say anything besides I was checking in to see how she was and offer to buy her lunch again this week. I knew it was sound advice, and it was what I needed to do but I told them both I was too afraid to call. I was too scared to find out. Tony said he was scared too. I knew he was just as scared as I was, but we had to find out. John suggested we have Andy call Michele's attorney and say he was confirming Friday's appointment. I didn't answer right away. It was a good idea, but I knew it had to be me that made the call. When I told John this, he said to take a few minutes and he and Tony were going to give me some space and go inside. Tony told John that coffee was ready and also said he would pour me a cup.

6

I sat there for a while by myself building the courage to call Michele. I could hear Tony and John talking in the kitchen and I was trying to listen to their conversation. They sat at the table, and I heard Tony say to John that he was worried. How could I know if something was wrong with the baby? John told Tony that he initially thought I was having an anxiety attack. He said with all that was happening, it was starting to get real. We were going to be signing the court documents and meeting with the judge. Talking about the due date and birthing options could trigger me for sure. Tony asked if what I was feeling was real. John explained that it was a real thing. He tried to tell Tony that parents have this intuition, almost like a sixth sense. He said it was like a heightened awareness or connection to their children. Curiously, Tony asked John if this was something he had. John admitted he and Alice always knew when something wasn't right with their daughter Debbie. Hearing John say what he said helped more than he knew. I wasn't sure he believed me at first when I said I wasn't high. What he was thinking as he walked down the drive made me feel better too. I was worried that he would just assume I was getting high or drinking but he really did believe in me. Tony was worried about our son. Hearing those words "our son" meant everything to me. Hearing all that helped boost my courage

7

I finally picked up the phone, which was at the far end of the living room sofa on an end table. I sat down as I waited for someone to pick up at the other end. Michele's mother answered. I said, "Hello Mrs. Gibons. It's Paige Turner," and asked if I could speak with Michele. As soon as she spoke, I could hear the resentment in her voice and thought right away Michele lied to me about her parents misjudging me. Like I do with Michele, I tried to keep it civil. I even said please to the bitch. I could see where Michele got her personality. "Michele isn't here. Why are you calling this house this early? What do you want? Are you starting trouble?" She wasn't letting up. I took a deep breath to maintain my cool before I spoke. When I did, I kept the tone even and civil, but I was very direct when I spoke. "Look Kathleen, I am not causing trouble. The reason I am calling this early is that I have been working so much overtime this week that I didn't think I would get a chance to call before Friday. I figured I would call now before I left for work. As for the reason I called. I am calling to make sure she and the baby are doing well. I would like to extend an invitation to Michele and Attorney Foster for lunch with my Attorney and me, my treat. I have been taking Michele to lunch after the doctor's appointments and thought I would do the same Friday after we meet with my attorney. So again, I ask if I could please speak to Michele so I can ask her." "Oh, I didn't know you were taking Michele to lunch like that, and you said you are at all the appointments?" Mrs. Gibons' tone softened. She hadn't realized I was at all the appointments or taking Michele to lunch. I told her I was trying to keep things as pleasant and civil as possible. I told her I wanted the next three months to go the same way. Michele wasn't being honest with her family– big surprise there. Mrs. Gibons told me that Michele was at her aunt's house in Quebec visiting with her cousin who invited Michele up for the week. She told me they hadn't seen one another since their High School Graduation. I thought it was odd that Michele didn't say anything to me. Then again, it's Michele so I shouldn't expect anything less. Mrs. Gibson said that she would be back in time for Friday. Then she asked if there was anything wrong. She said I sounded like I was worried about something. I told her everything was fine. It was just first-time dad jitters. She offered me the phone number of her sister in Canada so I could call if I wanted to. I wrote the number down, thanked her, then ended the phone call.

8

Tony walked over and handed me a mug of coffee. John asked if everything was all right. I told him "Yeah." He asked if I spoke with Michele. I told him who I spoke to, and that Michele wasn't there. I got the number for where she is, and she will be back in time for Friday. I know they already knew that; it was a small cabin it isn't like they couldn't hear me. Tony was the one who asked if I was going to call. I was sitting staring at the floor when I told him, "I can't. I just can't make the call."

199

Chapter 26

1

The portal brought me forward to Friday, August 14, 1987, the most miserable and God-forsaken day of my entire life. Tony and I were sitting at the kitchen table having coffee. Tony had asked how I was doing. He knew I didn't sleep at all Tuesday night. Surprisingly enough, I arrived on time for work on Wednesday. Both Wednesday night and Thursday night I was crashed by seven. I was exhausted from Tuesday night's lack of sleep and the extra workload at my job. I was feeling better this morning, I guess because I was going to be seeing Michele in a few hours and I would see that everything was fine. I was starting to think John was right. It was just a massive anxiety attack. I told Tony I was feeling better. He was glad to hear that. I wanted Tony to be at all the doctor's appointments with me and wanted him to come to the meeting with Andy and Michele today. As far as we both were concerned, he was going to be a dad too. Although we kept that part to ourselves. We didn't want anyone or anything to screw this up so the three of us agreed; it would be best if I went to all the appointments alone. Tony asked what time the appointment was today. He took the day off because, instead of our usual pizza night, we were going to John's favorite restaurant over in Yarmouth to celebrate and Tony wanted to do a little celebrating with just me for getting full custody of the baby. I told him we were meeting at Andy's office at ten-thirty to sign everything, then family court after lunch so the Judge could sign off. I told him that if all goes well,

I hope to be back by three o'clock or so. "I am glad you are okay, and I am hoping today goes even better than you hope it does." Just as Tony was saying that the phone started ringing. I smiled and said" Yeah, I am okay. Let me get the phone. It's probably John making sure I don't leave before he sees me."

2

I picked up the phone saying, "Hello". "Paige it's Michele" I wasn't expecting Michele. She caught me off guard. "Hey Michele, what's going on?" I was thinking to myself maybe she heard I called and wanted to take me up on my offer for lunch. She didn't waste any time, she got right to the reason for her call. "There isn't going to be a meeting today or any more doctor's appointments." I thought to myself, what the hell is she talking about. I don't think her words truly registered with me. I asked, "Michele did something happen while you were on your trip?" She was quick to reply, "You could say that." As soon she said that my heart was in my throat. That feeling from the other day came flooding back in and I could barely speak when I asked, "What happened? Were you in an accident or something? Are you and the baby, okay?" I still to this day can't figure out why I gave her the benefit of the doubt. I should have known right away. "Oh, I am fine." she said like everything was as right as rain. "The baby isn't." was said in a vile and ominous tone. I was starting to get scared, the hand that was holding the phone receiver to my ear started shaking. I tried to use my free hand to steady the phone receiver. "What do you mean the baby isn't fine?" Tony heard this and immediately got up and walked over to me asking, "What is wrong?" I didn't respond to Tony, but he knew something was wrong by the way both my hands were shaking. My hands were shaking out of fear, but I was starting to get angry with her the way she was toying with me. "What the fuck is going on Michele?" The words came out of her mouth so nonchalantly. "I gave you one last chance to marry me. You refused to marry me, so I terminated the pregnancy." I was dumbfounded by what I just heard. I couldn't process her words. I couldn't think, I just blurted out words. The rest of the conversation was all knee-jerk comments and unfiltered reactions to her statement. "What do you mean you terminated the pregnancy? What are you talking about?" She got nasty, "What part of abortion don't you understand?" was said with such sarcasm that the one rational thought I did have was that she was lying and just called to start shit to try and get out of the meeting today. "NOT FUNNY! You're in your third trimester, you and the baby are perfectly healthy so there is no way you got an abortion!" She wasn't letting up, "Don't believe me, call your attorney, Daddy's attorney probably called him by now." She was trying to get under my skin. Not only was she still being sarcastic, but she had that sassy tone she got when rubbing it in someone's face. "This isn't funny Michele; this is beyond cruel even for you. You got me your joke is over." "Like duh. Put two and two together. I went to Canada. I didn't have it done here." She is serious. Dear god almighty she is serious, that was all that went through my mind. "Why Michele why?" was all I could say. "I told you it's your fault for not marrying me," was what she said, but all I heard was it's my fault. I begged her to tell me it was a joke, and she didn't do this. I was pleading for her to tell me she didn't have an abortion. To prove just how sinister she was, the most vile and disgusting thing I have ever heard came out of her mouth. "What are you getting so upset for? It was just an embryo. It's not like it was a real baby. They just disposed of it like they do with medical waste." Hearing those unholy words was like getting punched in the chest by a pro boxer. I couldn't breathe. When I did catch my breath, I went into a blind rage and lost it. "SCREW YOU! THAT WAS A CHILD! You saw for yourself! You heard his heartbeat! You felt him kick! SCREW FUCKING YOU!". I was screaming into the phone. I lost all control as did Michele, "SCREW ME! NO SCREW YOU! I know you and that Jungle Bunny are fucking one another! There is no way I want you two faggots raising my baby! He's better off dead you would have just given him AIDS anyway. I saved him the suffering!" Those words were like dumping gas onto a fire and throwing in a stick of dynamite. I hollered into the phone, "You don't know shit! We're not faggots we are family. We don't have fucking AIDS! My son is not better off dead you're better off dead! You're going to wish you were dead when I get done with you! Michele took that as a threat there was real fear in her voice. "Stay away from me, you and that ni…" I cut her right off before she could finish saying it. "Don't you dare call him that!" I slammed the phone down. I hate that word but more than that I hate that she even tried to call Tony that. I never told him what she tried to call him because I think it would have hurt me more to say it than it would have hurt him to hear it.

3

The portal quickly shifted, and I was looking down into John's house. John had just picked up the phone and greeted the caller with, "Williamson's residence." He heard the caller at the other end say, "John it's Andy" Being one of John's oldest friends he gave Andy his typical jovial, "Good Morning Andy." followed with "Hey while it's at the top of my mind I want to ask both you guys to join us tonight for dinner we are going to the Rudder…" Andy cut John off. "John please just listen. You need to find Paige now. You need to find him before Michele calls or he leaves to come here." John's jovial tone was replaced with real concern. "What's wrong Andy?" Andy told John about the call he just got from Michele's attorney and why Michele went to Canada. When Andy was finished John hung up. "That rotten bitch that rotten mother fucking bitch!" I never heard John use anything fouler than smartass or that one time he called me a little asshole for the psych out. To hear those words come out of his mouth I knew the anger and hurt he felt was the same as if it had happened to Debbie. Without hesitation, John headed straight for the back door and down to the cabin.

4

The portal again shifted back to the cabin. In a rage, I slammed the receiver down. The rage was instantly replaced with shock and disbelief and not realizing I said the following out loud, "OH GOD NO! She killed him. she killed my little boy. This is all my fault!" Tony, failing to hold back his tears tried to comfort me. He reached out, with tears streaming down his face and pulled me closer to him. "NO this isn't your fault." I broke free of Tony yelling at him, "How can you say that! I refused to give her a second chance. If I had, none of this would have happened! Tony tried to say, "Paige that's not true" I just pushed past him and headed for the door. Tony begged me not to leave, to let him call John. "I want my son! Oh god, Tony, I can't do this! I can't fucking do this!" I stormed out of the cabin and damn near tore my car's door off the hinges as I got in. Somehow, in my blind rage, I was able to start the engine. With the engine roaring, I slammed the car into gear and spun the tires as I raced off, leaving a cloud of sand and gravel behind me.

5

John was just rounding the bend in the driveway up by the barn when he heard me start my car and race my engine. He tried to pick up his already rushed pace to try and stop me before leaving. Between being more than slightly overweight and being sixty-plus years of age, it was a futile attempt. Even if he was able to catch me or if I saw him in my rearview mirror I wouldn't have stopped. I was no longer in my right mind. John ran into the cabin just as Tony was hanging up the phone after getting no answer from John and now seeing why. Tony just stared at John with fresh tears running down his cheeks. "That evil monster John she is a demonic Tagati!" which was the worst demon in Africa. John was trying to maintain his calm and reason telling Tony, "I know, I know. Andy called me. Where did Paige go?" Tony told John he didn't know. He told John what I said as I was leaving. Tony knew just how devastating this was for me and was scared I would relapse. The same thought crossed John's mind, but he didn't tell Tony that. On his way to the cabin, John tried a few techniques to refocus his emotions and ground himself so he could think straight and be strong for the both of us. He had a hunch I might go to Andy's office hoping it was just a cruel hoax. Signing the paperwork today and giving up her parental rights means she lost all power and control over me. It means she lost the psychotic battle that was going on only in her head. He told Tony that was where they would start. John wasn't wrong.

Chapter 27

1

The portal shifted and I was looking down at Andy's office. I had come whipping into the parking lot, slammed my car into park, and went storming into Andy's office. I was so charged up on adrenaline due to the emotional rage I was experiencing, that I damn near tore his office door off the hinges. The woman who normally works the front desk hadn't arrived yet, but Andy was in his office with the door open. I heard him on the phone and went barging in. Andy was expecting me, and he knew I would be enraged. Not only did he expect to see me once I got the news, but John called warning him, before he and Tony left, to keep an eye out for me and try to keep me there till he got there. Andy had Michele's attorney on the phone when he saw me come in and quickly put him on hold. As I entered his office, I told Andy, "That fucking cunt better be lying!" I demanded to know what was going on. Andy didn't even try to tell me to calm down. He knew it would do no good. He told me who was on the other line and I needed to listen so we could find out what happened. He said he would use the speakerphone and begged me to just listen and let him ask the questions. Andy picked up the receiver and told Attorney Foster I was there, and he was going to put him on speakerphone. Andy looked past me, still speaking into the receiver letting Attorney Foster know that my family just arrived, and they would be listening in too. I think Attorney Foster wasn't happy about that, but Andy told him, "Tough shit" and that he owed us that much. I am also guessing he reluctantly agreed because Andy put him on speaker.

2

The three of us were silent. John and Tony took a seat, I was standing. I couldn't sit. With all the pent-up anger and aggression, keeping silent was going to take everything I had. Sitting still wasn't an option. "Robert, we had a deal. You and your client were supposed to be here today to sign all the paperwork. What the hell happened?" The first thing Robert did was try and defend his client which quickly backfired on him. Andy quickly told him that was the wrong thing to be doing, that his client had a long history of lying and manipulation, and that breaking our deal meant there was serious trouble headed their way. "Seems you and your client forgot about the police compliant," he told him. I shouted, "She better be lying! She needs to get her ass here fucking now!" So much for just listening and letting Andy ask the questions. I think the anguish in my voice made Robert realize what Michele had done. His tone changed when he told us that Michele wasn't lying and that she and her father were in to see him first thing this morning. He could see she wasn't pregnant and that she did terminate the pregnancy. He tried to apologize. He said my name and told me how sorry he was, that he was completely blindsided by this. He had no idea she was going to do this. I didn't believe him, and I let him know I thought he was lying. "You're her fucking attorney! How could you not know? You're supposed to know! We had a deal! We had a mother fucking deal!" Andy looked at me realizing I wasn't just going to sit there; it was my son. He saw I was a father in distress, not the teenager he met just a few months ago. Robert tried explaining. He said to us that Michele told her parents that it was a trip to visit with her cousin. He tried to explain to us that her mother had a breakdown when she found out. They had to take her to the hospital. None of us had any idea what Michele was planning. This was the point where, as the saying goes, I lost my shit. "That's fucking bullshit, all of it! Her parents blamed me! Well, fuck them! This is their fault! I want my son! I want my mother fucking son! Give him to me! We had a fucking deal!" John got up and tried to console me. Tony stood up and put an empathetic hand on my shoulder, I shrugged him off and didn't let John get a word in. "Tell that fucking cunt we're not faggots, we don't have fucking AIDS!" I was aggressively pacing back and forth screaming into the speakerphone. Spit was flying out of my mouth as I was hollering, "You know what your client said? She said she would have regretted having an abortion! She looked me straight in the eye when she said that! Then the fucking cunt goes and has an abortion–are you fucking kidding me!" I screamed, "Did you hear me? She said she would regret having an abortion!" Robert said he had heard what I said. "Good, now tell your client she is right she is going to regret it! I am going to make sure that cunt, her douchebag parents, and her two piece-of-shit friends regret this for the rest of their lives!" I slammed a fist into the wall and stormed out of the office. I pushed the door to the office open so hard I broke the stopper and the glass shattered when the door swung into the wall. John came running after me but again couldn't catch me in time. By the time he got outside, I was already peeling out of the parking lot.

3

I was still looking inside Andy's office. Robert was still on speaker phone doing what attorneys do. "Was that a threat? Did he just threaten my client? I will call the police." I could not believe what I was seeing. Tony had never been so assertive or commanding. In a booming voice that matched his large stature he said, "You will do nothing! You and your client have caused enough damage to Paige! You will do nothing!" Robert claimed he was going to handle this like a threat which I am sure he was going to try and use against me if I went ahead with the complaint and civil suit. Once again Tony laid into him, "You couldn't even handle your client and you let her destroy my family! Back off asshole!" Andy quickly took Robert off the speaker and picked up the receiver telling Robert, "You heard him, you will do nothing. We will handle it!" Andy hung up on Robert. John came back in telling them he couldn't catch me in time. He told them I took off and he had no idea where I was going.

4

I had no idea where I was heading. I just got out onto the road and started driving.

Chapter 28

1

I was watching myself drive aimlessly. I was doing that for hours on end that day. The pain and agony were building up so much pressure that my head felt like it was going to explode. I remember it felt like my eyes were bleeding, I was so blinded by rage. Several times I pulled off to the shoulder of the road and gripped the sides of the steering wheel so hard my knuckles turned white. I rested my forehead on the top of the steering wheel and screamed, "I wanted my little boy." My mind was tortured by everything that happened. I don't even know how I ended up where I was. I had no idea how I got there or even what town I was in until I passed the Town Office. Once I saw the name of the town, I knew who lived there. I saw a public pay phone by the Town Office and stopped, hoping some little asshole didn't destroy the phone book. Luckily, they didn't. I was able to find the address I was looking for.

2

It didn't take me long to find the house associated with the address that I stopped to look up. The house was a ranch-style house that sat on top of a small knoll with a daylight basement on the side where you pulled into the dooryard. There was a sliding glass door for the entrance to the basement. The side of the basement with the sliding glass door was a finished rec room furnished with a beat-up old sofa, dark paneling on the walls, a macrame owl hanging on the wall, shag carpeting on the floor, a wooden spool the power company uses for power lines, as a coffee table, a thirteen-inch color TV with the fake wood grain decal on the sides, and a stoner sprawled out on the sofa playing Super Mario Brothers. I didn't even give Josh the respect of knocking before entering I just walked right in. Josh looked at me and I could see the "Oh shit" expression on his face. Just the sight of me standing in his basement was enough for him to know something was wrong in a bad way. He asked, "Dude what's wrong?" in his non-stoner voice. I guess that voice was reserved for campus life and not used when he was within earshot of his father. I told him not to fuck with me and he knew what was wrong. He said he wasn't fucking with me and asked again what was wrong. I didn't get into it I just told him I needed something to take the edge off. He quickly told me no his father was home and insisted he would smell it. I told him I didn't want weed I needed something stronger; I wanted some coke. I wanted to do lines with him. He was shaking his head telling me no way we were not doing this again. That just made me more agitated. This time I wanted to get high and never feel anything ever again. I told him he had no problem with it before so there is no problem now. I got louder, "I know you got a stash around here. Come on dude, I need it!" Josh told me to keep it down or his father would hear us, saying his father would kill the both of us if we did drugs in the house. I shouted, "Just get me fucking high!" His father heard the shouting and yelled down demanding to know what was going on. We could hear him walking towards the basement stairs. Josh told him we were just playing a video game then turned to me and said I had to bounce and bounce now. That enraged me to the point I backed Josh into a corner and got in his face. Through gritted teeth, I told him this was his fucking fault, and this wasn't over. He stayed in the corner till I left. He was afraid of me kicking his ass. I was almost in my car when Patty came running up to me crying, telling me she heard what Michele did. News travels fast in the small-town gossip circles. She tried hugging me telling me how sorry she was. I sidestepped her hug then got in her face the same way I did with Josh telling her this was her fault too and she can go fuck herself. Patty backed away from me and went running to the sliding glass doors of the basement. I got in my car taking off to God knows where. Patty ran over to Josh crying and hugging him. Josh guided her to the sofa asking her what was going on. "Paige didn't tell you?" Josh was confused. I didn't know he truly had no idea what happened. I had no idea they stopped talking with Michele and were no longer close like they once were. "Tell me what?" he asked. Patty told Josh what Michele had done. Josh couldn't believe Michele went and had it done this late in the pregnancy. He knew Michele just fucked them over too. She broke the deal which meant there was now a real possibility of police involvement. Patty buried her face in Josh's hug crying, "What did we do? Oh God, what did we do?"

3

As I went tearing out of Josh's, who was my only source of drugs, I started driving again with no set destination. Then it hit me. I couldn't get high, but I could try getting my hands on a bottle of JD. I had cash for that on me. I needed something right away but the only place I knew I could buy underage was a small hole-in-the-wall state liquor store on the east side of the big lake. A lot of the students from the campus would go here because we never got carded. I needed to stop the pain, so I wasted no time and headed that way. It took just over an hour to get there; I parked and went into the store. I purposely left my wallet in the car, but I did tuck a twenty in my front pocket. Everyone who was underage would do that so when the clerk asked for ID, they would say they forgot their wallet. The clerk bought it every time. When I entered, I knew what I wanted and went straight for that shelf. I grabbed a bottle of JD and went up to the counter. I knew just about everyone who worked there including the manager, but this clerk was new, I had never seen him before.

He wasn't much older than me but old enough to sell alcohol. I put the bottle down and he asked if there was anything else. Without looking up I just shook my head no. He rang up the bottle and told me it would be $18.99, he just needed to see an ID. I told him I was twenty-three. I even threw a "Come on dude" in there too. I was expecting him to just say, "No problem," but he insisted on seeing an ID stating that he IDs everyone. I told him my wallet was at home and asked if he was going to make me go home and come back. I figured this would do it. But I was wrong. He politely said he was sorry, but he needed to see an ID. I was getting pissed, I needed to get fucked-up in the worst way. I struck out with Josh so there was no way I was I was leaving here empty-handed. I looked right at him and told him I wasn't in the mood for this shit, and that he didn't want to do this. He took a step back saying, "Sir please." I lost my cool and I slammed the twenty that was in my pocket on the counter. "There's your money!" I grabbed the bottle and told him to keep the change. He tried to say something, but I shouted at him, "If you don't like it call the fucking cops!" I took off. It was late afternoon, and I all wanted was to open that bottle and start guzzling it down in the worst way but my nineteen-year-old mind, or what little of it I had left, was convinced there was going to be a state-wide manhunt for me even though I paid for the JD. I was underage. I knew of a little, out-of-the-way spot where I could park my car out of sight, hide out till dusk, then head home.

4

I was looking down into the cabin and both Tony and John were there. I could hear Tony say to John that I had been gone all day and no one had seen or heard from me. John let Tony know that he and Andy made some calls to people they knew to let them know if they saw me. Tony's face showed distress. This concerned John, he could only imagine what was going through Tony's mind. John knew this was affecting Tony as much as it was me. John asked Tony if he was OK. The distress in his voice matched the distress on his face. He told John no, he wasn't okay at all. He told John that watching me take that call was the worst thing he ever experienced. He told John what it felt like; he could see my heart breaking. He felt so helpless just standing there not being able to do anything as he watched the soul-crushing conversation play out in front of him. Tony was scared that I was going to harm myself and he let John know he felt that way. John knew how devastating this was for me yet that was the one thing John was not concerned with. John felt I was stronger than that and shared that with Tony. The concern John had and didn't tell Tony, was his fear I would relapse, get high, and this time have to go to a facility. That he wouldn't be able to intervene, I'd have a nervous breakdown that I would not recover from, or worse; relapse to the point I would become hopelessly addicted to drugs. I would let the drugs destroy me and never recover. John knew he couldn't think that way right now, he knew he had to be there for us. Just then John heard my car coming up the drive and past the cabin. John had to be the most amazing person I ever met. He was feeling the same as we were and yet he put his own feelings aside and did everything he could to be the voice of reason, the calm in the storm, and to be the dad we both needed to lean on that day and for the coming months.

5

That morning when Tony and I were sitting at the table having our coffee, I was looking at the ultrasound that was done at the last doctor's appointment. I was looking at my little boy, he was the most beautiful thing I had ever seen. I was picturing myself holding him for the first time, thinking about all the dad things I was going to get to do, thinking that in just a few hours a judge would grant me sole custody once he is born. I was looking at the beautiful little miracle that I made, the life I created, not knowing I was moments away from the news that would shatter me, that would crush my soul, would make me feel like I died with him. The news would change me as a person, never again being the Paige I was moments before the call. That was what I was thinking about sitting there in the front seat of my car with the bottle of JD between my legs, looking at the ultrasound, and then the call itself was running through my mind. Where I parked I was hidden from sight. I wanted to gulp as much of the bottle as I could to numb my mind just so I could stop thinking. Every time I put my hand on the cap to open the bottle, I would hear John's voice in my head telling me how I had earned his trust, and I didn't give him reason to drug test. He was proud of me and so was Tony. They were proud that I broke my chemical dependency proving I could handle life without the aid of any drugs or alcohol. I don't know if that was the reason I didn't open the bottle and start gulping away or not but I didn't open it. I needed to get high and drunk in the worst way. I wanted to be high till the day I died. Never to be sober again was how I wanted to handle this. You could have performed surgery on me without any anesthesia and the pain would not compare to the mental agony I was experiencing. It would build up inside me till I burst into a violent rage: slamming my fists on the steering wheel and screaming at the top of my lungs till all my energy was drained. This went on for several hours while I waited for dusk before heading back home to the cabin. After I exhausted myself with the last outburst, I laid my forehead on the steering wheel and blacked out for a while. When I lifted my head, it was just after dusk. It was time to go home. I slid the bottle out of sight, started the car, and headed home.

6

When I arrived home, I drove right past the cabin and went straight to the barn. I don't know why I did that; I just did. Maybe it was because on the drive back I made up my mind that I was going to drink till the pain stopped. The barn just seemed to work. I got out of the car, reached under my seat, grabbed the bottle, and went into the barn. I was standing in front of the workbench with one hand wrapped around the neck of the bottle and the other hand gripping the cap. I stood staring down at the bottle. The rage was building up again, I let go of the cap, grabbed the bottle by the neck, and slammed it down on the workbench while screaming in my head, Just drink the fucking shit. I lifted my hand and slammed the bottle again screaming in my head god dammit just do it so it will stop hurting! I picked the bottle up and slammed it a third time, this time, I was silently pleading with myself, please, just open it and drink it. You want the pain to stop; please make the pain go away and drink. I could feel my chest heaving and my breathing was growing louder. My breathing became rapid, and saliva was spewing out of my mouth with every exhale. I picked up the bottle for the last time and instead of slamming it down, I cried out, "I want my SON!" and with everything I had I threw the bottle across the barn and started slamming my fists on the bench yelling, "NO! NO! That fucking cunt, we had a deal!" Tony and John were outside the barn–I had no idea they were there. Tony rushed toward me putting his arms around me and trying to embrace me. I raised my hands to his chest, clutched his shirt, and buried my face in his chest. I cried out in agony and despair, "She killed our son. Our little boy is dead." My chest started heaving as I groaned, "This hurts so bad, oh god it hurts." As I looked down through the portal, I could see John in the door of the barn, his jaw quivering as tears streamed down his face. Tony had tucked my head under his chin and squeezed his eyes shut as the tears streamed down his face. I was the only one who couldn't cry, all I could do was throw fits of rage. The portal gently shut, there was nothing more I needed to see here.

Chapter 29

1

John and I were in physical form again and I was angry at myself. I should have seen that coming, I should have known, I should have never believed her. John looked at me and said that he knew that face. It was the face I would make when I was angry with myself. The face I would make when I blamed myself for something I had no control over. I told John I should have seen it coming, how could I have missed it? John assured me that everyone missed it, her family, friends, even he missed it. No one saw that coming. I asked John why. I wanted to know what Tony or I had done to her to deserve this. John said the only thing he could think of was that whatever happened to her on that trip to Mexico was taken out on Tony and me. Me telling her "No" at the cookout was seen as a rejection and that was what triggered her. We became the ones she took it out on because we unknowingly set her off. My anger showed even more when I said, "Because I was wasted all the time, I made myself an easy target." With that, John placed his fatherly hand on my back saying he had more to show me. The mist swirled around us as the portal reopened.

2

The portal was showing me parts of my life that happened after that night in the barn. I don't know how long we were in there, but I do remember being so exhausted by the time we finally went to bed that night that we lay there like always, except I no longer felt anything at all. It was like my mind and body had shut down from the trauma and exhaustion of that day. In the days and weeks that followed, I was like a zombie, only going through the motions. My head was foggy and there wasn't much I remembered. One of the things I did remember was going to work the following Monday. John and Tony wanted me to take a few days for myself but there was no way I wanted to hang around the cabin. My friend at work, Hal Leonard, was a permanent full-time employee. Hal was a local guy and he and I were about the same age. Hal was taking night courses at the Community College in Old Port studying computer science. His parents refused to help pay for his college education believing computers were only a fad. They would go out of style faster than Bell Bottoms was what they told Hal. Hal and I always got along well when I was an occasional employee. Now that I was full-time for the summer and would be a permanent employee after the fall semester, we started becoming good friends. Hal was the one who put in a good word for me with the big bosses about coming on as a permanent after the baby was born. Hal was the guy who I always took breaks with and had lunch with. Whenever there were overtime hours or extra shifts, we would work them together. We were a great team, and we were both pretty stoked about working together permanently after the baby was born. That morning when I clocked in, Hal noticed right away I wasn't myself. He asked me what was wrong. At first, I told him it must be that summertime flu finally catching up to me, but I was fine to work. Hal and I took our lunch break in the break room. He noticed I hadn't eaten more than a few nibbles. "Okay Paige, let's have it," he said "You haven't said two words all morning, you're walking around with your head up your ass and you look like a fucking zombie. Dude this ain't the flu." I didn't answer him till he said my name again. I didn't tell him everything or get into the details, I just told him that Michele went and had the abortion. Hal smiled and said, "Dude, do you realize the bullet you just dodged? She did you a favor I didn't want to say this before but you're too young to be a father. You were going to ruin your life. Talk about catching a lucky break." I couldn't believe what Hal had just said. I was horrified. He had been so supportive and asked how the pregnancy was going all the time. He told me he was happy for me. To hear this come out of his mouth just blew my mind. I didn't say a word. I picked up my lunch, threw it in the garbage, and I went back inside. I told Personnel I was going home sick and left. I didn't bother giving notice. I just stopped showing up to work. That was the point where I completely shut down and stopped talking. I reminded myself this is why I bottle shit up. After I left, a supervisor went to Personnel to tell them what he overheard and that I lost the baby. Personnel called John, since I didn't reply to the messages they left on our answering machine, he was my emergency contact. They told John what happened and what was said and asked if they should mail me my paycheck. I received my check the following week with a note inside, "Sorry for your loss. Come back when you are ready, you will always have a job with us."

3

The portal moved forward a couple of weeks and it was pizza night. Tony and I had finished up our first week of classes. John was concerned with how things went. He didn't know how I would react if I ran into Josh or Patty. He was also concerned about Tony running into or having classes with Michele. John asked me how my week went. I knew what he wanted to know, and I told him no, I didn't run into Josh or Patty this week and I wouldn't have to worry about that at all. I told John about what happened when I was at the campus bookstore getting my class schedule and buying books. Steve Blackburn walked up to me and asked if I needed a roommate this year because his roommate was a no-show. Last year Steve lived in the dorm room next to the one Josh and I had. He was in a couple of Josh's classes last spring and would occasionally toke up with Josh. He told me he was supposed to be rooming with my old roommate, but he ended up dropping out about a week ago. He didn't know why Josh dropped out. I did leave out the part about Steve telling me he was bummed out because he heard Josh liked to get high and watch his girlfriend go down on another guy while he fucked her. I figured that was something no one needed to hear. When

Steve said that I told him he was a total fuck tard and walked away. Later that same day I found out Patty dropped out at the same time; she was supposed to be in my English Lit. class but never showed up. It was thirty years later when I found out why Josh and Patty didn't return. John was relieved to hear they wouldn't be back and was just as relieved to find out Michele didn't return either. Michele was supposed to take the fall semester off because of the pregnancy but thought she might try and return for the wrong reasons now that she wasn't pregnant. She ultimately dropped out of school and a couple of years later, I found out she had taken off after she and her father met with their attorney and hadn't been heard from since. That was about all John could get out of me. John knew I would have opened up and talked but after what Hal said he knew it was going to be a while before I would talk to anyone.

4

The next time the portal moved, I was looking at a ride we took a month and a half after classes started. It was later in October of that year. It was Saturday, October 24, 1987, to be exact. Tony and I were sitting on the big rock at Rattlesnake Pond looking out over the water. Columbus Day weekend was usually peak foliage time. This weekend being two weeks later, the trees would be bare, but the foliage was still full, vibrant, and bright. The leaves around the pond hadn't started to fall yet. It was as if the colors were alive and wrapping around you as you sat there captivated by the breathtaking beauty of it all. We had gone on several rides since that devastating day back in August, but much like everything else, I was just going through the motions. A huge part of me died with my son, there were no feelings or emotions. I was just existing. It was the worst feeling to just exist like that, completely detached and devoid of all passion and the sensation of life itself. Any ride we took before this day was just a blur to me. Today was different. Sitting on the big rock was different. I was noticing the colors, no, I was feeling the colors. It was overcast, damp, raw, and cold this October day, yet a warm sensation surrounded me. I felt as though I was being embraced by someone or something as we sat mesmerized by the spectacular display of color. It was the first time in two months I felt anything. It was Tony who finally broke our silence, "I have never seen the foliage so radiant and the colors so intense. No matter the time of year this is my favorite spot in all of Maine." I don't know why but I started to slowly open up. I was still mesmerized by the colors as I stared out onto the pond which mirrored the surrounding foliage on its glass-like surface. I said to Tony, "I wanted to take our son to this spot." Tony and I both knew our son would have loved it here. Tony said that he was sure our son would have loved this spot. I agreed we would have made lasting memories here with our son. We sat in silence again; this time it was me who broke the silence, "You and John keep asking if I am okay." Tony turned his head to face me saying they both knew I would answer when I was ready. I turned to Tony so we were talking face to face when I said that I wasn't okay and didn't know if I ever would be. Tony admitted he wasn't okay either and Michele had taken a precious gift from us. I revealed a little more telling Tony that it was more than that. Michele had taken every first away from us. Holding him for the first time, watching him take his first steps, hearing him call me daddy, walking him to his first day of school. I told Tony we would never hear him call you Baba Tony or John, Opa. She took our entire life with him away. He and I both knew that was something I could never forgive her for. I could see the tears welling up in his eyes when he told me he could never forgive her either. I questioned why. Why would she do this to us? Tony just shook his head. Somehow, we both knew we would never know why. I was at a point where I felt like I had lost everything including Tony. I was expecting him to tell me that he had enough and that I should move back into the dorm after Christmas break when we returned for the second semester. I thought to myself, let's just get it out in the open now. I said to Tony that since we met it had been one horror show after another. That I have only brought trouble to his life so if he didn't want me around anymore just say so and I will go without a fight. There was a look of shock on Tony's face when he said that I had no idea how much good I brought into his life. I just couldn't see the good, so I asked, "Yeah like what good have I brought?" He put a hand on my shoulder and using a very matter-of-fact tone, let me know that before me, he was alone. No one would talk to him, he had no friends, he was lonely, I was the only person who was nice to him, and he never knew what happiness or joy was. Because of me, he discovered who he was and we created a home together. He never knew love at first sight existed till he saw me that day at the cookout. It's not that I didn't believe him, I thought he was just trying to spare my feelings because of what happened. One of the things I loved about Tony was he was always honest and sincere especially if it was something he was passionate about. I just wasn't sure about anything. I questioned him saying, "Even with all this shit that has happened?" I instantly regretted saying it till Tony took my hand in his and spoke. He told me that everything that has happened has brought us closer together and that it deepened our relationship. He said his love was so deep that he couldn't picture life without me. He needed me in his life. He promised we were going to get through this together. I squeezed his hand. "You really mean that don't you?" He did and, he meant it when he said, "Andrew Paige Turner, I want to spend the rest of my life with you. I promise you we will be married right here on this very spot." Those words melted my heart, I squeezed his hand even tighter as we sat side by side, shoulder to shoulder. I laid my head on his shoulder and he turned, kissed the top of my head like he always did, and rested his chin on my head. We sat like that till the sun started to set before heading back home.

Chapter 30

1

The portal brought me forward to the next day. It was late morning, and I was sitting on the front porch doing some reading for my English Lit. class; it was raining out. No matter the season, when it was gloomy, my favorite place to be was on the porch enjoying the rain. My second favorite place to be on a rainy day was walking in the woods, which we were going to do when Tony was done in the barn. Tony was up at the barn making his after-ride tweaks to the choppers. The rain started just as we had gotten into bed the night before. The light pitter-patter sound the rain was making on the roof and the soothing rhythm of Tony's heartbeat were hypnotic and lulled me right to sleep. It was the first good night's sleep in quite a while. This morning, I wasn't myself, but I was feeling a little better after sleeping soundly and knowing I hadn't lost Tony too. I ate normally for the first time in a long while. The sound of the falling rain on the leaves ablaze with autumn colors drowned out John's approaching footsteps. It was his yellow raincoat that caught my attention. The yellow raincoat made him look like a clean-shaven version of the Gorton's Fisherman. "Hey, mind if I join you?" "Of course you can, it's not like you even need to ask." John stepped in saying he was just at the barn talking to Tony and had heard we had a good ride yesterday. I replied that this was my favorite time of year to ride. There was a moment of awkward silence. John was hoping I would say more but I didn't. "Come on let's take a walk. There is a trail around back, it's a shortcut to Big Lake Variety. I'll buy you a Moxie and a Whoopie Pie. I wasn't up to talking, which I knew was what he wanted to do, but how could I turn down a Moxie and a Whoopie Pie? I got up and went inside to put on my orange safety vest. October is bow and arrow season and even though it was Sunday, you could always count on some asshole being out in the woods on the one day a week you could not hunt, and he was probably hunting with a shotgun.

2

Just like the day before, the foliage was stunning. It created such a picturesque scene, sort of like the scenes used for jigsaw puzzles depicting a cabin in the woods surrounded by brilliant fall foliage. I got the same warm feeling that I felt when I was sitting on the big rock with Tony. The trail was wide enough so we didn't have to walk single file. John was setting the pace, and I figured this was so he could walk and talk without getting winded. I was right because not very far into the walk he started talking. He said he knew that I was not okay and he wanted me to know that even though I don't see it now, I would be okay. I didn't want to talk but I found myself opening up just like I did the day before with Tony. I told John, "I need my dad right now and there is no way I can turn to him." John knew I was right and understood why I was keeping everything including my relationship with Tony from them. I knew if my mother ever found out I was dating a black girl in high school her first words would be, "You're fucking a N…!" using the "N" word I hate so much. "You're no son of mine!" and would disown me. I can't even begin to imagine what would be said or done if she found out I was in love with a gay black man. I vividly remember the time my father slammed a car door on one of my legs in one of his fits of rage. God only knows the drunken outbursts he would have over this situation. We walked a little further before I told John that I was sorry. He looked at me puzzled and asked why I was apologizing. I told him I let him down. Still puzzled, he asked how I had let him down. I told John that I had broken my promise to him and Tony. I went to Josh's house looking for drugs and not just weed. I told John I went there because I knew

Josh did coke and I wanted to snort lines. When I struck out, I went and bought a bottle of JD intending to drink till I passed out or emptied the bottle, whichever came first. John had no idea I felt that way and he wanted to reassure me that I didn't let him down. He knew I didn't need that burden, and I needed to know he wasn't disappointed in me. John said, "Paige you didn't break your promise." I told John he was just being nice and giving me a free pass. John assured me he wasn't giving me a free pass, he was being honest. I told John the only reason I didn't get high was because Josh's dad was home. John told me he had gotten to know me very well and said, "I know you would have walked away just like you did with the bottle. I know you would not have gotten high even if Josh's dad wasn't home." I said, knowing how I desperately wanted to get high that day, "Well that makes one of us," John told me to quit beating myself up like that. I still needed some reassurance that I didn't let him down and John gave it to me. He told me again, "You didn't get high, you didn't even open the bottle. Paige, you didn't let me down." Just as he said that, we came to the other end of the trail at Big Lake Variety. I was glad. I needed a break to clear my head before we walked back.

3

We went inside. The seating area was empty, the breakfast regulars who were the heathens and never went to church on Sunday, were gone. It was still too early for the Sunday-after-church lunch regulars to trickle in. We were the only ones there, but I just wasn't comfortable continuing our conversation inside the variety store. I walked down to the back where the beverage cooler was and when I came back from the cooler with three Moxies and three Whoopie Pies from the bakery shelf, he knew I was going to bring one of each back for Tony. John was by the coffee station pouring us both a cup of coffee in to-go cups for the walk back. The owner was working today though his grandson usually ran the store on the weekends for his grandparents who had run the store for almost fifty years. John made small talk as the owner was ringing up our stuff. He said, "I see you're working today." The owner replied like all the old timers do, "Ayuh." Then he proceeded to tell us that Junior got himself all stove up in some pucker brush when he was out hunting yesterday. Damn near lost an eye. He told us some flatlander, probably a Masshole from Taxachusetts, thought he was a deer and shot at him." So numb nuts dove for cover and landed himself in the pucker brush. Mutha took him into Old Port Medical but the boy gotta see a specialist on Monday for his eye." Shaking his head the old man said, "He still has one good eye, don't see why he couldn't come in today." He finished ringing us up and said, "All that for under five dollars, can't beat that with a stick." I smiled, thanked him, and picked up the bag with our stuff in it as the owner said, "Ayuh. You fellas have a goodun." We got outside, shook our heads, and laughed. "Masshole", "Taxachusetts", "stove up", and calling his grandson "numb nuts", he had a way with words didn't he," John said. I replied "Ayuh." Even though I was still devoid of emotion, it felt good to laugh.

4

Every day I tried to put on a brave face and live life like we always did before that dark day, forcing myself to smile, pretending to be okay. I didn't have much to say at pizza night, I forced myself to enjoy the rides on the choppers and even when Tony and I made love, I put on that false mask, pretending I was fine so he wouldn't worry about me. I told them I let it all out in the barn and I was okay now. They both knew better. They saw how I barely functioned in everyday life. They could tell I wasn't feeling anything, and I had shut down, void of all emotions and feelings. I wasn't fooling anyone but myself and I realized this when John told me at the start of our walk that he knew I wasn't okay, he didn't need Tony to tell him. He said that he knew. We didn't talk on the walk back till we got to the halfway point on the trail. That's when I told John that I was hurting badly, it was sheer agony. I told him the mental anguish and emotional torture had caused me physical pain to the point I had to take ibuprofen to ease the headaches I was getting. John said he understood just how much pain I was in. He and Tony were devastated–they shared my pain too. They understood it was different for me because I was the baby's father, but we were a family, and families hurt together. I told him I wanted to talk, and I was going to try before classes started but... I couldn't finish. I thought the reason I shut down was stupid. John asked, "But what?" I told him the reason was stupid and I was kind of ashamed of it. John said he knew what Hal had said to me. All of it. He said he knew I had shut down and stopped talking because of that. He didn't blame me one bit. He told me my reason was valid, not stupid. I told John it pissed me off so bad that I just had to leave. "How could anyone think my son was ruining my life? He was my son, he was my life, and there was no way my life was ruined because of him. My son was my world." After Hal said that I couldn't work with him. I couldn't even look at him without losing my shit." After a few huffs and snorts I said, "He was supposed to be my friend." John said he got it, what was said was not called for. It was cruel and heartless. He was worried that what was said would have caused me to shut them out too. He was worried I would push him and Tony away. He was glad it didn't. I nodded in agreement; I had nothing to add. As we continued walking, we didn't say anything till we were just about back to the cabin. I stopped at the mouth of the trail and told John, "I know I need to talk about this and maybe it is time to start. Just not today." John smiled, "Today we eat Whoopie Pies."

5

We did just that, we ate our Whoopie Pies and drank our Moxie on the front porch in our soaking wet clothes telling Tony about Junior and his hunting accident. We were simply enjoying a little family time. Later that evening as Tony and I were lying in bed, I gave some thought to what John said on our walk and it felt good to at least get that part out. As I lay there my thoughts shifted. I started thinking about what Tony said to me the day before, how he couldn't picture life without me, that everything that happened drew us closer together, and how he wanted to marry me in our favorite spot, started to bring back that feeling of love and passion for him that I thought I had lost. I reached down to take hold of him and swore he could read my mind. He

226

was already ready for me. I looked up at him and we started kissing. As I pulled him on top of me, we held our bodies together. The passion and deep-rooted love I had for him came flooding in. It felt the same way it did the very first time we made love. I couldn't stop thinking about what he said as we passionately made love in many ways that night. Later that night when we were lying there just holding one another, Tony said, "That Whoopie Pie was very good but nothing beats a good cannoli" I couldn't stop laughing! "Yeah, tonight's cannoli couldn't be beat." God how I loved him. I rested easy that night knowing my little family was there for me.

Chapter 31

1

Before the portal closed, I remembered lying with Tony in bed the next morning. It was time to get up and get ready for classes, but we didn't move, we just stayed in bed all day. We kissed, we made love, we held one another. We knew the events and the things that were said over the weekend including this day together were the reassurance I needed to know that my family was there for me. Together we would take the first step towards healing and moving forward on this new path that was forced upon us. The healing was going to be a long and painful road but now I was ready.

2

The portal now showed brief glimpses of what followed. We played hooky that morning from classes. I saw the first pizza night we had after John and I took that walk. That was the night I started to talk. I still believed it was a cruel hoax, that Michele was still pregnant, and her parents didn't want me to have the baby, so they lied to their attorney. Maybe he was in on it, but I refused to believe my son was gone. I believed they lied to me so Michele wouldn't have to sign the papers giving up custody. I was convinced they lied to me so the baby wouldn't be raised by a couple of faggots. They lied to me cause her father hated me and he hated the fact I stood up to him and won. Even though there were times I referred to my son in the past tense, I never really believed Michele had the abortion. That was the night I had to face the hard truth; they didn't lie to me nor was it a cruel hoax. My son was truly gone.

3

The portal shifted again. I don't remember the reason why, but I was home alone. I had lit a fire in the fireplace, and I was sitting on the sofa holding a file looking at some papers. I watched myself get up and start pacing around with the folder still open in my hands. I could see the anger on my face, and I could also see what I was looking at. It was the ultrasound images of my son. I could hear myself yelling at him and blaming him for dying on me. I knew it wasn't his fault, but I was only nineteen, still just a kid, and I didn't know how to control or deal with the anger. Out of anger, I blamed Andy because it was his "stupid mutha fucking plan." I blamed myself because I was a druggie. I told Michele, "No" but didn't have the balls to back that up and I let her do what she did to me. The anger just kept building and building till I finally lashed out and crumpled up the images, throwing them into the fire. I slammed my fist on the wooden mantel yelling at my son for dying on me. I was yelling, "Fuck you Andy and your stupid mutha fucking plan!" I yelled at myself, "It was just a stupid fight you fucking waste case. What the fuck you pussy, why did you get high like that." I yelled at Michele, "You evil fucking cunt we had a deal we had a mutha fucking deal." The anger was overwhelming. It was sheer uncontrollable rage that was coming out of me. It was one of the roughest nights I had since that night I had the first round of withdrawal. At the following week's pizza night, I discovered I wasn't alone in my anger. All three of us were angry and we blamed Michele. Tony and I were angry with Andy because his plan failed. I was the only one who blamed myself and my son. I was afraid to talk about this. I thought Tony and John would hate me for getting mad with my son for dying on me. In a moment of angst, I blurted out that I was mad at my son for dying on me. I told them I didn't care if they got mad at me; it was the truth. They didn't get mad. John was glad I told him that. He said the only way I was going to heal was not to hold anything back. Tony stood up and came over and wrapped his arms around me hugging me, and so did John, he hugged the both of us. The anger was the hardest to deal with and I never really moved past it. Looking down now, I still hate Michele and what she did. I am still angry, and I can never forgive her. I did stop being angry with my son that night, there were times I begged him to forgive me. My son was still inside his mother's womb and here I was blaming him for what she did. I had a hard time getting over being angry for thinking such a foolish thing. I never told Andy how I felt, but I did stop being angry with him too.

4

The next shift in the portal showed me at John's woodshed. I was working on splitting the pile of unseasoned firewood and stacking it. I wasn't alone in my work; John was helping me stack while we were talking. Pizza night was more group therapy time for us to work things out together. There were times I was talking with John the way I wish I could have talked with my dad. I heard myself say to John, "If I only said to Tony, let's go try the new Chinese food place instead." and "If I had only stayed and had breakfast with you that next morning. If I only went to breakfast with you or at least sat down and talked when you returned my jacket." I even tried, "If I only walked across campus and talked to the shrink. If I only said "no" to Michele and prevented her from doing that to me. If I only had a set of balls and manned-up right from the start of it all." I talked about how I told God that I was going to throw the bottle out the barn door and never touch drugs or alcohol again and in exchange, he was going to give me my son back. If I had only said that out loud instead of in my mind he would have heard me. John's reply to me was simple yet powerful enough to have stuck with me for years, "Paige, there are things in life we have no control over, sometimes very bad things happen to very good people." On the next pizza night, Tony had his list of "If I had only…". "If he only made me stay for breakfast" was a big one because he felt it was his fault I left. It was also the night we both were told, "There are no 'ifs or 'what ifs', there is only what happened." Even though his words stuck with me, John and I would end up having this conversation again in a very different time and very different place.

5

I did have my good days, and there were some days, even a pizza night or two, where things were a little bit light-hearted. Then there were those days when I felt disconnected, feeling nothing. There were mornings where I should have felt good but when I was driving to the campus, I would get this overwhelming feeling of sadness and being alone even though I wasn't. The portal showed me the time when I was in my favorite class, but I couldn't engage. I had no interest, so I sat staring out the window having no idea what that day's lecture was about. There were pizza nights where I would only eat a few bites. There were days I realized that I knew it wasn't a hoax or lie. I knew this wasn't an elaborate scheme to steal my son from me because they found out I was gay. It was the days I knew I would never get to hold my little boy. The days when I would never be his daddy. I only had to say those things to John once, then any time I was having a day or few days like that he already knew what was going through my mind. He knew those were the days I needed a dad and not a therapist. Those were the days Tony would hold me just a little closer, a little bit tighter, and he made sure I knew I was loved. I wasn't alone. Tony had days like that too and I always made sure I held him a little closer, a little tighter, and let him know just how much I loved him. I never let him leave for class or work or let a day go by without telling him how much I loved him. It was days like that when I needed to say it and he needed to hear it.

6

The portal shifted again. It was the early part of May 1988, and I was looking down at pizza night. John and Tony had just taken a seat as I was coming in with the pizzas. Setting the pizzas down, I announced before taking my seat next to Tony, "Tonight there is going to be no talk of the past two years. This weekend is all about Tony's graduation. Absolutely no tears." John was quick to agree saying there was nothing that we needed to talk about that couldn't wait. I was still standing when I declared May

6-9,1988, is Tony's weekend. It's all about the Tones. John laughed saying the proclamation had been made. I opened one of the boxes and let the graduate have his choice of the first slice. Tony was grabbing the first slice saying how excited he was to be spending graduation weekend with us. He admitted he wished his parents could have been there to see him graduate. John told Tony while patting the leather case that was on the floor next to him, not to worry. He has plenty of blank tapes and a brand new camcorder to record the graduation ceremony. "Your parents won't miss a thing." I was so happy for Tony and I was feeling pretty good. In fact, I was feeling some semblance of my old self so I leaned over and said to Tony, "Hey maybe we could try out the camcorder in the bedroom later." Tony rolled his eyes. "Paige, there is no way John is going to want to record that." I almost fell out of my chair laughing when John told Tony not to worry "The camera came with this nice tripod accessory." John started to laugh at Tony's reaction. "John Williamson, what in God's name am I going to do with you both!" As hard as he tried not to laugh, Tony couldn't hold it in any longer and laughed with us. I saw Tony's eyes tear up. John asked him what was wrong and why was he crying. "These are tears of joy! Paige is being a smart-ass again. That is the best present I could ask for." As the portal was closing, I remembered that it was a long, emotional, roller coaster ride of a winter. That weekend was a needed change of pace. It was the weekend I started re-engaging.

Chapter 32

1

As the portal shifted, I saw the brief moments leading up to the first full week of July. I saw how I was becoming more and more engaged with my life. Although I was taking baby steps forward, I was still moving forward. My relationship with Tony was growing deeper. I understood now that not only were we going to get through it together, but we shared a lot of the same emotions and were in this together. I did see moments when I was disengaged or overwhelmed with sadness, but those moments didn't last. They were becoming a lot less frequent and severe. Most of all, I was getting back to being as close to my old self as I probably was going to get.

2

The portal shifted and came to a stop on July 8, 1988. Tony and I were in the cabin waiting for John to arrive with the pizzas that he was picking up on his way home from Old Port. I was setting the table when Tony asked me where I wanted to go riding this weekend. I told Tony I was thinking of maybe going up to Rattlesnake Pond. My reasoning needed no explanation, but I gave one anyway. "There is barely any traffic and virtually no one around, plus, I love hanging out at the pond. Tony walked up behind me, wrapped his arms around my waist, and said, "The pond, sure, that's the reason you like it there." I started laughing because he wasn't wrong. The pond was a good mile down an old, abandoned logging road off a barely traveled country road in one of the many disorganized territories in the Western Maine mountains. So, in the summer going skinny dipping in the pond became one of our things. Since we were naked one thing would lead to another. In my defense, I told Tony, "I am riding on top of a six-hundred-pound vibrator so a little "bow chicka wow wow" in the woods was a given." Thank God the surrounding forest couldn't talk. Tony was so happy to see me laughing and wise cracking again. It took damn close to a year, but I was starting to live again. We were still laughing when we heard John come in. "Knock Knock, pizza is here." Tony told John to come in. I was expecting Tony to release his embrace before John entered; Tony and I never showed physical affection in front of John. Tonight, Tony held me tight saying he was so happy to see me laughing and joking again. He gave me one of his, what I now call trademark kisses, on top of my head, before letting go and taking a seat. John didn't seem to mind either. As we were grabbing our slices John was saying how crazy it was in town and all the traffic that was still here from the fourth of July. I agreed with John adding that it took me forever to get home. We always started pizza night off with small talk just to break the ice so to speak, before John would ask what we would like to talk about. Tonight, Tony spoke right up and said if I didn't mind, he wanted to talk about him tonight. I welcomed that right away telling them both that any night we don't talk about me is a good night. Tony said this would affect me too but was only temporary. I sighed, rolled my eyes and said, "The one night I am off the hook, and it immediately goes right down the shitter. Nice going boner killer." John cracked a smile at that and even chuckled but did say, "Let's hear what he has to say." Tony reached over, took me by the hand and said that he told his parents about us. My jaw just about hit the table, "DUDE! It would have been nice if you gave me a heads up. I don't need your parents hating me too." Tony quickly put my fears to rest, or at least one of them. "No, my mother wants to meet you. She said she wants to meet the person who has made me so happy." John said he liked the sound of that, but I still wasn't convinced. I said to them, "He didn't mention his father. I bet that went over like a fart in church." They both could sense the fear I still had.

Tony admitted his father was disappointed not because of me but because he would be the one to break the family tradition of families getting together to pair their children off for marriage. John had asked if that angered his father. Tony said that his mother always thought that was a foolish tradition, telling someone who they love and who they will spend the rest of their life with. Father likes the tradition but not if it causes me to live an unhappy life. He wants to meet you too. I breathed a sigh of relief saying that it all worked out and we were back to having a good night, too bad that was short-lived. Squeezing my hand a little tighter, Tony said there was more. His voice carried a serious tone when he said he didn't want me to get upset but there was something else he needed to talk about. I immediately had that sinking feeling and wanted to end pizza night right then and there. I just couldn't handle any more bad news. I looked at Tony and asked, "What now?" Tony explained how his parents were being reassigned to Johannesburg on a more permanent basis. Right away the news hit me hard, "Great here it comes I am losing you too." I tried to let go of Tony's hand, but he wouldn't let go of mine, promising me he would be allowed to stay till the end of summer and that I wasn't losing him. It would only be temporary. He said his parents know that he hates Africa and wants to stay here in Maine with me. He said he was only going back so he could get a permanent visa. This time I did pull my hand away and I was angry when I said, "Why the fuck can't you just do that here? Can't the people they work for just get it done?" Tony reached over and took my hand once again promising me again, it would only be temporary. He did the best he could to explain a process that could take up to six months and a process that he had a hard time understanding. John tried to help the situation by telling Tony he already had a place to live because he had no intention of letting anyone else rent the cabin. John told me to just stay in the cabin till Tony got back. There was no need to move out or go back to the dorm in the fall. Tony said he loved that idea, and he did need someone to take care of the choppers until he got back. John assured me that it was all going to work out. Somehow, I knew better, and I couldn't help feeling like I was driving Tony away.

3

I laid in bed that night asking myself why I kept losing the ones I loved. What the hell did I do that was so wrong that it caused my son to be taken from me and now Tony?

4

The portal shifted and brought me forward a month in time to August 1988. The company that I had worked for last summer called me during the holiday break and asked me to come back and work for them. They told me Hal had moved on to their MIS department which was in another state. Since he was gone, I agreed to work for them over the holiday break and the summer again. I loved the four-day work week schedule; the pay was great and I enjoyed working there. I was looking down at a perfect summer day. I remember that Friday very well. John and I were hiking some trails that he had been wanting to hike for some time. We had gone to breakfast shortly after Tony left for work then headed over to Bradbury Mountain in Pownal to hike the trails in the park. We made it to the top, and as John had said the view was worth the hike up the small mountain. I told John he was right, the views and the trails were awesome, "But something tells me this is more than just a, 'Hey it's a beautiful day'. Let's hike Bradbury Mountain." John smiled saying it was a beautiful day and he had always wanted to hike this mountain, but I was right, he did want to talk to me but in a different location, away from the cabin. I knew that's what he wanted. It was just like the day we took a walk in the rain that Sunday back in October. I hadn't done much talking about Tony leaving at our weekly pizza night. I would always talk about something else like work or any topic that avoids discussing the elephant in the room. I told John that since we were the only ones there, I guess it would be fine if we talked. John started by saying he knew I had a tough year academically. He knew my grades slipped from a 3.8 to a 2.5 which pretty much was the same as going from A/A- work to a C average. I did well considering what went on. I was still passing, still able to get financial aid and not even close to academic probation but scoring well below my normal performance. I told John that I caught hell from the 'rents about it too. They were not happy unless there was a screaming match. John wanted to know if I told my parents why I had such a hard time this year. I told him, "Hell no!" Not only would that be a disaster, twenty years from now my mother would still be throwing it in my face about how badly I fucked up." I told John there was no way in hell I was telling them anything about what happened. I would rather suffer in silence. John asked if I had told them about Tony. I said they had no idea about my relationship with Tony, the choppers, or that we are living together. Telling them is just another disaster waiting to happen. We took a break from talking as other hikers started reaching the top of the mountain. We decided to take the back trail back down. From what the Park Rangers told John, not many hikers know there is a back trail leading you to another trail that runs around the base of the mountain. We headed that way and got a few hundred feet down the trail before John started talking again. He asked what my plans for the fall semester were. John offered the cabin to me if I didn't want to go back to the dorm. I don't think John was expecting me to say that I just needed a break, that I gave things a lot of thought and I was taking next year off. I told John I needed to re-group and take some time for myself, focus on myself, and start my junior year next fall. I can honestly say I wasn't expecting John to be so supportive. I was expecting some pushback because John was focused on my academics too. Maybe the reason I was expecting pushback from John was because I was used to constant pushback from the 'rents. Every time I tried to make a choice or decision on my own, the 'rents would have a meltdown. I was never allowed to make my own choices. I had to follow the orders they would command me to follow. I was pleasantly surprised when he said he thought it was a good idea to take some downtime, focus on me, and re-group so I can start fresh for when Tony gets back. I wanted to say, "If he comes back," but I didn't. Maybe I should have so he knew how I felt. Instead, I told him that work has a location close to where my parents live and they asked if I would head up a project for them. When the project is done, I will transfer back home. John asked if I would be staying with my parents since the location was close to them. I told John I was reluctant to but there would be so much overtime and weekend work I would be hardly there. I wouldn't have to pay rent so I could bank plenty of cash to pay for my tuition and not have to answer to the 'rents about school. John did agree this wasn't the best idea but being able to pay for, as he would say, "my own schooling," would be smart. I did reiterate that with all the overtime and weekend hours, I wouldn't see them much. John expressed concern about our no longer meeting weekly. He didn't want that to stop. He told me he knew a diner on the New Hampshire border where we could meet. The food was good, and the booths were private so we could talk. I was glad he brought that up. I told John I would do that if he agreed to something. John listened while I told him that I knew he was being my therapist all this time because that was what I needed. I also said I knew that he was being a father figure, a dad, and a friend because he knew I needed that just as much if not more. I went ahead and did something I hate doing because it shows my vulnerable side. I told him, "No more therapist. I will only meet with you if you promise to be a dad to me, be that father figure I never had. That means more to me than you know. I just want a dad in my life, and I want it to be you." I could see him get a little misty-eyed when he said, "Yeah I can do that." By this time, we were back by the parking lot. John said," Come on, I will buy you and cup of coffee on the way home." I smirked and said, "I was kinda hoping we would stop and grab a beer but hey, coffee works too." John shook his head and laughed saying, "You're something else you smart ass."

5

The portal shifted and brought me to the Big Rock at Rattlesnake Pond. Tony and I were headed into the pond for a swim. This was the last weekend we spent together. He was leaving Monday morning to meet his parents in New York to fly back to South Africa and I was heading back to my parent's house to get settled in and begin the project for work. We left first thing that Friday morning and planned on camping out the whole weekend at The Big Rock. Even though Tony said he was coming back after getting his Visa, John still wanted one last pizza night. We ended up doing two pizza nights. One a day early and the other late Sunday evening when we got back from our weekend ride. They both tried to get me to share how I felt about Tony leaving, but I just didn't want to talk about it. I kept telling them it's only six months and it will go by fast. It will give John and me some time to talk and work through all the past traumas. I added that Tony and I would be able to start our new life together with a fresh clean slate when he returned. I kept my real thoughts bottled up–I didn't think he was coming back, that he was using this as an excuse to end things with me, and that it was my fault because of the shit shows that went on even though I had no control over what happened. I was watching both of us splash around in the pond without a care in the world or a stitch of clothing on. We swam out to the middle of the shallow pond which was maybe fifteen feet at its deepest point during spring runoff. Being late summer it was closer to ten feet. Tony would tread water holding the both of us up. I would wrap my arms around the top of his shoulders, and we would start making out. Tony would put his arms up over his head and we would do a slow sink to the sandy bottom in a lip-lock. Once we hit bottom he would bend his legs into a squat. I had to wrap my legs around his waist so he could push off the bottom and bring us back to the top without letting go of our kiss. After we caught our breath, we would do it again and again. After a while, we both were worn out, so we swam back to the big rock, got on top, and lay in the sun drying off. Tony, being a man of few words, usually wasn't the one to start the conversation but today he did start the conversation. He did something he hadn't done since the night I got jumped. Tony sat up and said, "Andrew Paige, sit up I need to tell you something." He hadn't called me that name maybe once or twice since I said he could call me Paige–everyone else does. I sat up as Tony took me by my hands and guided me to sit in between his outstretched legs facing him. My legs went over his hips on each side of him so they could wrap around. Holding my hands with our fingers interlocked he asked if I would just listen to what he had to say. I agreed, taking a deep breath and bracing myself figuring this would be the break-up speech I was expecting. He made sure we were looking one another in the eye before saying what he wanted to say, "Andrew Paige, I know you think I am not coming back. That I am leaving you. I need you to know I do not want to leave. I do not want to go back to Apartheid, or the violence, or being hated because of my skin color in the country where my ancestors are from. I want to stay here with you, but I have no choice in the matter. I will not be granted a visa if I do not follow the proper process. Believe me when I tell you Mother and Father have tried but our Government Officials in South Africa will not budge on the matter." I did not know how hard his parents were trying to keep Tony from having to leave. He continued telling me, "I told you last fall this is the spot I want us to get married and we are going to do just that. John has a friend who is a Justice of the Peace and has already volunteered to perform our Commitment Ceremony right on this very spot. Andrew Paige, I am not leaving you." Tony didn't start crying but I could see his eyes tearing up. I didn't have to see his eyes tear up to know he was telling me the truth. Before I could speak Tony continued. "I want to make this official. Andrew Paige Turner, would you do me the honor of becoming my committed life partner and marry me? Promise me that we will spend the rest of our lives together the way I promise you I will." I was so shocked. I wasn't expecting him to do that. I let go of our hands and wrapped my arms around him pulling him close, holding him, and not ever wanting to let go. I told him, "Yes to all of it." We sat there holding one another until Tony said, "I have something for you." We got up and, holding hands, we walked down to the choppers. Tony let go of my hand so he could reach into the front saddle bag and pull out two clatter rings, both on chains to wear around our necks under our shirts yet close to our hearts. He slipped mine over my head and then slid his over his head saying now it is official we are engaged to be married. We didn't do any more riding that afternoon and we didn't come out of the tent until the following morning.

6

Neither of us wanted to leave and head back to the cabin but it was time to go. We took our time on the way finally arriving at the cabin in the early evening. John knew Tony was going to propose to me and was waiting for us to get back. He heard us coming up the drive and met us at the barn wanting to know how it went. Being the smart ass, I tried to act like nothing happened but I was so elated that Tony and I were engaged to be married, I couldn't pull it off. After I told John about it, Tony and I were both starving and since we emptied all the food from the fridge and freezer because we were leaving, Tony suggested doing another pizza night. We were all glad we had one more pizza night, it was time spent together, and we all needed that extra time together. When we finished eating, Tony handed over the keys to the choppers and the paperwork giving me ownership so I could take care of them until he got back. I decided to keep both choppers. I was riding my favorite one when the accident that brought me here happened.

7

The mist cleared out from around us and John and I were back in physical form. I thanked John for sparing me the long and sad goodbye. I didn't want to see the tears from him or Tony again. Watching Tony cry always broke my heart and that is when it dawned on me. I asked John if he noticed it too. John wasn't sure what I was talking about, so he asked me to explain. I said, "Looking back at everything that happened, being attacked, getting dependent on pot and alcohol, the intervention, losing my son, and then having to say good-bye when I lost Tony, I got angry. I threw things and yelled and screamed in anger. I burned the ultrasound images of my son; I did everything but cry. I never once shed a tear. How is it that I couldn't cry for my son or anything else. How cold must I be, never shedding a tear, not even for my little boy? Right on cue, the fatherly hand of support gently squeezed my shoulder, "There is something I need you to see."

Chapter 33

1

Once again, the mist engulfed us, and the portal opened. I was looking down at the little diner John and I would meet at every week. It was the first week of the new year. The diner was just on the other side of the draw bridge on old Rte.1. I was running a few minutes behind, and the draw bridge was just starting to come down. Tony had been gone for five months. John was reading the letter from Tony that arrived the day before. Finally, the bridge was back down and the road reopened. I was only five minutes late which wasn't bad. Sometimes it can take up to an hour or more depending on whether the gears that raise and lower the bridge get stuck. Today there was no such issue.

2

John had re-folded the letter and slipped it back into the envelope. I came into the diner. John and I had not seen one another since a few days before Christmas. The New Year had just started a few days before our usual lunch day. It was a couple of weeks since we had lunch, and I was happy to see him. As I was taking my coat off and sitting down, I was asking John how Christmas and New Year's went and did he get a chance to visit with his daughter, Debbie. He told me the holidays were great, and that he got to spend a lot of time with Debbie since they are talking regularly again. John asked how my holidays were, and I told him that I chose to work the holiday because the pay was awesome. I said with all the overtime coupled with the holiday

242

hours and bonuses, I will now be able to pay cash for college and have some money left over for a honeymoon next summer when Tony and I get married. John thought was great and said, "Speaking of Tony, I got another letter from him." John handed me the envelope with the letter in it. We all thought it would be best for Tony to send all the letters to John's house because my parents didn't know what happened nor did they know about Tony. We all thought it was best to keep it that way. Not only that but the few pieces of mail I did get had been opened by my parents. God only knows what would have happened if they opened a Tony letter. I opened the letter and started reading. As I was reading, I could hear his voice in my head with that accent that I loved.

Dear Andrew Paige and John,

This letter is going to be brief. The revolt against Apartheid is causing a lot of chaos and violent clashes. Once again, we must move to a safer area. Even though Visa applications have stalled, Father is still making arrangements for my return. It won't be much longer, and I will soon be home. I will send an update and our new address once we get settled. Paige, I promise we will be together. I miss you and love you very much. I miss you too John you are family to me, and I love you like my own family.

Love Tony

As I was putting the letter back in the envelope, I didn't realize I said out loud, "I am counting the days Tones, I am counting the days." John smiled, assuring me it wouldn't be long now. I told John that I hoped so because I was so ready to move back in with him. John asked if everything was okay with my current living situation at home with my parents. I told him, "No it wasn't", but that wasn't the reason. I was missing Tony in the worst way and wanted him back. John asked what was going on with my parents. I told him everything was going well when I first moved back. It didn't take long before the shit show started again. The shit hit the fan when my parents found out I am gay. I don't know how they found out but they did. Things got so bad that I just packed up the few belongings I had, put them in storage, and I am now staying in the garage apartment the head of personnel has at their place. She offered the place to me when my mother called telling them she kicked me out because, as my mother put it, "He's a fucking queer." Now that he is homeless you need to fire him." When I went to work that morning, I got called into Personnel and she told me what had gone on. She also assured me my job was safe and offered me her garage apartment to stay in until the project was over and I headed back to Maine. John didn't like the sound of what happened, "Oh boy that's rough. I am sorry, that happened." I told John that the project was ending much earlier than expected and the transfer had already been processed. I will be back in the Old Port location in two months or less. John was happy to hear that and offered up the cabin saying it was mine if I wanted it. I told John I appreciated it but I would rather get a place of my own, I just can't be there without Tony. John told me he gets it because he can't bring himself to go back to the old neighborhood when he goes and visits Alice's grave. I was glad he understood. After the waitress brought out our order, John said he needed to change the subject. He told me that Andy called and wanted to know if you still wanted to file the complaint against Michele. Andy had told John that Michele's parents didn't know where Michele was. Michele's parents said she had taken off shortly after she hung up the phone when she made that call to me. He said her father had overheard what she said to me and lost his cool with her. After he chewed her out, Michele threw some clothes in a bag and took off. She quickly realized that even her father had his limits, and certain lines couldn't be crossed. She was no longer Daddy's little princess. She had lost her power and control over him too. Her parents had not heard from her since. John did tell me Andy could track her down if I wanted. I sat silently for a few minutes trying to work up the courage to give Andy the go-ahead. I just couldn't and I told John that if I did that, I would have to relive the whole thing all over again. "No, I just can't." John nodded in agreement. I had a feeling he didn't want me to do it either. I don't think he wanted to see me go through that again. He went on to tell me that Andy had heard from Michele's parents along with Josh and Patty. They were asking how I was. They wanted to talk and make peace with me. Without any hesitation I told John that I didn't want that, I didn't want to see or hear from any of them again. John said he didn't blame me at all, it was perfectly fine, and he would let Andy know. Surprisingly enough the conversation didn't ruin my appetite. After we finished eating, I said to John, "I just couldn't stop thinking that what if I had just married her like she wanted." John told me to stop beating myself up over it, no matter what I did there would have been no good outcome. He felt no matter what I did she wasn't letting me have my son. It wasn't worth getting stuck here. I knew he was right. No matter what, she was determined to destroy me, and my son was the tool she would use. I just couldn't help it. I couldn't get the thought out of my head "What if I just married her".

3

The portal did its shift. John wanted me to see something else. When the portal reopened it brought me forward to April of 1996. It was a sunny and warm spring day. John and I had breakfast that morning at the Old Port Diner and we were up on the east end of Old Port sitting in the park which just happened to be John's favorite place to go. It was also the place he called his thinking spot. It was his favorite place to go when he wanted to be close to Alice. When Alice was alive, they would spend weekends and vacations at the cabin all through the spring, summer, and fall before building the house. He and Alice would come here. and Alice would sit under the big tree painting the ships as they came in and out of the harbor. John would sit in the exact spot we were sitting in pretending to read but he would be watching Alice paint. He told me this was the spot he came to when he made the decision that I earned his trust and to take the step forward and stop drug testing me. He said he likes to think Alice helped him make that decision because he felt so close to her when he was here. "Still missing her, aren't you?" I asked. He said he sure does miss her. I told John I could never figure out why it is that I miss someone I never got to meet or even hold for the first time. I told him I miss my son so much and think about him every day. John knew I did, he couldn't believe it had been nine years, ten since he first met me. Even though we had a good conversation, I was on the quiet side at breakfast that morning. John knew there was something on my mind. I finally came out with it and said, "I thought things had finally gotten better, that life was getting a lot easier until the other day at work." John asked if I wanted to talk about it. He asked what happened. I told him that one of the women at work who was out on maternity leave brought her newborn son by for everyone to see. She asked if I wanted to hold him. I told John that it took everything I had not to tell her, "I couldn't even hold my own son why would I want to hold yours." I told John that I thought I was past all this. John said that after all this time he still had bad days too. He told me that there is no expiration date or closure for grief. There's just the beginning, the middle, and the rest of your life. I told John it got me thinking about Tony again and how closure would have been nice. I told John that I never told him this before but every night for two years I would fall asleep with my head on Tony's chest listening to his heartbeat. There were nights that if I didn't have that, I would not have slept. Without a doubt, it helped me get through it all. I told John that after Tony left, it took me a long time to learn how to fall asleep again. John not only knew how I felt but he knew what I meant by having to learn how to fall asleep with no one next to you. John turned to face me and said he didn't know how he knew this, but he just knew. "What do you know?" I asked, "Did you hear from Tony?" John hadn't heard from Tony; it was just his intuition. His instincts were telling him that something caused Tony to not come back. He didn't know what, but he knew it was something serious. I had come to know that John's instincts were always spot on. He said Tony and I would be together again but not right now, for now, I owe it to myself to be happy and live my life. I was reluctant, but I did tell John that I had been seeing this guy for a few months now. He was the first guy I dated that didn't make me feel like I was cheating on Tony. I wanted to try dating, but I felt like I was betraying him. This time it isn't like that at all. John encouraged me to give it a chance. If I like the guy, it is okay to be happy. I told John that I did like Mike. John told me to give Mike a chance and when it is time for Tony and me to be together again, it will all fall into place. I didn't say anything else, just sat there thinking about what he said. After a few moments, John looked down at his watch, "Look at the time. Debbie's flight will be landing shortly. I have to get going to pick her up." As we were getting up and headed to our cars, I asked John if she was flying out next Sunday. He told me she was and that he had to leave the house at five a.m. to bring her to the airport. Rolling his eyes he mumbled, "Lucky for her I am an early riser." "Let's do this," I said to John, "I will pick you both up and after we drop Debbie at the airport we go get breakfast. I am not taking "no" for an answer." John smiled asking what the occasion was. I told him that life got so busy that we haven't done much more than talk on the phone since the new year. I miss hanging out with my dad every week. I will be unpacked and settled into my new house soon, so I thought maybe he would like to come out and see it. I was thinking about asking Mike to join us for breakfast so John could meet him. John loved the idea and told me five a.m. sharp because we both knew how Debbie would get if I was one second late. I hung out for a minute watching John walk to his car and drive off. I was so glad I made time for him that day, it was the last time I saw him.

4

The portal shifted quickly bringing me forward just a few days. It was early Tuesday evening, I was feeling great and loving my new home. I was looking forward to this weekend. Mike was due back from his business trip Friday night, and he was coming out Saturday morning to see the new house, spend the weekend, and meet John on Sunday. Now that the snow was gone and the ground was thawed, I was planning on tilling the garden area this weekend. I had just finished painting the three rooms I wanted done before the new furniture I bought arrived. I was sitting at the kitchen table mapping out the garden and deciding what to plant next month when the phone rang. I was surprised, it was John's daughter calling. I thought to myself she must have gotten my new number from John which I gave him Sunday at breakfast. When she spoke, I could tell right away something was wrong, she was upset. Debbie told me that when her father didn't come out of his bedroom for breakfast, she went in to check on him. She couldn't wake her father up; he had died in his sleep. I was completely caught off guard by the news. I was so stunned I didn't know what to say. Debbie told me it was a heart attack, and they figured it happened shortly after he went to bed. We didn't talk for very long because Debbie said she had a few calls to make, and I couldn't speak after hearing the news. Debbie let me know that Friday morning she was having a brief viewing and small service for his friends here in Maine before taking him back home to be buried with her mother like he had wanted. I told her I would be there Friday morning and let her go so she could make her calls. I hung up and sat there at the table in complete shock and disbelief. It wasn't long before I went into denial. I got up and made myself something to eat, finished my garden plan, and went to bed like nothing happened like I never got the call. The next morning the furniture arrived, and I told the guys I was glad to see them and my dad was coming over Sunday to see my new home. After the delivery guys left, I went through the house and cleaned it from top to bottom for Sunday.

5

Friday morning rolled around, and I saw myself getting ready for John's service. I was putting my suit on tying my tie and getting ready to go to the funeral parlor but in my mind, I was thinking I was just going to meet John and Debbie for breakfast. I arrived at the Funeral Parlor and Debbie greeted me as I entered. We hugged and exchanged condolences. I went over to the casket to say my final goodbye. Debbie said that since John considered me family, I could have a few private moments with him. I was good at going through the motions while still being numb. Even seeing him in the casket it was not registering that John had died. Even though that was the case, I made sure I said what needed to be said. I told John that if it wasn't for him and Tony I wouldn't be here today. I told him he was the reason I had become the man I am today. If it wasn't for him, I don't know what would have happened. I said, "Thank you for being my dad, my mentor, and most of all a true friend when I needed one. I love you Dad and am going to miss you." In the decade that I knew him, calling him Dad was something I wished I had done when he was alive. He truly was a dad to me. When I finished, I let Debbie know so she could let everyone in and start the service. I had already taken a seat when Andy Harwich came in and sat next to me which still made me uncomfortable. I know Andy did what he thought was right and the plan he came up with was the only option I had so I wouldn't lose my son. But it was still his plan, and it failed. Even though I was not angry with him, I just could not warm up to him after that. I know it wasn't his fault and no one saw it coming but deep down inside there was a small part of me that held it against him. His partner sat on the other side and tried to make small talk by saying, "Look, a thorn in between two roses." Andy rolled his eyes saying, "Great, another lawyer joke." I just gave a polite smile. After the service, Andy walked out with me asking if I had a minute, he wanted to talk to me. We talked out in the parking lot briefly. Andy said he never got the chance to tell me how sorry he was about what happened. The last time Andy and I saw one another in person was that day in his office when I shattered his front door. Any communication after that was done through John, I think it was because Andy was afraid he would be making things worse. I also think he felt guilty about what happened and felt some of the blame landed on him. He said he completely understood why I didn't want to file the complaint against Michele. He wanted me to know he made Michele's father pay for the door saying that was the least her father could do for you. I honestly didn't care and was not sorry I broke the door, but I instead thanked him for doing that. He wanted me to know something else. He said that it hurt John to see you go through all that. You were like a son to him. He even told me he wished you were his son; he thought the world of you. He threw his arms around me hugging me tight telling me he was truly sorry and wished for the whole thing not to have happened. He let me go and he walked off. I wasn't trying to be cold towards him I was just numb and I think he got that. I hung out for a bit, I wanted to watch the hearse leave to take John to be with Alice again in their final resting place. I took the chopper to the Funeral Parlor. I don't know why I didn't take my car; I didn't think about it I just did it. When the hearse was pulling out, I got on my chopper and followed the hearse to John's house for one last time. I waited out at the head of the dooryard for the hearse to come back out. When the hearse came back out, I followed along to the state line where I stopped and watched it continue down Rte. 95 until it was out of sight before turning around and heading home.

6

By the time I got home, it was the afternoon. My suit was a little worse for the wear. My white shirt was ruined from all the springtime bugs going splat as I cruised home, and my tie was looking tattered from flapping in the wind and my shiny dress shoes were no longer shiny or even worth trying to polish. After I finished changing clothes, I thought it would be a good idea to call Mike and tell him breakfast on Sunday is canceled but to still come out on Saturday. I called knowing I was going to get his answering machine. When I got the beep to leave a message I said, "Hey Mike it's Paige. Just wanted to let you know plans for Sunday have changed. We won't be having breakfast with John. He died the other day." Saying it out loud was what it took for me to realize John was gone. I don't even remember saying, "Oh my god he's gone. My dad is gone. I have to hang up I can't talk right now." I hung up not realizing the message I left. I walked into the living room, sat on the sofa, and looked around at my big empty house knowing I was now alone–my little family was gone. I started crying. I couldn't stop. I was sobbing so hard not even John could have consoled me if he was there. I couldn't control myself, and I just couldn't stop. I couldn't stop because my son was gone, I would never get to hold my little boy, he was gone forever. I failed as a father. I couldn't stop because Tony wasn't coming back, I would never see him again, I drove him away. I couldn't stop because the man I considered my dad, the one person who believed in me no matter how far I fell, the one man who was the positive role model young people needed, and who truly cared about me like a dad, my last and only link to my son, He was gone and I still needed him. My little family was gone and I was alone and had no one. I couldn't stop sobbing. I sat alone for hours on the sofa sobbing late into the night in the dark alone. I was so exhausted I sat back and finally cried myself to sleep.

7

It was well past midnight when I fell asleep. I woke up the next morning after only sleeping for a few hours. I was emotionally drained. I walked out to the kitchen and looked out the window at the meadow and trees that were turning green, then looked down and saw the river was still running high from the spring runoff. I stood staring out the window. I didn't even know what I was looking for, I do know I was wishing the past decade was just a hellish dream. I was so preoccupied that I never heard Mike's car pull up nor did I hear him knock at the door. He saw me standing at the kitchen sink through the glass door and let himself in when I didn't respond. He knew John was like a dad to me so he figured I would be one hurting unit; he wasn't wrong. When he came in, he put his hands on my shoulders and asked how I was doing. I didn't say anything as I reached up to brush his hands off, I wanted to tell him to leave. I was tired of being hurt and losing the people I loved. I was afraid to fall for Mike because I was afraid to lose him too. I was going to end things before I could get hurt again. When I started reaching up it was like John was in the room and I could hear his voice in my head as if he was standing right there talking to me, "Paige, you have been through the beginning and the middle, now it's time for the rest of your life. If you like Mike and he makes you happy give him a chance, it's okay. You owe it to yourself." Instead of brushing his hands away, I gave them a gentle squeeze. He stepped in closer and wrapped his arms around my waist. He leaned in and kissed the side of my neck then rested his chin on my shoulder. From that point on, that is how we would start every morning for the next twenty-five years we were together.

Epilogue

The mist cleared out and John and I were back in the meadow that overlooked the pond and the babbling brook with the forest and mountain scenery that reminded me so much of the Maine landscape. John motioned for us to walk down to the brook. There was a bench by the brook that looked like the bench we sat on that day back in April of '96 and had what was to be our last father-son chat. I told him that it reminded me of that bench and day. John made me laugh when he told me he was late picking up Debbie that day and boy did she give him hell. We both sat and took in our surroundings; this spot was so calm and peaceful. John wanted to sit there for a bit because there was a lot that he had shown me, and he wanted me to take some time to reflect and to process it all. I agreed with John that it was a lot to process, but I did get it and once again he was right, I needed to stop beating myself up and forgive myself. I realized I had the deck stacked against me from the get-go. As we were sitting there, I told John how grateful I was for that day on the bench with him. After he died, I had never felt so alone. We talked for a bit. John told me that the "powers that be", here in the light, know I can't find it in myself to ever forgive Michele for what she did. The "powers that be", knew I had every right to refuse the meeting with Michele's parents and with Josh and Patty. They only wanted me to forgive myself. They said I had proven myself and you knew what they were talking about. I did know what they were talking about. I told John a while back when I was in Old Port that I came across a kid maybe just eighteen years old living on the street. I swore it was Josh, the kid looked exactly like him back in the day. I ended up approaching him and saying he looked just like my old college roommate, and I told him Josh's name. He looked at me and asked if I was Paige, which shocked me! I wasn't expecting it to be Josh's son. When he told me who he was I was curious why he was living on the street. He started from the beginning telling me how when his dad was just about two years old, he was at Woodstock. His dad's parents and Patty's parents were very close friends and hippies back in the Sixties. He saw pictures of his mother and father in diapers hanging out at Woodstock, which was something I would have loved to have seen; my old college roomie and his girlfriend running around in diapers. He went on to tell me his grandmother, Josh's mother, was a big reason why they had to make the famous announcement at Woodstock "Don't eat the brown acid." She took a hit and almost instantly had a bad reaction which she never really recovered from. When she finally got out of the hospital, both Josh's parents and Patty's parents joined a religious detox program which ended up being a cult. He went on to tell me that since they were from a small Maine town it didn't take long for Josh and Patty's parents to find out what was going on at Mercy College. Michele's parents filled them in. Both sets of parents found out and forced Josh and Patty to join the cult and get married since they were already having sex. Josh Jr. went on to tell me how when he came out to his parents, Josh Sr. said it would be best if they allowed him to just "run away from home." They told Josh Jr. he needed to do that because the cult would have put him through a violent deprogramming to make him straight again. They knew they couldn't beat the gay out of somebody. They protected him by having him run away from home. Patty told Jr. about me and how they were forced into the cult. Patty also said for Jr. to look for me hoping I would help him out. I did help him out. I let Jr. stay in the guest quarters that were in the old barn. He got his GED and then attended the local Community College earning a degree in social work so he could work with at-risk LGBTQ teens. Eventually, he would bring the kids out to the farm for day trips. Mike and I got the idea that since we had no heirs, we should set up a trust and estate so that after we passed on, Jr. could convert the farm into a safe house for those teens. That is exactly what we did. I didn't punish Jr. for what Josh and Patty did to me. I knew it wasn't his fault and I respected what they had done to get their son safely away from the cult. After, I told John we needed to talk for a while about what I saw. Before Tony, I was becoming someone I wasn't and didn't want to be. The influences in my life were shaping me to be not only someone I didn't want to be but what others wanted me to be. Tony was the first person I met who didn't tear me down or belittle me because I was different. I could be myself without judgment and he could be himself without judgment. It was the first time in my life I experienced unconditional love and of course, I was now seeing why I needed to forgive myself. I couldn't deny it, John was right, it's time to forgive myself. It was time to be at peace with myself. I needed to see it from a different view to understand the true nature and reality of it all. I said to John, "Now that I am making peace with myself, I guess my final Journey is over." John replied that it wasn't over just yet. I asked him what else there was. As soon as I said that I felt two hands gently squeeze my shoulders and that trademark kiss on my head. I jumped up spinning around exclaiming, "TONY" I jumped into his arms and held him tight. I couldn't believe it was him. I held him until the tears of joy stopped and I could speak again. When I could speak, I said I couldn't believe it was him and how I missed him and that there wasn't a day that went by I didn't think about him. Tony knew I thought about him every day since he left including that morning when I was gazing out my kitchen window waiting for Mike to come down for coffee for what became our last ride together. He told me he knew that I would always think about him and said, "You're probably wondering why I didn't come back". Of course, being the smart ass I was I replied, "Now that you mention it, the thought did cross my mind once or twice." He smiled knowing I waited for a long time for him to come back even after the letters stopped. I asked him to tell me what happened. Tony told me that when they arrived in Africa things were so unstable that they couldn't stay in one place for very long. That is why he didn't send any more letters. He and his family had to move often to keep themselves safe. Finally, in the spring of 1990, they were able to settle in a town called Durban. In July of 1990, his father was finally able to secure his visa and travel arrangements. Tony said he was set to arrive in Maine the same day we met for the very first time. I couldn't help myself, I had to say, "You mean the day you opened the barn doors to show me your...." Tony quickly cut me off, "Andrew Paige Turner, what in God's name am I going to do with you. " We both laughed. I loved when he used to say that. Tony continued telling me that he was finally able to mail us a letter telling us the good news, but they had no idea that the rioters had moved into the area. He was walking to the post office to mail the letter when he heard gunshots. Immediately, chaos ensued and he got caught up in the mass panic of the crowded streets. He was trying to get to safety when a kind woman took him by the hand and led him to safety. He said, "That is how I met Alice." and he told me he never felt the bullet. I told him I had no idea what happened; I thought I had driven him away. He told me John had eventually arrived and the four of them had been waiting for me. I was confused. The four of them? I said. "You, John, and Alice are three who is the fourth?" Tony said he would tell me who else but there was something we needed to do first. The fog started swirling around us and in an instant, we were completely engulfed. As fast as the fog appeared it disappeared with the same speed. It was autumn, my favorite season. The colors were spectacular! The blazing reds, brilliant yellows, bright oranges, and the splash of purple here and there were breathtaking. As I was looking around, awed by the new surroundings, I realized where we were. Tony and I were standing on the Big Rock at Rattlesnake Pond. Tony put his hands on my shoulders and said, "I made you a promise. It is time I kept that promise." John joined us on the top of the Big Rock and asked if I was ready. I took one more look around and saw Mike on the other side of the small pond. He was standing holding hands with someone who I had never seen before. He looked as happy as I was, he gave me a nod and a thumbs-up with his free hand. I told John I could never be more ready. It was so fitting that John was the one who performed our private ceremony. John had Tony and I exchange the traditional wedding vows, and he married us. You could feel the excitement and energy of celebration in the air. It was like the universe was our witness and John presented us as a married couple to the universe. I looked out to see Mike waving and smiling as they walked off hand in hand. I noticed the wedding band on his ring finger that was not there before. It was time for him to go be where he was supposed to be with the person he was supposed to be with. I was happy for Mike. I will always cherish our time together and will always have a place in my heart for him. As they walked off, I watched them fade away, and I knew it was time for us to do the same. Tony turned my attention to a woman who was standing at the base of the big rock with her back to me. He said someone had been waiting a long time to meet you. I naturally assumed it was Alice but didn't understand why she had her back to me, and where was this fourth person? As we approached, the woman began turning around and as I was about to say, "You must be Alice," She turned fully around, rendering me speechless. I froze in my tracks. I was paralyzed, I couldn't breathe, my jaw started to quiver, and the tears started streaming down my face. John had walked down behind us and was now standing next to me on the opposite of Tony. Both John and Tony took one of my arms and raised them so Alice could lay my son in my arms. I was so overcome with emotion that John and Tony had to help support me because I couldn't stand and needed to sit down. I sat at the base of the big rock doing what I thought I would never do, hold my son for the first time. I was so overcome with emotion, I couldn't stop crying. I couldn't believe I was holding my little boy. I told him how sorry I was that I failed him. I told him I tried so hard to protect him. I kept saying over and over, "I am sorry, I am so sorry I failed you". I couldn't say I was sorry enough to him. Tony sat down next to me putting his arm around me and holding me close to him telling me it was okay. He knows I did everything I could, and it wasn't my fault. He said Alice has been watching over him. When I finally was able to gain my composure, Tony said it was time to look into his eyes so he could tell me his name. I looked into the eyes of my beautiful little boy and told Tony that he was right; his name was there. I said, "Everyone, meet Andrew Adama Williamson Turner, daddy's perfect little miracle." After a few moments, John said, "Come on. it's time to go be a family." We started walking down the trail. I stopped. I sang out very badly, "HEY HEY MOMMA said the way you move gonna make you sweat gonna make you groove! Hey, look Tones he yawned, I told you it would work." Tony shook his head and rolled his eyes "It's like living with a twelve-year-old." The mist swirled around us, and in the distance I could hear the heart monitor make its final beeps then flat line. The day I got to hold my little boy for the first time, the day I thought would never come was finally here. It was time for me to go home to my little family.